The Daughters of Swefling

Swefling Eleanor Archer

Barbara Grantham Hicks

The Daughters of Swefling
Swefling Eleanor Archer

Copyright © 2014 Barbara Grantham Hicks

All rights reserved. No part of this book may be reproduced in any form by any electronic or mechanical means including photocopying, recording, or information storage and retrieval without permission in writing from the author.

This is a work of fiction. Any reference to people who lived and their actions, particularly in relation to the characters in this story, and places referred to, come entirely from the author's imagination and should not be considered factual and/or true (except where known facts exist).

ISBN-13: 978-1499262834
ISBN-10: 1499262833

The Daughters of Swefling

Swefling Eleanor Archer

Sunday May 12 1616

We have been at sea for seven weeks and seen nothing but the ocean and the sky in all that time. The sea is sometimes grey and full of foreboding, the sky matching it, increasing the fear we feel of the might of God's creation through which we sail. At other times the sea is blue, as deep a blue as the sky above devoid of a single cloud. And yet our small ship, the Agnes Rose plows on, riding the steep waves and the endless rolling motion with ease and confidence.

We are seventy souls, risking our lives on the soundness of our vessel and the sea knowledge and skills, of our Captain and crew, and we sail the vast ocean seeking our fortune. We left Ipswyche, in the fair countie of Suffolk on a fine spring morning and sailed down the River Orwell to the sea bound for a new life in the America's. And we are only [Now] a matter of weeks from our destination. What trepidation there is? Amongst the women and children it is expected of course but the men and boys, despite their bravado, and excitement and boastfulness, attempt to hid their fears but not as well as they believe.

I should start my tale at the beginning. My name is Swefling Archer and I was born in the village of the same name, in Suffolk, the only daughter of John Archer, a skilled carpenter of limited means and Ales, daughter of William Cobbold of Swefling. How my parent's should ever have met, much less come together in a love match, is as much a mystery to myself, as to my maternal grandfather on the day they declared their feelings for one another. That my mother saw in my father her knight in shining armour as in days of old, even though he possessed neither horse nor armour, is in no doubt nor the fact that my grandparent disowned her when they wed and she a maid of sixteen years.

My grandfather, although I never knew or met him, was a powerful man and used to much influence in the countie. He used his position to persecute my father in his given trade, so that by the time my younger brother Philip was born, we lived in an area of Ipswyche beside the cemetery of St Mary le Tower church, and close to the quay. From that vantage point we saw ships coming and going for ports and places we hardly ever heard of. It was here that my father found much work and although we remained in our poor accommodation, at night I oft times heard my parents talk of their plans and dreams to remove us all far from a land where a man is condemned for where he is born in the social scale.

My father was fortunate in his trade to work on refitting vessels that came to the port and became employed similarly on the Agnes Rose. In exchange for his services, we are most fortunate to sail to our new life in the luxury of a tiny cabin of our own. The other passengers are obliged to find space where they are able, below decks, in the confined and crowded area amongst cargo and supplies. Even so, our cabin is cramped with five adults as we are, but at least we have beds and paliasses, although my two brothers John and

Philip, aged seventeen and fourteen sleep on a narrow bunk whilst I share with my parents, lying at their feet and frequently find myself disturbed in the night time when they undertake their marital relations.

...

We were most surprised moments before our vessel began her voyage to be hailed from the quayside from a fine carriage that slid to a halt at the gangplank. A smart, clean and important lady alighted and forced her way on board much to the amusement of all around her.

"My ladie Mother!" my own mother cried to her own dismay fearful perhaps the elder woman would topple over into the river.
"I was not about to permit you to depart without a word or sight Ales" she said nodding to father and glancing at us. "I wish you John, to protect my daughter, with your life if you must and my grandchildren likewise"
"I will endeavour so to do Lady Cobbold"
"So be it" she declared "Boys!" she addressed my brothers, "I am your grandmother, fetch the trunk from the carriage. Be quick about you"
"Yes Madam" John said so full of surprise he delayed, momentarily watching the woman.
"Go!" she urged.
"You must be Swefling" she said to me.
"Yes Madam" I nodded and curtseyed and lowered my eyes out of respect.
"Good. Ales" she said turning once more to my Mother "I cannot give you a vast sum or chattels but there are items of use and value in the trunk, keep it safe. John, I give you coins to help you on your way" and she handed father a black leather pouch that even to my unknowledgeable

eyes seemed ~~quite~~ *most* heavy. "Careful!" she called out to my brothers, who tottered quite dangerously on the gangplank before lowering the fine wooden box with brass handles, onto the deck.
"I have no words sufficient to thank you" Mother said.
"Then say no more Ales. This is an address where you may write me when you are able, I will not allow your father to deny me that" and she handed Mother a slip of parchment, "I must be gone" she gave Mother a brief hug, and a kiss on her cheek and without another word headed down the gangplank to the carriage. "Out of the way William" she growled to a young boy whose head had stared out of the door while grandmother was with us "Drive on" she called to the coachman when she was settled, and she was gone as quickly as she had arrived.

"Any more last minute callers" the Captain called, a hint of a smile on his face I thought, and as there were not, he gave the order for our vessel to be prepared for departure. "John get the box stowed" Mother urged for apart from anything else it was in the way and thus it takes up much valuable space in our cabin.

...

Over the weeks of the voyage our company of adventurers have become acquainted with one another and generally our relationships are pleasant enough, although beneath decks I expect, arguments are frequent. There are a few females on board, for men and boys make up the majority of the passengers. These folk are not as fortunate as us, with a father and sons with a skill and trade, for many we discovered are to be servants, their indentures over many years, arranged to pay their passage. One or two others though are similarly skilled as father and three declare they are to seek their fortune but we have never yet discovered how they intend to do so.

There is a woman on board, we have befriended, Rebecca her name is, a girl in reality only a few years my senior I believe, with two daughters already and very close to another delivery. We have spoken oft times but she is shy and clings to her husband, a fine looking man to my thinking, as if she is fearful his eye will be turned from her. She is pretty and comely and wears her pregnancy well, which surprises my mother on such a voyage and the upheaval she suffers, and the melancholic air about her.

Rebecca's husband is a Suffolk man, like father, and goes by the name of Crispin Martin. He is a carpenter by trade, as my father and brothers, and spends much time in my father's company and I ponder that they may previously be acquainted but it is not my place to enquire. My mother who is always a kindly woman, has taken Rebecca under her wing and as a consequence, I am often instructed to amuse the daughters while they converse. I am free though to wander the deck in my own time and especially after our service of this Sabbath morn, when I begin my tale, I leant at the side of our ship as we scudded along, arm in arm with my father.
"Look father" I said pointing to movement in the water not too distant from our bow "What are they?" for even as we watched several large, dark grey creatures with pointed noses left the water and flew into the air before descending to the depths of the ocean once more.

"I believe they may be called dolphins" he said as I stared in awe.
"They must be the most beautiful creatures in the world.

Look father they fly again like birds. Will there be dolphins in America?"

"Perhaps there will be, one of the sailors says they are friendly creatures"

"They might be with us all the way. Is it much farther do you suppose?"

"So many questions" father smiled at me. He is a young man still for I was born when my parents were only two or three years older than I am now, and I am just sixteen. "A number of weeks yet, but the weather is warm and we may enjoy our voyage and with God's good graces, we shall gain strength. We shall have much to occupy us on our arrival"

"I hope it will be so, father. The Agnes Rose is so small and all alone in the ocean. I can't wait to arrive. Will we have a house to live in?"

"We shall not know until we arrive, If the weather is kind, sleeping under the stars will not be harsh and we shall be content"

"But what of the wild animals and the natural people. Mr Martin says they're very fierce"

"He was saying so to worry you my dear"

"But why father?"

"To tease" he smiled.

"Hmmm" was my unladylike reply "It is not nice to tease. I feel sad for his wife, she is most unhappy now in her pregnancy"

"Do not over concern yourself, your mother comforts her"

"I wouldn't want to be sailing the oceans and about to have a child and with two at my side. Mr Martin is wrong to bring her"

"It is the way of the world my dear. You'll see once the child arrives, Mistress Martin will smile"

I left the matter rest there for who was I to know any

difference.

Wednesday May 20 1616

The storm blew itself out during the night and we woke in our beds, our stomachs still uneasy, but unlike many of our companions below decks I have subsequently discovered, thanks to our Lord, none of my family have been ill. I moved, stretched and found there was space against the wall. I sat up immediately aware Mother was nowhere to be seen.

"Where's my mother?" I asked a measure of concern at her absence.
My father woke and opened his eyes.
"Mistress Martin was in need of her assistance in the night with the birthing" he said.
"In the storm? Father how awful, should I offer aid also?"
"Mother suggested you might care for the daughters"

...

I went below decks and found the noise of the ocean most frightening and disturbing. I searched for my mother anxious to be in the open as soon as I was able and I found her with another woman. They were on their hands and knees scrubbing at the deck, amid terrible smells of sickness and people confined under decks for the several days the storm had accompanied our vessel.

"Mother. What are you doing?" I asked, horrified to see her so.

She looked up and smiled briefly.

"It has to be done Swefling. We're near finished"
"Father said Mistress Martin was birthing her child, is she well?"
"She is delivered of a fine son" was all she said which surprised me for my mother was one who loved to talk, not gossip you understand but she enjoyed good conversation "Mistress Martin would be thankful for you to take the girls. They are together, just beyond the partition"
I smiled at my mother as she stood, looking flushed and weary, but perhaps it was the feeble light of the candle [lantern] that made it so.
"Go rest Mother" I suggested nevertheless.

I walked to the area where the family lived on the voyage and found them as mother predicted. Mistress Martin lay on a mattress, tears rolling down her face as she fed her new child at her breast. Mr Martin sat beside her watching, looking most perplexed and melancholy at the same time. The two girls, Lucy who I believed was three years and Joane barely one lay weakly at their mother's side.

"I've come to take the girls to the deck" I explained my presence.
"My wife thanks you Miss Archer" Mr Martin looked at me "Go" he told his daughters.
"I'm sick" the elder girl moaned.
"Fresh air will be good for you" I smiled at her reaching out my hand to her.
"Father!"
"Go Lucy, leave your mother in peace" he began crossly, ending more kindly with a smile. I picked up Joane and taking Lucy by the hand I led them onto the deck and found many folk taking the air now the sea was calmer.

My father and brothers were standing at the side as we approached and I told him the news of Mistress Martin's delivery.

"My mother was on her hands and knees scrubbing the deck" I told him "She should rest, not be clearing up after others"

"Swefling your mother is a good soul. She wishes to help"

"She should not clean the deck from sickness of others"

"It's women's work"

"Father! Not my mother"

"I'll go find her"

"Make sure she rests" I said and saw a most peculiar expression on my father's face. I was not implying anything at all, but he was not to know that.

"What your mother and I do is our concern Swefling" he said quite firmly and quietly.

"I meant" I began to reply angrily "I'm sorry father" I softened immediately "my mother looked tired and feverish"

Father nodded

"I'll see to her. Be not concerned my dear" and he patted my arm as he left.

Lucy and Joane remained beside me throughout the day and I returned them only in the early evening after supper when Joane fell asleep in my arms. Mistress Martin was dozing when I arrived but woke briefly when her daughters lay down beside her.

"Do you need anything?" I asked as I found covers for them.

"Thank you Swefling, no" she said softly "except for my husband, where is he?"

"Would you like me to find him?"

"I would be much obliged" she smiled, but as I left, the

baby began to whimper and as I turned back to help, I saw her wipe a tear away and heard a despairing sob.
"I'll find your husband" I said and hurried onto the deck.

My parents were in a heated debate and I remained some distance away half listening and looking around for Mr Martin who I couldn't see at that time.

"I said no Ales" my father said "we will not relinquish our cabin, so hard won, to the woman. I have you, my dear heart and my own children to consider"
"But John, she is so poorly. We must help her"
"You devoted the night to her. What more can you do?"
"Let her have the cabin, sweetheart, for a night until she is recovered"
"And where will we rest?"
"Swefling will remain with Mistress Martin and the children. We shall be comfortable enough below decks"
It was at that moment they noticed I stood listening to them.
"All well Swefling?" my father asked.
"Mistress Martin requires her husband"
Father nodded.
"I believe he's on the deck yonder. Tell him, tell him to move his wife to our cabin"
"Father!"
"Thank you sweetheart" Mother smiled at him and squeezed his arm.

I left my parents smiling at each other and climbed the ladder to the higher deck and found Mr Martin staring out over our wake trailing far behind us. He glanced over at me as I approached.

"I shouldn't have brought my wife and daughters with

me" he said to my surprise.
"We're almost arrived my father says. It will be a great adventure" I smiled.
"My wife does not believe so" he said mournfully "where are my daughters?"
"I took them to your wife. She wishes for you at her side. My mother says your wife is to be moved to our cabin and we'll go below decks" I said attempting to show my disagreement.
"It's unnecessary"
"Mother insists" I replied "You're to take your wife and child"
"Thank you"
"What is wrong with your wife?" I asked then.
"She always cries in the first days. It's her way"
"Oh" I said "perhaps you'd best go to her"
I remained on the deck staring at the ocean as Mr Martin had, for some time as the darkness began to fall and turned when I heard footsteps approach and father joined me.
"All done" he said "you'll sleep in the cabin"
"I'd rather be with you and mother" I said.
"Mistress Martin will welcome your company Swefling"
"Yes father" I replied accepting the inevitability of the situation.

Saturday May 23 1616

Dawn was breaking when I felt a hand on my face and opened my eyes to peer straight into those of little Lucy Martin.

"My Mother is gone" she said.
"What do you mean gone?" I asked as I sat up, bumping my head on the ceiling of the small cabin bed.

"She went with the baby" I swung my feet to the floor and reached for my skirt pulling it on quickly and wrapped a shawl about my shoulders against the early morning chill.
"Get back to bed" I told Lucy "I will fetch your Mother"

The girl dutifully did as she was asked and I hurried outside not knowing quite where to go. I turned for the main deck expecting Rebecca had gone for fresh air from the oppression below deck. I recalled now, the long evening before as I'd lain in my bunk, my back to the room Mistress Martin cried bitterly. Her infant child and youngest daughter joined her and nothing Mr Martin could do or say could stop the sound. Mr Martin seemed uncertain how to console his wife and gave up the effort with words but I heard murmurings and a kiss now and then before thankfully I dropped off to sleep dreaming of a green land and blue skies.

The sun was rising above the distant horizon when I came onto the deck and looked around but could not see Mistress Martin. Perhaps she wasn't there after all, maybe she was below with her husband. One of the crew caught my attention and as I turned to where he pointed I saw on the upper deck Mistress Martin leaning over the rail.

"Find Mr Martin, please" I called to the sailor and clambered up the steps holding tightly to the strong ropes at each side and even as I arrived I watched unable to do a thing, the distressed woman climbed the rail and sit astride, her back to me still.
"Mistress" I whispered softly "Don't, please don't" she turned then and looked at me, such a sad expression on her face I'd never thought to see on anyone.
"I…. I must" she said "It's the only way"

"No, your daughters need you, your husband too"
"I make them sad"
"Please, it's not so. They care for you" As I pleaded with her I heard footsteps behind us. Mr Martin spoke to his wife, and I felt my mother's hand on my shoulder.
"Rebecca, come back" he pleaded her.
"Don't stop me Crispin. I thought you were a friend" she said to me "But you delayed me"

She turned and even before her husband could reach her she swung her other leg over the side, hesitatingly still, staring at the rolling ocean but with a sudden movement as Mr Martin leant out and caught her skirts, she slipped from the rail. Mother and I crossed just at the moment to see the fabric of her skirts torn asunder as the poor woman, clutching her infant child to her breast, fell from her husband's grasp into the deep waters of the ocean. I turned into my mother's arms, sobbing at the scene we had witnessed and she consoled me, speaking softly and calmly. I felt other hands about me as my father came upon us and took mother and I in his arms whispering words of comfort.

At length we drew apart and looked towards Mr Martin staring out over the ocean himself. My father went to him and reached a hand on his shoulder.

"I'll not follow her" he said a smile momentarily on his face "but with God's grace she will be at peace"
"We shall pray for her soul and that of your child" My father said "come away now"

Monday 31 May 1616

This last week, following Mistress Martin's death, has been most awful and a very subdued and melancholy mood came over our little vessel. It wasn't so much the death itself, tragic though it was, for death is a common occurrence that visits our lives frequently. In my own family we'd lost three infants before their first anniversary, but it was the unnecessary way Mistress Martin and her son departed. The girls spent much of their time in my company but Lucy was a most angry and bitter child blaming me for what occurred, reminding me I had told her I would bring her mother to her. Joane was less troubled although undoubtedly she missed her mother greatly. My own mother and the other women on board helped console the children though they spent their days with me. Their father they saw now and again, but he frequently declined their company.

My father spent much of each day with the new widower reminding him, I was certain, of the responsibility to his daughters and to our expedition. For although we were joining an already existing communitie Mr Martin's skills as a master carpenter was as much in need as father's, to the development of Jamestowne.

...

Great excitement fills our minds. The reason was occasioned two days since, a week to the day after the tragedy, by the lookout high on the mast. It was as the sun was setting that he called down to us that he could see land far into the distance. We gathered at the prow of our vessel and saw nothing except another glorious sunset reflected in the vastness of the ocean still before us. Even so a happier mood descended on our ship; a fiddler brought out his instrument and there were foot tapping rhythms, some singing and even dancing.

We were returned to our cabin and early yesterday morning I rose from our cramped bed and headed on deck as the sun rose over the ocean behind the Agnes Rose. I made my way once more to the prow and saw for the first time in my life the land of America. We were close, so close I believed I could soon reach out and touch the trees and shrubs at the waters edge. Beyond it though the land fell away and a wide expanse of water showed itself once more.

I watched as the light grew as we sailed beside the land on our left and saw the changing colours and forms as they took shape out of the darkness of the night. Birds flew up from the trees but everywhere there was silence, even the noise of our sails seemed reduced now. There was an ethereal feel to the new day as might have been experienced at the dawn of time. Pristine land, never before perhaps touched by human kind.

The sun rose higher in the sky and I moved to the side of our ship and clutched at the rail feeling excitement and awe as slowly and inexorably the day began to take shape over the virgin land and I tried to imagine the life that lived unmolested in the forests and clearings. But I realised, as I mused that this was not virgin land empty of human kind at all, for it had been peopled for 1000's of years by naturals, or natives perhaps they were named now. Even so it was unknown to those of us who came from across the ocean. And it was here, still some distance across the mighty bay we now entered and thence along the James River, we would make our homes and live and eventually die and hopefully leave our descendents with as best a start as we were able, in a new land.

"Are you well Miss Archer?" a voice suddenly brought me back to the present. I turned as Crispin Martin stood beside me.
"Oh, Yes" I sighed "thank you I am, Mr Martin. I was just marvelling at this beautiful land and thinking how very pleased I am to be here"
"You are not fearful of the dangers?"
"I don't believe so, my father will protect us and if I am fortunate I will find a good man for a husband and when it's my time to die I trust I will be ready, whenever it comes. No, I am not fearful. I am excited, anxious to step on the land of America where I will make my home"
"You are much a dreamer Miss Archer. It is a joy to behold. My Rebecca was no dreamer at all. She feared everything"
"Yet you brought her on this voyage"
"I have no defence. There is much to hope for, land and wealth and freedom we could never find in England, but she was fearful. Perhaps I was wrong, but my daughters at least will have a chance"
"I'm sorry for your loss all the same and your girls. Lucy misses her mother greatly"
He nodded, leaning on the rail beside me but didn't reply.
"Oh look" I said pointing into the distant shore at four legged shapes at the edge of the tree line.
"Deer by the looks of them" I was told "there will be plenty to feed us, we shall not starve. I'm sorry Rebecca didn't live to see this, but this is a good decision, the right decision"
I had to agree that perhaps he was right but I didn't say so and soon after I bid him a good day and returned to my family.

June 12 1616

We are arrived in Jamestowne and find a busy communitie of soldiers and craftsmen, several women and numerous children. There is a barrack building for the soldiers and single men, a church and about ten or so cottages in the oldest part of the village and several newer ones, some in the process of construction in the area beyond the original pallisaded settlement, all now surrounded by a high fence of various construction.

The Agnes Rose sailed to the jetty protruding out into the river, during the mid morning. We were all eager to disembark but arrangements had to be made and whilst father, John and Philip along with most of the men went about their business, we remained on the ship for several days, although we were allowed a brief excursion as I detailed above. Some changes in circumstances had prevailed since the outset of our intention to come, for the previous Master Craftsman of carpenters was deceased having ventured into the wilderness one afternoon and got into an altercation with some natives and been killed.

As my father and Mr Martin had their papers and my brothers were journeymen carpenters they were soon inundated with work but first my father declared their task was to complete accommodation for ourselves. In the meantime we repaired ourselves to a pair of quite poor dwellings near each other and the work on larger premises was commenced. Mother and I shared our chores, as was our wont in England and I cared for Lucy and Joane who much enjoyed being off the ship to run around with much freedom. When I wasn't with my mother I was also charged with keeping Mr Martin's cottage neat and tidy and undertaking his laundry and cooking, but as he and his daughters spent much time with our family there was little extra to be done.

My father, soon after our arrival acquired an acre of land beside the river and near to the settlement. It became our practice as the warm evenings of the summer came upon us, we gathered together in our field at the end of the day and spent the remaining hours of daylight clearing the land. As the sun fell behind the tall trees each evening, we would finally take our ease, drinking ale and chatting and laughing after the hard work of our labours.

Our lives followed a similar pattern for six days of the week until Sunday, when all labour ceased except for the women who produced the food for the communitie. After church and a long two hour sermon, it was a time of rest, of meeting with new found acquaintances and reading. I spent many afternoons writing my journal for I was too exhausted at the end of each day. On other occasions mother and I walked beside the riverbank searching for plants for the medications she could manufacture.

I was in an interesting situation for I was, it transpired, one of two single females in the communitie at that time, the other being a girl of a similar age to mine by the name of Amey Butler, and the two of us became most friendly. As a consequence of our circumstance we were forever confronted as we went about our business by any one of the numerous single men of a great variety of ages, physical appearance and circumstance. It became a great annoyance to me for whenever I ventured out alone there would be a least one male coming alongside wishing to converse, and some being overly familiar with words and hands. My father advised me on several occasions, he was spoken to with propositions of marriage for me. I am eternally thankful he declined on my behalf, for I had been brought up by my parents to believe I had as much a right to determine who I should wed as my spouse. As a result of this situation, though I was only able to run errands in the company of a member of my family. My brothers on occasions were not pleased to have their sister, with them even if there was only one other single female for them to impress.

One afternoon I walked with Mr Martin to the field, with his daughters when we were approached by several of the younger men intent on fun and mischief as they proceeded to tease and plague me.

"Let Miss Archer be" Mr Martin turned on them.
"She's no spoken for" one declared with more bravado than usual and I wondered if he had overindulged with the ale.
"'It's not your concern" Mr Martin declared.
"How are you to know?" he was asked.
"Because I say so. Now leave us be"
"Miss Archer will you be spoke for?" I was asked.
I looked at them and back to Mr Martin uncertain if I should speak.
"You heard Mr Martin" I said nervously.
"Let us pass" Mr Martin told them as the girls began to cry at the group of men and as if by magic they drew aside and let us on our way.
"Thank you" I said as we hurried to the field where the family were gathered. When I later related the incident to father he declared it was time to speak with the town council.

"This cannot be allowed to continue" he said as we sat with our ale as the sun went down. "I will insist they issue reprimands and if they are not able to resolve the matter to our satisfaction we shall leave the town and take our chances beyond the confines of Jamestowne"

"But where will we go John?" mother asked "there are grave dangers in the wilderness"

"I will not have my daughter molested. We came to America for a good new life and freedom for all of us"

I had never heard my father speak so vehemently and in my defence and I was most pleased and proud of him and I did something I have never done since I was an infant. I got to my feet and crossed to him and wrapped my arms about his neck and kissed his cheek.

"Thank you father" I smiled and sat down beside him and rested my hand on his knee, as he held my hand.

"You are my flesh and blood Swefling and until you wed I will protect you from any danger, from wherever it so comes"

Sunday September 12 1616

Life has been so busy in recent weeks, I have been too exhausted even on a Sunday to write in my journal until this day. In June two events occurred to take the interest of the single males away from Amey Butler and myself. The first occurred after father spoke as he promised to the council who duly issued an instruction and called all the young men together, for it was mostly them and gave a warning of most serious consequences should such harassment persist. I am pleased to report that I am no longer pestered by groups of young men, although more friendly and simple conversations have taken place, one in particular with Amey Butler's brother, Andrew who works in the carpentry shop. But I am in no hurry to form a lasting attachment with any member of the opposite gender just now.

The other event that occurred was the arrival of a vessel from England. The Patricia arrived full of settlers and thankfully, mother and I and the other women of our community saw to our satisfaction, numerous females, the majority of whom were single. However whilst many of them had arrived to become brides there were some who had no intention of becoming one man's wife but were willing to share their charms with those who would pay. I am in no position to judge another, but I do believe that to have the love of one man is preferable to the attention of many. I trust these women will not live to regret their decisions and way of life.

…

There is much activity within our communitie to gather the harvest as this month passes and the necessary requirement to preserve what meat the hunters return with, to ward off a winter famine. We are advised the cold, deep snow oft times remains throughout the dark days from November until March, without respite. Winters would appear to be far more severe than ever had been encountered in England, so with such information we make necessary preparations. Whilst all this activity takes our time, my father, brothers and Mr Martin continue their carpentry work, spending many hours on our own house before the cold sets in.

The frame of the two storey building we are to occupy was soon erected; two rooms down the stairs and two up. It will be spacious even for our growing numbers, for Mr Martin and his daughters have removed themselves already from their cottage and live with us to conserve supplies and effort and share the warmth. We are exceedingly overcrowded with eight of us in two rooms but we manage as we may. Whilst our carpenters, when they have completed the structure of our own property moved onto other tasks, those more able to build chimneys, wattle and daub the walls and thatch the roofs came and used their skills and gradually as the winter came upon us the house began to resemble a place we could live in.

October 1616

We have removed to our new house a week since and we are well settled. Mother and I spent much time marvelling at the smell of new wood and the fine craftsmanship of our own menfolk and those of our town. Soon our pots and pans and jars were tidied away on the shelves father put up and the basins and bowls and platters and spoons and knives in their places and we are well satisfied.

Father, my brothers and Mr Martin spend their evenings now the harvesting is completed and the nights soon dark, on making furniture for our use. We have a table and benches and a growing number of beds to sleep on, all made comfortable with the linens we brought from our house in Ipswyche and those in the chest grandmother deposited on us on the Agnes Rose. Mother and father settled themselves into the small room leading off the main room down the stairs, where we prepare the food and eat and sit in the evenings. Up the stairs in the two rooms above, my brothers and Mr Martin share one, and Lucy, Joane and I the other. I am delighted to have such a room even though I share with the young girls for I have a place to hang my Sunday dress and second shift. Very soon father made me a bed of my own and at night before I fall asleep and in the mornings when I wake, I love to spread my arms and legs out and feel the space that is all mine, that I do not have to share with anyone.

Often times at night I lie awake in the darkness, day dreaming well not so much dreaming because I am awake and not day for it is night time but I feel as happy as I have never been before, excited at the great adventure mother and father have brought us on. Sometimes I wonder what it would be like to be wed and to sleep with a man and do what I have heard and felt my parents doing onboard the Agnes Rose, and all other married people I expect. My thoughts at such time often drift to Andrew Butler and more frequently to Mr Martin, asleep I suppose on his mattress against the same wall as I lay. I reach out from under my quilt and touch the wall wondering if he may sense my thoughts but of course I will never know and perhaps it is best.

Outside of our house, father and Mr Martin and my brothers fixed up a small barn for the milk cow we acquired and the chicken coup. At the side there is a workshop and between the two and the house there is a covered area where our water barrel is stored and table and bench and an outside oven. Mother is determined that on fine days in the future we will launder our linens and bake outside in the fresh air and eat there too. And so in a very short time we have become very settled and organised, happy and surprising content.

December 31 1616

Christmas was an occasion when the entire communitie, now numbering over 800 souls I was told, came together for the church services giving thanks to our

Lord for his son's birth and for the provender of the new land, our safe keeping and good lives lived. The festivities were most enjoyable and many of the single men spent much of the twelve days in a state of intoxication. Those residents with family about us, celebrated together in our homes and on 12th night in one of the large barns in the new part of towne. The perfume of herbs and spices filled the air and hot punch and ale filled and warmed our bellies with the platters of food we brought with us and shared and there was music and Christmas singing and dancing.

I was taken to the floor many times by some of the young men of my earlier acquaintance and in particular with Andrew Butler, the one I'd spoken to alone earlier in the summer. I danced with my father and Mr Martin also but my brothers refrained to escort me. It was a wonderful evening and I do believe I have never enjoyed myself more. And as we walked to our home at the end of the evening snow began to fall about us and we arrived with red faces and rosy noses and ready for a hot wine punch. We sat in the parlour around the fire on the benches or the floor, and before we headed for our beds, father led us in a short prayer.

When he was done and we raised our heads and opened our eyes it was clear he wanted to speak further.

"I was greatly feared when we thought to come to America my dears" he smiled at us, his eyes shining brightly "but you came willingly and we've made a good start in this land. We have a fine house about us, a fire in the hearth, food in our bellies, all the work we could ever wish for and good friends and companions" he said to Mr Martin "we could wish for no more than a long and happy life in this place we now call home" And father raised his glass full of wine and called for us to join him in a toast for our own good fortune.

March 1 1617

Despair has haunted us over recent days. After a freezing winter full of snow as cold as we were told it would be, my darling mother was laid to rest just yesterday. My father is disconsolate and I have no notion how to help him for I am devastated myself at her passing. She was my closest friend, my confidant, my inspiration and she is gone from me, from us all, in the cruellest of ways.

As always as was her nature, Mother was giving aid to the sick in their time of need and visited a family in ill health and caught a fever from which she never recovered. It seemed no more than a common chill and she should easily have got well for she was in rude health, well fed and a healer but nothing she could tell me would help her and she died in father's arms yesterday in the morn at day break. I rose as always to make up the fire for the breakfast and heard a strange pitiful sound emitting from my parents room, not the usual noises I'd grown used to on the Agnes Rose when I shared their bed, but altogether a most mournful sound. I slowly opened the door to their room and found my father sitting on the bed in his nightshirt holding mother tightly to his chest, kissing her face and crying as he rocked backwards and forwards.

"Father, what is it?" I asked taking a step towards the bed. He shook his head unable to speak and I knelt on the bed beside him and reached a hand to mother, feeling no life in her at all.

"Oh father" I whispered, crying now and burying my head against them both "What will we do without mother?"

Sometime later the rest of the household came upon us, curious they hadn't been summoned from their beds for the start of the day. My brothers stood watching, concern on their faces but showing little emotion and of the two girl's, Lucy understood well enough but Joane not so. Only Mr Martin knew the trauma my father was going through for he had felt the sadness and despair so short a time before. It was he who arranged for a woman to lay mother out for her internment, for no one else was capable. I stood at the side of the room, not able to help but watching as mother was washed and clothed in fresh linen and her long dark curly hair brushed and tied back.

"Your mother was a beautiful woman" the woman told me when she was done. I knew she was trying to be kind but I didn't want to hear such words, I wanted my mother back and I remembered my flippant words on the Agnes Rose when Rebecca died and I retorted that all around us death was always with us. It helped me not one bit now for my mother was dead but the woman was talking still "she must have been very young when she birthed you"
"She was" I replied "eighteen years when I was born, I believe"
"And you the second one. Such a waste of a life"
"Have you nearly finished" I asked not too kindly I thought, even though I knew she had, but I wasn't particular how I appeared to others.
"Yes dearie, will you be alright on your own?"
"Yes" I said and added a thank you to my remark.
"I'll call later with food for the wake, your father will arrange the ale I suppose?"
"Would you speak with Mr Martin. I don't know what my

father has done"

...

We walked through the snow covered paths to the church, my arm through my father's, my brothers beside us, Mr Martin and his daughters a step behind. A sad little procession following my mother's body. As we passed the houses, many mourners came out and joined us. We entered the church for a long service which became so tedious I wanted to scream out for it to end, for my mother was dead and I wanted to go home. We shivered in the churchyard after, where the priest spoke more words of wisdom and read from the good book, and after we'd sprinkled earth on the coffin my mother was laid to rest in the cold snow covered ground. My father told us he wanted to remain at the graveside for a time and we left him with the vicar and returned to our house, which was now bursting with folk come to offer their respects with a glass of hot toddy and a piece of cake. They were gone and father was yet not returned.

Mr Martin was on the point of commencing a search for him, when father arrived, with the vicar, both very much the worse for alcohol. The churchman was able though, to explain they had shared a glass or two of a very special reserve of French brandy. My father was in a bad condition and I attempted to insist he lay down, to which comment he declared he was never going to sleep in his bed again without his wife.

I told him not to be so foolish and with the help of my brothers, we took him to his room as meekly as a lamb and even as they removed his boots and tucked him into his bed, he was fast asleep.

The vicar after finishing a glass or two of sack declared it was time for him to leave but it was clear he was in no fit state to be out on his own. My brothers saw this as their opportunity to leave the house for the evening and John suggested they escort the vicar to his residence. I wished them well not pleased I was to be left alone but sat at the table picking up a half full glass of wine that sat unfinished by my elbow.

Mr Martin spoke quietly to his daughters and helped them to their beds leaving me leaning heavily on the table all alone. I laid my head on my arms, crying again for my loss, for my father and the changes that had befallen our lives, but most of all I cried for my mother. I didn't hear Mr Martin return but felt him sit beside me and place a hand on my back.

"Miss Archer" he whispered "do not distress yourself so" and he drew me close to him, his arms about me as my sobs ceased. I felt calmer and comforted and I thanked him for his thoughts and kindness.
"It's a small recompense for your family's kindness to myself" he said "you should go to your bed, the pain won't be gone in the morning but it will be lessened"

We stood together and I laid my head against his chest, as I might my father, and felt his heart beating as he held me. I looked up at him through tear stained eyes as he bent and briefly kissed me.

"Sleep well Miss Archer" he whispered releasing me "I'll sit with your father"

I nodded and climbed the steps to my room and soon lay on my thick straw mattress. I pulled the quilt over me and to my surprise I began to feel quite sleepy and very soon I drifted off.

...

I woke ~~this morning~~ and lay in the early morning gloom feeling warm and comfortable in my bed, my mind going over the events of yesterday and I realised that Mr Martin was correct, I felt a little less pain than before, not much but different, perhaps it was because my mother had been laid to rest that the healing could begin.

I heard voices down the stairs, deep male voices not loud but the low murmur of conversation and was glad Mr Martin was with father. They are of a similar age I estimate, for my father is thirty six years and Mr Martin about thirty or so he told John and Philip, and they will be company for each other. Yes, I decided it would be good, both widowered within months, they would help and talk and comfort each other, in the way men do. My mind slowly then began to return to the end of last evening, when Mr Martin had comforted me and held me and kissed me. Just a whisper of a kiss it was. No more probably than a comforter's kiss, but I liked it well for I'd never been kissed by a man before, except by my father. And I didn't feel at all the same when he kissed me. What did it mean? I wondered.

I gave up on my thinking when my stomach began to gurgle and rumble and the thought of food encouraged me to rise from my warm cocoon for I'd eaten very little the previous two days. I dressed and brushed my hair and proceeded down stairs and found father and Mr Martin at the table, the fire burning brightly in the hearth and a pot of coffee already brewed.

"Father" I smiled as I kissed his cheek, pleased to see him out of his bed after his drinking "how do you feel?"
"I have a pain in my head" he smiled briefly back at me.
"I'll find mother's remedy" I said, suddenly mentioning her bringing everything flooding back into my mind. Father took my hand and squeezed it.
"Coffee and breakfast will be just right Swefling" he said "but I thank you all the same"

I realised breakfast would take longer than usual as on the last two days, whilst Mother began to cook I'd milk the cow and collect the eggs and now I'd have to do everything, but it was the way it was to be. I found my coat and socks and boots as the two men watched me, questioning my actions.

"The milk won't get into the jug on it's own, nor the eggs in the basket" I grinned and went outside closing the door after me.

...

The day passed in many ways far worse than the previous one for there were so many chores to be done and so much I didn't know how to do, for mother had not shown me just then, as she wasn't expecting to be leaving. For instance I knew she brewed the ale and made butter and cheese and baked bread and cakes, well I could cook of course but I was never certain when a task should be done. I worried constantly that day without her but at supper time the food was on the table and the cleared plates from the four males in the house gave me some reassurance that perhaps all was right in that area.

In the evening when the dishes were washed I joined the men of my family and sat on the floor beside the fire and began to fall asleep in the warmth and comfort of the room.

"Swefling" my brother John spoke, waking me suddenly "have you darned my hose, I can't find them"
"What hose?" I asked.
"Mother always did them immediately" he told me.
"I'm not your mother"
"Can't cook like her either" he said. At that remark tears began to come into my eyes and as I wiped them away father spoke up in my defence.
"Leave your sister be. She's had much to do today"
"So have I father" John replied "I worked all day too and I mean to go out"
"Well mend them yourself" I said feeling more confident now.
"It's woman's work"
"And so is taking a belt to your backside" I suggested.
"No it isn't foolish woman"
"Be quiet the two of you" Father told us "find other hose John, Swefling will do them when she has a moment"

March 20 1617

Our house has not been a happy place over the last few weeks. My brothers and I are constantly at odds with one another and Mr Martin's daughters crying at the upset. Only poor father who has lost his wife, and Mr Martin, seem able to carry on their lives, working hard, long hours, returning exhausted at the end of the day to supper and then turning out to the field as we all do, to prepare the soil for planting, with barely a complain.

But the situation with my elder brother and I is resolved the Sunday just gone. John complained over the lateness of our meal and then refused to eat it, telling us all it was unfit even for the swine in the forest. I looked at him in much anger and upset and found to my extreme annoyance tears began to trickle down my face. I calmed myself and placed my spoon on the table and rose from the bench.

"Sit down Swefling" father told me softly "eat your food. It's good enough for me"
"Thank you father" I said and nodded to him but fled the room and the house, hearing raised voices behind me. I ran a few steps, then walked more slowly and evenly and headed through the gateway and out towards the river, where mother and I liked to go.

I sat on a fallen log in the sunshine, and watched little wavelets form in the swell of the fast moving river, before me, heading forty miles or so to the ocean, but my thoughts for some time were blank. I made no effort to prevent the wind from the blustery breeze coming off the water, blow about my hair, which had escaped my cap, hoping the freshness would clear my muzzy head. I knew, when I began to appraise my situation I had no choice whatsoever in my circumstances. I could not escape, there was nowhere and no one to escape to and my father needed me to keep house. I had been thrown in this situation before my time, helping my mother was different. We'd shared the chores together, and when we had a dreary task to complete we would take a moment to smile or laugh to make the work seem pleasant. But she had been taken away from me and I was thrust into her role. It would never change for me now, for the rest of my life until I died, because when I wed I would change one household for another. I resented the fact my mother was dead. I was angry, very angry and wanted to hit out at the unfairness of it all and of being a female. Why me? I asked looking skywards as if the answer would come to me, why my mother?

My tears fell freely now and I thought about others who shared our house and resented exceedingly Mr Martin and his daughters. Why did I have to care for them as well. The girls always crying, and Lucy as awkward as the day is long, but I also remembered they too had lost their mother. We were not alone. Life is often very short and we accept it, or I believed it was so, it was just so difficult when it was my own mother.

I was busy wiping my eyes on my apron when I became aware I was no longer alone for sitting beside me was my brother John.

"What do you want now?" I asked harshly.
"Father said to come and find you" he told me, holding out my cloak, which I took gratefully for I was quite chilled. I caught his glance as I slipped it over my shoulders and pulled it close around me and saw as much sadness in his eyes as were in mine.
"It's so unfair" I said.
"I'm sorry" John said, an apology from him worth his weight in gold pieces.
"It's not what I mean" I said "mother shouldn't have died, I miss her so" I cried again.
"I know" John said reaching his arm around me and holding me against him "we all do" I heard him sniff and saw out of the corner of my eye his hand reach up and wipe away a tear and I felt comforted that someone else felt the same. I looked at him and through my tears I smiled.
"It's not only you who shed tears" he admitted.

"I'm sorry I argue" I said "and I can't cook and mend" John laughed softly.
"There's not a thing amiss with you're baking Swefling, just it's not mother doing it, but I'll be away soon, so you'll have one less to bother with"
"Oh don't you leave as well" I wailed.
"You'd stop me being wed would you?"
"You're to be wed? Who too?"
"I haven't asked yet, but I'm hopeful. The wheelwright's daughter Amey Butler"
I nodded.
"She's nice, I like her, but you don't have to leave"
"Swefling the house is overcrowded fit to burst with the Martins' there. Father will negotiate the cottage near the church for us, 'til we get established, if she'll have me, until I am of an age to apply for my land grant in a year"
"You'll be a farmer John?"
"I mean to try" he grinned "I'm glad we're here in this land, we could never have such opportunities in England and so much space for us all"
"You're a dreamer, just like me"
"Maybe, like father with such a dream to bring us here, but we're practical too, we won't starve. We'll make a good life and you'll be wed soon enough"
"Oh me. Who do I get to meet, I hardly get out of the house now"
"Well there's Amey's brother Andrew" he reminded me "and I've seen Crispin Martin look at you with affection ….. and some longing" he laughed "and a ready made family" he teased.
"Sometimes I wish those girls didn't live with us, well Lucy, she is so awkward and cantankerous"
"You mean you're not?"
"Don't start again" I said softly nudging him with my elbow. "I suppose I should return and apologise to father"

I said, as I rested my head on my brother's shoulder "I'm glad we had this talk"
"And now you'll darn my stockings!" he laughed as he stood holding a hand out to me.
"You'd best be wed very soon then I'll gladly give them to Amey, my wedding gift to her" and feeling much happier and somewhat relieved we headed back towards our home.

As we turned through the gateway of the old part of Jamestowne we came across the object of John's desire and her own brother Andrew, out for an afternoon stroll.

"Miss Amey" my brother grinned at the young lady, bowing formerly as I giggled at his antics "A pleasure it is to be sure to be seeing you"
"Thank you Mr Archer and yourself, and Miss Archer, Andrew and I are to take a stroll to gather flowers for the table, perhaps you would care to join us?"
"I'd be delighted" John said glancing briefly at me "but my sister has to return home"
"Perhaps I might escort you to your door, Miss Archer?" Andrew Butler enquired. I was pleased to agree and we changed partners and with a brief if somewhat stilted farewell we headed in opposite directions.

When we reached the house, I was not then inclined to go inside and end my liaison with Mr Butler and sat on the bench at the side, in the sunshine.
"You may join me if you wish" I smiled at him, looking uncertain whether to go or stay, but he sat and we began chatting, at first of our brother and sister and then on other matters until we were disturbed by Lucy and Joane running out of the house, presumably on hearing our voices.

"I'll be leaving Miss Archer" Andrew said, rising "thank you for your company and conversation"

"And yours Mr Butler" I smiled and watched him for a short time as he walked away. He turned once and waved and I returned the gesture before turning my attention to Lucy and Joane.

We wandered into the house and found father and Mr Martin sitting comfortably at the table, one reading a newssheet, the other a book. They looked up when we entered .

"All well Swefling?" father asked a smile on his face.

"Yes thank you father, all well"

"And who were you conversing with outside?"

"Just Andrew Butler"

"Just Andrew Butler eh?" father teased a smile on his face.

"I cannot stand here and gossip with you father" I smiled "I have dishes to do" I giggled, happier than I'd been for many a week.

June 3 1617

Life is very strange isn't it? There I was at the end of March in the first bloom of being courted by a young and very personable man and now I am to be wed to another. Am I a fickle female? Perhaps I am, but life's twists and turns never let us know where they will lead us.

A number of weeks since, on my birthday May 14 when I turned seventeen, I was alone in the house kneading dough for bread, it being a rainy, blustery day outside and not conducive to working in the covered area as mother and I liked to do. All the men were at their work and for once Lucy and Joane were visiting with the vicar's wife, who told me I was looking very peaky and needed time away from the girls. I was deep in my thoughts and it was thus a few moments before I became aware I was no longer alone and Crispin Martin had returned to the house and was standing at the door watching me.

"Why are you here? Has anything happened to father?" I asked startled to see him.
"Your father is well when I left him. I have words I wish to speak with you" he said drawing closer to me "Miss Archer, I've a mind to take a wife"
"Oh, will you be removing yourself and the girls?" I asked supposing that being the reason for our conversation.
"No" he replied slowly "Miss Archer, I thought to ask you to be my wife?"
"Me? Why?"
"Why?" he asked surprised "you care for my daughters and …… and I believe I love you"
"Love me?" I asked a giggle escaping as I felt suddenly hot with a flush "lust you mean" I suddenly realised how brazen I sounded. "Oh!" I looked at him but for some reason resumed my earlier thought "It's lust Mr Martin"
"I cannot deny I have known a willing woman, and today is the anniversary of Rebecca's death. A year is a long time to be without, so perhaps some lust will be in my mind"
I laughed embarrassed as he moved a step closer towards me.
"You don't need to wed me to satisfy your lust Mr Martin, I mean you could seek one of the women at the tavern or the barracks, they would surely satisfy your needs"
"No doubt they would but you will have seen my eyes on you"

I stared at Mr Martin not so much confused for I knew clearly to what he was referring but uncertain if I should make reference. Despite my turmoil I did.

"Yes I've oft times seen the way you look at me when no one else is about. I believe on occasions you forget who I am"
"I don't believe I forget Miss Archer" he smiled at my effrontery "But I see I am undone"
"I trust not Sir" I giggled glancing at his breeches "perhaps more discovered"
"You have a fine way with words. So what will be your answer?"
"You'll not consider the fine ladies of the towne?"
"I wish for more than a quick coupling with a stranger and the sharing of a bed. I believe it would be most enjoyable if you were to agree to be my wife"
"I am but seventeen years this day Mr Martin. I am unfamiliar with the world of men and their desires"
"You mean you would consider my offer?" he asked standing very close me as I made a feeble attempt to continue working the dough. "I could show you Swefling" he said using my given name for the first time. I felt his hand hesitantly on my waist, as he leant towards me and kissed my neck. "You could decide afterwards to accept or not" I felt his hand on my arse caressing me as I stood stock still, and I couldn't deny I enjoyed his attentions. I felt his mouth on my neck and I turned my head slowly and he kissed me on my lips. "Would you care for me to show you?" he asked again, a hand at my breasts caressing them as he continued to murmur and kiss me.
"What if I decline afterwards, I'll not be a maid or if I get with child"
"It is my intention to persuade you to my way of thinking Swefling" I nodded and Mr Martin continued his business.

My hair became lose and my cap fell into the flour and I laid my hands flat on the table to steady myself, desperate for him to continue.

"I'll not hurt you" he whispered. But he did. He stopped as I cried but the pain was passed and to my surprise I began to feel a wonderous sensation come over me as he moved, so much so I gasped with delight and moved with him.

I cannot recount further our coupling for decency sake but soon other feelings overcame us and Mr Martin cried out and all but collapsed on me, murmuring my name over and over. I opened my eyes, and saw just my hands imbedded in the dough on the flour board. I sighed deeply and smiled and looked at him steadily as he repaired his apparel.

"Will you be my wife?" he whispered standing exceedingly close once more but not touching me at all.
"I have a question" I said softly but feeling strangely powerful by the experience of being taken in such a fashion and more particularly because I had enjoyed it.
He nodded looking at me uncertain of my feelings.
"Ask" he suggested.
"If we are wed would you sometimes have me in your bed?"
He looked at me in complete and utter surprise, then laughed, a happy joyful laugh and his face lit up in a broad smile.
"Wherever you wish, sweet Swefling and most often" he told me.
"Then I'll be your wife" I said finally removing my hands imbedded in the dough and wiping them carefully on my apron.

"Perhaps I might kiss you" he said becoming emboldened himself and placing a hand on my shoulder.
"I think that would be perfectly in order Mr Martin"

And he did.

June 8 1617

"Mr Martin has asked for your hand" father told me a number of days later.
"Yes father, he said he would" I replied looking up from my scrubbing the cuffs of his shirt.
"Do you care for him?"
"I believe so, he has a nice look about him" I replied wondering if I was being given a choice.
"It's a beginning" father smiled "he cares for you"
I looked at my father steadily, then lowered my gaze to his shirt in my hands.
"He lusts after me" I said very quietly.
"I considered 'twas so, but mayhap he has other feelings also. Has he made advances to you? You are at liberty to decline. Do you remain a maid?"

I looked at my father again not certain how I should answer but I, like my brothers had always been reared to be honest and truthful.

"He has made advances and I'm no longer a maid"
"Ye'd best be wed if it be your wish" He replied with no malice or disappointment in his voice for it was the way of the world.
"Father, may I ask a question?"
"I'll answer if I am able" he replied leaning on his work bench, stopping the turning of a piece of wood.
"Did you love my mother?"

"Love her?" he asked seeming surprised at my words. "She was my beloved wife and I miss her. She gave up her life of riches to be at my side and I lusted after her and we were sixteen years" he laughed.

"Will you wed again?" I asked smiling now.

He shook his head and I thought I saw a tear in his eyes.

"One wife in a life is sufficient for me" he said evenly.

"Then I think you loved her but whether Mr Martin and I feel that way I do not know"

"You'll be a loyal wife to him Swefling I know that. You're mother taught you well and perhaps in time such feelings will arrive for you"

"Thank you father" I smiled and reached out a wet soapy hand to his. He clasped it in his own and we smiled at each other.

"You're a distraction with your questions" he smiled kindly at me "I'll never get this wood turned by Christmas at this rate"

"Yes father" I grinned at him fully aware as he was, it was his questions that had taken us away from our chores.

July 1 1617

My brother John and I were wed on the same day, June 29 and as fine a summers' day as anyone could wish for. There was much celebrating and feasting provided for by the Butler family and ourselves on the open area in the old village and in the evening there was dancing and much drinking before folk wearily made their way to their homes.

John and Amey removed themselves to the cottage father and Mr Butler acquired for them, only a step away from the celebrations whilst Mr Martin, Crispin I mean, though it sounds peculiar to me even now to write his name, and I processed with Papa and the girls to our house. My brother Philip being somewhere with Andrew Butler and would no doubt return later with a sore head.

There had been some reorganising at the house as well, for father decided he would remove himself up the stairs to the bed Crispin had used and Crispin and I would use father and mother's room, which seemed entirely satisfactory. I took Lucy and Joane to their beds as I did most nights and for not the first time there was much reluctance on their part but in time Joane gave me her customary hug, while as always her sister declared I was not her mother and she would not hug me, ever. I smiled at her with no interest in arguing on this occasion and returned down the stairs to find my new husband and my father on the back porch enjoying a quiet smoke they'd taken up since our arrival and watching the smoke curl away into the night. I stood in the doorway observing the two men and smiling to myself as tiredness surprisingly drifted over me.

"We were just remarking" father said when he noticed my presence "perhaps we should find a woman to help with the chores. You'll have less to be doing with John away with his wife, but even so"
I looked from one to the other and stood between them.
"Thank you I'd welcome the help. I'd like to get a garden planted"
"What fripperies are you planning?" father asked a grin on his face.
"No fripperies" I laughed "I mean to grow herbs and plants for medication that mother told me of. One of the books grandmother Eleanor placed in the trunk was full of receipts"
"Well if you're to cure us from ills and sickness then

certainly"
"And fruit, like an orchard. Blueberries, loganberries and raspberries grow wild but it would be easier if we had them on our land"
Father nodded
"And have you discussed this plan with your husband?" father continued.
"No, I ...." I stuttered a reply "I just assumed"
But I saw them both smiling and realised I was being teased.
"Well if you're going to amuse yourselves at my expense I'll go to my bed" and as I spoke I found myself growing appreciably warm with embarrassment and deliberately refrained from glancing at my husband.

Father reached for my hand as I turned to leave and smiled up at me.
"I'm pleased for you to be wed Swefling. Mother would feel likewise. Proud of you too"
"Thank you father" I whispered and bent to kiss him on his cheek "good night"

I closed the door to the bedroom and leant against it excited at the prospect of my first night as a married woman but also exceedingly nervous. I had no reason to be for I knew Crispin was a good man and we had already encountered one another but even so this was different.

I removed my clothes and found the fresh shift I'd kept especially for this night and slipped it over my head and brushed my hair. I lay in the bed wondering if Crispin would keep me waiting long but enjoying for the moment the freedom and space of being alone. As I revelled in my mood I heard the door open and close and saw Crispin standing by the door.

"Why are you in the dark?" he asked "I can't see you" and he found the tinderbox and lit the candle before I could answer. "You looked most enchanting and beautiful today" he said "I thought how fortunate I am you agreed to be my wife"

As he spoke he began to remove his clothes with no sign whatsoever of wariness at all.

"Thank you for saying so" I replied softly.

"Are you alright Swefling, you sound quite different" he turned as he spoke and I saw his naked body for the first time and in the candlelight it shone and glistened like smooth marble, "are you nervous?" he asked, pulling the sheet back and sitting down on the mattress looking at me.

"I am a little" I confessed.

"You don't have to be. You weren't before" he grinned "do you want to go to the parlour and make bread again" he laughed trying to ease me. He took my hand in his.

"No" I smiled at the thought "I'll stay here"

"Well you did ask to have a bed and here we are. Would you like to remove your shift?"

"Do I have to?"

"No, but you might like to, shall I help?" he offered.

"I can manage" I said.

"I know you can, but I'd like to do it" he said "come here" and he tugged my hand and I slipped across the bed and knelt on the edge beside him. "Come stand before me Swefling so I may see you" he whispered as he also stood and as his arms slipped around me he lowered his head and kissed me in such a different way from before that I felt quite breathless when his lips left mine.

"I think I do love you" he said "I know I have a great feeling for you and I'll be a good and dutiful husband and never do you harm"

"Thank you" I said "I like the way you kissed me then" I replied not knowing my own feelings or daring to speak of them.

"It pleases me to hear you say, let me take your shift away now" he whispered and easily pulled it over my head and threw it across the room. He took hold of my hands as he looked at me and smiled before pulling me into his arms once more, our naked skin touching in so many places. He felt warm and his skin soft and I placed my hands around his back as he moaned and rested his head in the crook of my neck holding me tightly.

"Can you feel me Swef?" he whispered hoarsely "tell me what you feel"

"You are hard, but your skin is soft, like silk. It's nice"

"Shall we lie on our bed?"

"Oh Swefling" he sighed "What a beauty you are" he said as his hand found it's way over my person and I moved with pleasure of my husband.

"That's my girl" he whispered.

"Cris" I whispered wanting more and trying to convey so.

"Open your eyes" he whispered breathlessly and as I looked at the expression on his face I knew I was giving as much as he and I felt totally overwhelmed.

On and on we continued on our journey. For me it was a journey of discovery and I wanted it to continue forever but it was over and gasping for breath, kissing and smiling at the same time, we slowly came back to earth.

"I never knew" I breathed eventually "there could be so much, so great excitement in the world between a man and a woman" I smiled wanting to run outside and proclaim my discovery to all.

"Are you saying you enjoyed our union?" he asked delighted I thought but there was some surprise in his

voice.
"Yes. "I sighed "Was I alright? I mean…" I asked suddenly nervous once more.
"Ssshhh" he whispered lying still "you are wonderful. I've never had so much joy. We shall be very good, we're good now and we've only just begun Swefling"
"Will you do this often?"
"We'll do this often. Together" he sighed slowly as he lay on his back beside me.
"Are you alright?"
"Oh Sweffie, I could conquer the world with you beside me" he grinned.
"Such a powerful thing isn't it?" I laughed, wanting him again but he turned towards me and pulled me into his embrace.
"Ssssh now, and sleep a while" and I did his bidding and closed my eyes sighing as I held tightly to him.

July 31 1617

Several weeks have passed and I have felt such a growing love for this man whose bed I share, love that he could bring such feelings to me and I am able to return so completely, but love for him as a man as well, in ways I'd not noticed before. He is kind and amusing and makes us laugh many times at the table over our meal. He is a good friend to my father and brother and works hard every day with them and our house is full of love and joy.

The only cloud on our happy, busy lives is Lucy for she remains a difficult child even to her father but especially to me. I feel for her for she has suffered much in the four years of her life and now she believes I am taking her father away from her. This is not so and we are forced to ignore her tantrums when we are able and get on with our lives, for they are most hurtful and destructive.

As father suggested we found a suitable woman to help with the chores and thankfully young Lucy and her get on quite well. Mary Waters arrived on a ship with her husband at the end of last year but he died during the winter and she has since been employed in another household before she came to us. It was a most unsatisfactory placement she told me for the father and two adult sons were constantly at her person, but with us she is settled and has become a good friend to us all.

There has been a tremendous debate in town about the planting of tobacco for there is a great demand for it in Europe, in the smoking of pipes and by other means, for recreation. Father looked at the possibility of growing the plant ourselves, but reasoned that with the limited time available each day, once the carpentry work was finished there would be insufficient hours remaining to work the land for growing tobacco to sell. We were hard pushed to work in our field to grow crops for our food and to care for the animals without growing tobacco, which apparently requires much labour and attention despite the financial recompense.

"But perhaps one day we shall get our land and think differently" Cris said to me one Sunday afternoon a few days ago when we returned towards the house after we checked our acre of land and found the maize nearly ready to harvest.
"I thought you liked the carpentry?" I asked surprised at his words.
"I do, but if land is available we ought not let it pass us by"
"But what will we grow, we have all we need with father's acre?"

"But it's your father's Swef not ours. Don't you want to own land. It's what we came to American for"

I grinned at him then.

"I've got all I came to America for"

"What's that?" he asked clearly not aware I was teasing him.

"A husband, good weather, a fine house and plenty of food"

"I see, I hope in that order"

"Of course, though it's a difficult choice between a husband and food" I giggled.

"I will have to remind you again of the benefits of a husband" he laughed.

"Not in the middle of the day in the field, everyone will be searching for us"

"That's why we need some land so we may hide from prying folk" he grinned taking my arm in his "but for the time being we'll have to make do with your father's acre"

"You know the tobacco people are saying they need lots of workers, if that is so more and more will arrive and Jamestowne and the colonie of Virginia will just grow and grow"

"It's called progress Swefling, everything changes in time"

"I don't like change, there's always conflict when there's change and people disagreeing"

"Oh dear, you are finding difficulties but I can change that. Come along wife" We were close to the house and were pleased to have it to ourselves, for once inside he dragged me into our room and firmly closed the door after us.

"Sunday afternoon alone with my wife" he smiled taking me in his arms "What an heaven sent opportunity not to be missed"

"Opportunity for what" I giggled as my petticoats suddenly found their way to the floor "Oh dear how did that happen?"

"Very careless" Cris laughed as the same thing happened to his breeches. He walked backwards dragging me with him to the bed and fell down pulling me on top of him holding me firmly against him.

"This is a very interesting position" I giggled "I wonder what we should do?"

"I'll leave it to you Swef I'm suddenly tired"

"Not you" I laughed as I kissed him.

"In the sermon this morning" I giggled. "Reverend Whickham preached against fornicating on the Lords Day"

"I'm not fornicating" he said, "I don't know what you're doing"

"I'm doing nothing but lying here" I giggled but even as I said the words I moved.

"Swefling" he gasped, a huge grin on his face "What are you doing?"

"I'm not sure but it feels very good" I sighed feeling waves of joy through my body until I thought I could not go on.

"Don't stop Swef, please don't, not yet" he cried and I looked down at him as he lay on the bed his arms outstretched, his eyes closed and a smile on his face.

"I'm dead and gone to heaven for my sins" he said suddenly, opening his sparkling eyes.

August 19 1617

The weather has been dreadful over the last few weeks, wind and torrential rain, flattening the corn and making the ground of our acre a quagmire, so we are unable to even begin the harvest.

"If we don't see the sun before long" father said mournfully as he stared out from our awning between the house and the workshop, watching the latest downpour, "we shall go hungry this winter"

"Oh surely not father" I said, "there'll be hunting and fishing parties going out"

"Well that's as maybe but with seven hungry mouths in the house to feed, we'll have to be careful"

"It's not like you to be so low" I said, slipping my arm through his "and there's plenty of time for the weather to improve"

Father turned to me and smiled.

"You're probably right Swefling" he grinned briefly "I'm just feeling a little melancholy this day"

"But you're bound to be father, it's only months since Mother's passing. You'll get days like this"

"You're a thoughtful girl Swefling. A girl no longer but a married woman now, are you happy with you're husband?"

I smiled broadly.

"Oh father, you know it to be so. He's a good man and I love him well"

"I am pleased for you" he said patting my hand "and you make us all contented, you're a good girl. We'll be fine in the winter, don't you listen to me" and he wandered off in the workshop where I heard him talking in low tones to Crispin as he took up his work once more.

September 15 1617

The weather has improved of late, and we've had two glorious weeks of sunshine and whilst much of the corn and maize was ruined, we have harvested what we were able and sent it to the miller to be ground into flour. It is an arduous task I believe without the aid of a windmill or watermill but the miller at least will not go hungry in the winter for most folk paid in kind.

We harvested the root vegetable we had become acquainted with since our arrival and found the potato versatile and filling, we have onions and beans as well, added to our larder, so perhaps we won't starve in the months ahead after all. Following the arrival of the more clement weather Mary and I take Lucy and Joane with us to the edge of the forest collecting berries and nuts that grow in wild abandon and profusion, but our excursions meet with disapproval.

"I don't care for you being out in the wilderness alone and unprotected" Crispin told us one day when we returned with our baskets brimming with blackberries, blueberries, huckleberries, passion fruit and plums ready to be preserved or made into pies and jams.

"We're safe enough I'm sure, there's always folk about" I said, "everyone is gathering for the winter"
"We can't survive on fruit alone" he said.
"If there's nothing else, preserved fruit sitting on the table will be all that will keep us from starving" I replied a little testily now "why are you so ungrateful?"
"I'm not. It's a man's work to provide the food for his family" Crispin told me, as he sat at the table. I gave him what he often described as my old fashioned look and crossed the room and stood behind him resting my arms on his shoulders and kissing his ear.
"You're always telling us this is a new land and new beginnings for us all and so it is. Women are allowed to help now"
"Who says?" he asked, a smile forming on his face.
"Why Swefling Martin of course" I giggled, "It will be set in the Charter of the Assembly whenever, if ever, it comes into existence"

"I see" he said slowly taking my hand and leading me round to sit on his lap "and I suppose you intend to sit with the assembly?"
"Oh no! I shall be too busy cooking and cleaning and washing and gathering food and having babies"
"I see" he said again picking up only on my last comment "having babies is it now?"
"Only one at a time" I giggled.
"And when do you propose to begin this new occupation?"
"Possibly next April time" I grinned at him. Crispin looked at me steadily staring into my eyes. "I think so" I whispered. Crispin's smile widened, as he pulled me closer to him and kissed me.
"You'd best not be man handling my daughter like that in public" father laughed as he came into the room.
"Oh I had to, she tells me she's with child"
"Swefling is this so?" father asked sounding quite delighted.
"I believe so father, next year in the spring."
"What good news this is" he said patting us both on our heads.
"I don't want a brother or a sister" we heard a voice call out from the bottom of the stairs. We turned and saw Lucy sitting there with Joane watching us.
"Why ever not?" Crispin asked holding a hand out to her, which she patently ignored while Joane scrambled over and climbed up onto our laps.
"My mother is your wife not her"
"Lucy, we've been over this before. Stop. I'll not tell you a further time"
"I don't care I don't want one" and with that Crispin's eldest child stomped up the stairs.
"I do" Joane said "a baby for us"
"Indeed yes" Crispin smiled at her taking his glance from the disappearing Lucy to his younger daughter "and we

must be very good for your step mother and help her"
"Yes father and you likewise"
"Of course me" and we returned to the happy thoughts of our new arrival and were able for a time to put Lucy's words out of our minds.

...

As September wound to an end Mary and I continued to venture out collecting various plants and nuts to store away and our larder was becoming quite full, which was very reassuring after the poor summer and our earlier expectations of food shortages.

"I heard the Indians grind nuts to make flour" Mary said to me one afternoon when she, Joane and I walked out of the towne walls into the forest "and use something called chicory to make a coffee drink"
"Do you know what the plants look like?"
"I believed so"
"Perhaps we could locate some chicory and mix it with the coffee. It would last us until the supply ships arrive in the spring. I know Crispin and father are concerned but there is so much food growing wild, we just have to learn and understand and we need never grow hungry"
"We need a way to preserve the harvests though, unless they go hunting for meat every week, it wouldn't last"
"But we have snow and ice. We keep some things in the cold larder why couldn't we store meat in the snow?"
"How do you mean?"
"Well we could get Cris and father to dig a hole and pack it with snow and stuff cuts of meat in there"
"I never thought of that. Or they could build a box. If it's locked the animals won't get inside either"
"And we have salt" I reminded her "the Indians must do something to preserve flesh, they surely they don't go

hunting every day?"
"We have much to learn from them" she said suddenly showing a surprising observation.
"I can't understand why no one else sees it" I said.
"Because they're men and they have to control everything. They don't see the Indians as having thoughts and ideas and they think they know best about everything"
"But we know what rubbish that is Mary, my little finger has more sensible ideas than some men I could think of" I giggled.

March 1618

Despite our best endeavours there are food shortages in Jamestowne as the long bad winter continues and many of our neighbours who unfortunately were not as prepared as we, ran out of staples before Christmas. It was not in our nature to see folk starve and so we offered help where we were able, to our own detriment as it transpired. Word began to circulate that we had food stored in an icebox and despite our most careful precautions one morning we rose to find it had been ransacked and the entire contents gone.

"Oh how can folk do this to us?" I wailed, more tearful than I would have expected to be but I was after all in the sixth month of my pregnancy and was often visited with melancholy and disturbed at the changes to my body as my belly grew large and ungainly and certainly cumbersome.
"Folk only think of themselves" father told me, "but worry not Swefling we'll go hunting on the morrow and see what we may find. We have a duck hanging in the workshop that was missed by the thieves. It will go into the cook pot and feed us and winter will soon be done

with"

"We've come to no harm Swef" Crispin consoled me "but we'll be on our guard in future and consider a more secure place for the icebox another year"

I had to be reassured with their comments but I must confess I was highly suspicious of almost everyone and for a week or two I was very reluctant to share any of our limited provender with anyone who wasn't family and that was exceedingly difficult, for it went completely against my nature. But I resolved my difficulties in church the following Sunday and silently begged forgiveness for my uncharitable thoughts and was much relieved as the weather began to take a turn for the better.

April 1618

Slowly the cold dull days of winter have passed and new life comes over the land. The trees begin to bud and there is a hue of green about them, shoots begin to appear in the dark earth once the snows disappear and the bright flowers of spring are everywhere on the still virgin part of our acre and in any corner of ground by the houses and in the forest, all is in bloom. Familiar plants from home abound; the lily of the valley and the daffodil and rhododendron, magnolia and sweet yellow jasmine all make the spring a colourful and welcome experience.

Mary and I have begun to take ourselves off for a short stroll most afternoons usually with just Joane for we can rarely prise Lucy away from the house. It is as if she has a fear of finding her father gone if she is out and often trails around close on his heels, much to his growing impatience, but she is very much afeared I repeatedly try to tell him.

Mary, Joane and I on the other hand enjoy the outdoors and often return with flowers for the table, much to the amusement of Cris and father, and we have begun to dig up fresh growing plants and their roots to put in our own plot at the back of the house, so in future we will be able to grow our own herbs and food.

But life is hard and the days long for us all. Crispin, father, John and Philip in the carpentry workshop, labour day after day or out in the town building frames for new houses or any task that requires their skills, which leave Mary and I to maintain the household, care for our live stock, the cows, sheep, swine and chickens mostly, we milk the cows, collect the eggs and churn the butter. We gather the wool from the sheep and Mary combs, spools, spins, weaves and bleaches the cloth for clothing. We hem sheets, piece quilts, make candles and soap, and chop wood. Well Mary chops just now, but we share the tasks between us and of an evening when our men head for the acre, we go with them taking sewing or just sitting for a time watching or helping where we are able.

It is a hectic round of chores and tasks essential to our survival and although I am often tired these days, I wouldn't exchange my life for anything else. Nor, I must add, could I have survived without Mary, who in such a short time has become very dear to me and I begin, almost, to see her as my mother and I am pleased to feel that way.

April 30 1618

I am exhausted but deliriously happy for this morning as the sun rose across the land, my son, my first born child arrived. Mary said I was excellent but I cried and complained over the hours and hours before the birth and although she smiled and said it would be easier the next time, I vowed there and then I would never have another child.

Of course I haven't told Cris this and now, since I have held the tiny infant in my arms, perhaps I will change my mind but not today. When my son was moments old and I was comfortable in the bed and he had been fed and slept soundly in his cradle following his hard work in getting here, our peace and quiet was invaded by the three large men of our family. His father, grandfather and uncle all exceedingly anxious to greet the new addition to our household were not the least concerned, how far from birthing convention we had all strayed in our new lives. For I knew even for my own parents, when my brothers and I were born, mother was isolated with only the company of other women for upwards of a month. She, like all women in England, and many perhaps here in Virginia were not even permitted to attend the baptism of their infants but I would have none of it.

"He's tiny" Philip my brother stared at his nephew, inspecting the baby most carefully from all sides and angles.
"He seemed like a giant to me" I sighed grinning at them all "You may hold him if you wish"
"No! No! Not just now" my brother backed away, before the child was forced upon him, but Cris and father had surprisingly no such qualms and although they were nervous, having held tiny babies in their arms before, did so willingly. While they were sharing the pleasure between them Joane slipped into the room and climbed onto the bed beside me and snuggled into my arm.

"Mother Swefling" she whispered very softly "Do you love me still, and Lucy too?" she asked her big brown eyes staring up at me.
"Of course I do, you're my girls" and I drew her closer still "where's Lucy, is she coming to meet her brother?"
"She doesn't care for babies she says"
"Well perhaps when he's older then" I smiled "would you like to see him, your brother?"
"Oh yes" she giggled and Cris bought him round to her and crouched down whereupon she leant forward and kissed her brother on his head, as if she was kissing a snake.
"He won't bite you" Cris told his daughter, but she wasn't to be persuaded otherwise just then.

Much later after I'd been left alone for a time and had a sleep, Mary peeped her head around the door and stepped into the room leading a somewhat reluctant Lucy by her hand.

"Lucy" I smiled "you've come to see your brother, he will be pleased"
"He won't know" she said looking at him intently. "He looks like father, not you"
"Of course he does. What have you been doing today?" I asked trying to get her to talk.
"Nothing"
"Lucy" Mary spoke to her "we did, we went for a walk this morning and you collected something, tell mother Swefling what it was"
"I picked some flowers, Mary made me, but I knew you wouldn't want them, so I threw them in the necessary"
"Oh Lucy, I love flowers, thank you for the thought"
"May I leave now?" she asked edging towards the door.
"Of course, thank you for coming to see us"

"I came to see him" she said looking at her brother again. "Well thank you all the same"

October 15 1618

I woke with a suddenness that scared me to the core this morning, which was most unusual for I had never previously been a nervous individual, but there were so many reports of incidents involving the natives that I expected their presence at any moment. Cris and father's concern at our venturing out gathering wild berries and nuts had much to answer for. However, on this occasion I realised it was unlikely to be Indians and even as I reached a hand out to Cris, found him already rising from the bed.

"What is it?" I asked looking around as if the answer was in the room.
"I don't know" he said "stay here" he told me as I began to climb from the bed myself. I was stopped in my tracks as it were, with one foot on the floor when the noise that woke me came again. It was a thundering roar that seemed to shake the entire house and everything around. "Oh God save us" I whispered, as all around us I heard the voices of folk outside in a state of panic and concern, much as there was now within our house.

Cris pulled his breeches on as several smaller, but similar booms filled our ears and he opened the door to leave.

"Be careful" I urged him as he closed it after him and I heard his voice and that of my father.

I crossed the room to my son who slept peacefully

on, undisturbed by the commotion and reassured I pulled a skirt over my shift and padded barefoot from the bedroom into the parlour and found Cris, father and Philip at the back door looking towards the old towne where a pall of thick black smoke drifted skywards, intermingled with the orange and red glow of flames.

"What is it?" I asked as I joined them.
"I'll go and see" Philip offered, being young and interested in any excitement.
"I'll join you" Cris said, turning back to me standing in the kitchen with Joane and Lucy, who had clambered down the stairs with Mary.
"Don't leave me father" Lucy began to wail.
"I have to Lucy" he said ruffling her hair, "you'll be safe with Mother Swefling, and grandfather and Mary"

Cris patted my arm as he passed by into our room and emerged soon after fully clothed and after giving me a brief kiss, left the house with Philip, joining many of the menfolk of the neighbourhood.

"What is it father?" I asked as I joined him and Mary outside as the early sun shone down on us.
"Some big commotion near to the barracks I suspect" he said.
"But what could have caused such a sound?" Mary asked.
"Perhaps the gunpowder store in the arsenal within the barracks" father told us.
"Oh no! How could anything have caused such a difficulty? Perhaps the Indians natives came after all" I said.
"Cris and Philip will investigate and tell us" father told us and as we stood and watched the sky to our left become obscured by the smoke, I heard a crying inside the house and wandered away to greet my son, calling me to his

side for his breakfast.

...

We waited throughout the morning for Cris and Philip to return and thought at one stage to wander to the old towne and see for ourselves the cause of the troubles, but father firmly forbade it.

"We all have chores to occupy us" he said and walked away to the workshop. Mary and I grinned at each other, shrugged our shoulders and did as we were told, looking up from our cleaning every so often though to see if the smoke and flames had reduced, which except for a thin wispy trail of smoke, now thankfully drifting away from the towne, it had, but more importantly looking for Cris and Philip to return. we were

Eventually as the midday meal was on the table, we saw them in the yard, covered with dirt and soot and looking as filthy as I've ever seen them. We made them wash and get out of their dirty clothes before they were allowed into the house and they then told us, as we sat at our food, what they had seen. They confirmed there had been a mighty explosion in the arsenal, exactly as father had suspected.

"It is a shambles, the building is half demolished" Cris said, "and several soldiers are dead"
"We helped clear the debris as we were able and searched for the injured. We found three men" Philip said, not so much shocked by what he had observed but more subdued than was usual for him.
"Are they cared for?" Mary asked.
"The women in the barracks are tending to them" Cris confirmed "One of their homes has gone. We will all

assist replacing what they have lost" he added, to which we agreed, for this was how our community was able to survive by generally helping where we could.

...

In the early evening after supper before the sun went down, we wandered to the old towne to take a look ourselves at the devastation and were much surprised at what we saw for the end of the barracks were gone and all that remained were smouldering and blackened timbers. Even the over hanging trees had been caught in the blaze and they were scorched and bare. The same was true of the cottage that was lost, but bizarrely we saw a bench that had stood outside the property, like most of them where folk would sit of an evening and converse with the neighbours, was intact and completely untouched by the conflagration and set down very close to where it had formally been. The remainder of the barracks and some of the cottages had suffered damage, lessening the further away from the blast they were and could all be repaired, Cris and father decided, it being their trade of course.

In time we wandered away, along with many others who came to look at such a major incident in our usually peaceful towne, and in time as the night fell we returned to our home.

August 4 1619

A group of our menfolk gathered in the church today, it was the sixth consecutive day they had done so and now agreements have been reached. For weeks various leading citizens in towne have been passing word of their wish to begin a council to pass laws for the whole of the community and asked both Cris and father to join, being craftmen and well respected amongst others. The two of them spent some time one evening discussing the matter believing it incorrect both should be present and Cris quite soon declared he had enough to be dealing with, with me and his children, though I was thankful to see a smile on his face as he spoke, so it was decided father would attend and see what the plans transpired to be.

Father wandered to the church at the appointed time last Monday with Richard Butler, my brother John's, father in law, full of anticipation and expectation, and on his return that first evening he declared he was sworn in as a representative of the First Assembly of Virginia as our colony was now to be known, named for Her Majesty, God rest her Soule, Queen Elizabeth.

At supper this Saturday evening father said there had been much prevaricating by many of the men present, but in time the rules that governed our community were incorporated in the Assembly and they began to look at the wider world of commerce which didn't concern us personally but certainly did in a community sense for it concerned tobacco.

The law, which was passed stated that tobacco could not be sold for less than 3/-d a lb. It seemed completely beyond me and quite strange to pass such a law for if traders were not willing to pay such a sum what would the growers do? But father explained to me, that as there was a great desire for tobacco in Europe and Jamestowne was the only port of entry into Virginia we could set our own prices. Nevertheless it still seemed to me to be a strange thing for the main tobacco producer was Mr John Rolfe on his Bermuda Plantation and he also sat on the Assembly so why he needed to control prices I could not understand, but I saw the wisdom in saying nothing else on the matter, and by then of course father and Cris had moved on to discuss other matters.

August 31 1619

A strange thing happened today in our towne. Mary and I were taking a constitutional this afternoon with Lucy, Joane and baby, when a ship flying a flag we were unfamiliar with tied up at our dock. We watched for a time as much activity abounded on the landing and the vessel. We were joined after some minutes had elapsed by Richard Butler and his son Andrew, who I remembered from before I wed Cris I had been drawn towards in friendship, when my brother courted his sister.
"Where's she from?" Mary asked. announced
"A Dutch ship" Mr Butler senior replied "There's Mr Rolfe, perhaps the cargo is for him"
"There's a number of dark skinned people on board, father" young Mr Butler said and even as he spoke about twenty men and women were led off the vessel and stood looking nervously about them. Soon after Mr Rolfe returned to the dock himself with a man we took to be the Master of the vessel. They shook hands and Mr Rolfe departed leading the group of men and women behind him.
"Negars" Mr Butler said "I hear in the islands many are sold to work the sugar cane"
"You can't buy and sell men and women" I said "It's against God's will"
Mr Butler looked at me with barely an expression on his face.
"Men have bought and sold others for always. Slave's they will be"

"But not in America"
"Mr Rolfe is always recruiting workers for his tobacco. Indentured servants from England usually, perhaps that's what he's doing"

I looked at him unable to hide my thoughts from my countenance that told everyone not only did I not believe him but I believed it to be totally wrong.

As the procession moved away and through the towne, we separated and made our way home and later that evening over supper when we gathered at the end of our day, I told of the arrival of the black people.
"And mother Swefling spoke with young Mr Butler, father" Lucy announced as if it was the most important event of the whole day.
"Did you Swefling?" father asked an instant before Cris was able to mention it.
"I did yes" I confessed, "He was with his father. We were observing the going's on at the dock"
"And did you speak with him?" Cris asked.
"I said she did" Lucy told everyone.

And much to my annoyance at myself as much as Lucy for causing such a disturbance, I repeated our conversation with Andrew Butler, which Mary added parts to and thankfully the matter was dropped. But later in the quiet of our room, as we lay in our bed, Cris raised the matter again.

"Swefling" he began, his hand resting on my arm "you do not regret wedding me, do you?"
"Regret? No! Of course I don't. Why should you ever consider it so?" I asked naively.
"You spoke with Andrew Butler"

"Am I not to speak with men of our acquaintance Crispin?" I asked finding an agitation rising within me.
"I have no wish to restrict you in that way, but I know he liked the look of you"
"And so did you and I married you" I reminded him, my mood fading as fast as it had risen "and anyway why would I look at another man when I carry your child"

Cris looked at me for several moments and nodded a smile on his face as he drew me closer.

"I should not doubt you, I'll not again" he said which was as close to a confession and apology he'd ever likely give.
"You'll have no need to doubt me ever" I confirmed.
"And we're to have another child? When will it be?" he asked sounding quite delighted with himself.
"In the spring I believe" I smiled kissing him.

May 31 1620

Cris and I have a daughter and she has just this afternoon been baptised Swefling Ales. She is a delightful child, dark eyed with lots of light coloured hair just now and very noisy and demanding. Her arrival on May 9 was straightforward and Mary, who now lives with us in our house, was with me all the way through and we were well prepared, reading extensively Mr John Gerard's excellent herbal book for remedies, grandmother had left with us.

The reason Mary removed herself to our house was that she was being much pestered by all manner of gentlemen and those not so gentlemanly to become a wife, there being still an acute shortage of single women in our community. It seemed every day as she walked from her lodgings in the old towne to ours, not more than

150 yards, she would be approached and accosted and one morning a man in a very drunken circumstance even so early in the day, molested her person. She arrived at our house in a state of complete nervousness and anxiety and once she was becalmed and had consumed a large glass of brandy, I insisted she should seriously reconsider the invitation we had made several days before, for her to remove to our house. Space was no longer the difficulty it had been previously for our accommodation was growing in our home almost as fast as our own family, as over the months of the winter, father and Cris added an additional large room at the back with an upstairs. With thankfulness Mary gave notice at her lodgings and in company of father who pulled the hand cart, they bought her small bundle of possessions and very soon she was settled in.

In the weeks before my delivery, Mary and I spoke often of tasks we had to perform as the spring arrived in planting and seeding the garden, where amid the vegetables we grew, onions and potatoes, and beans and of course the fruit, we had many more herbs to watch over and sweet smelling lavender and rosemary, comfrey and fennel amid the flowers. In the kitchen we asked Cris to construct a small narrow cupboard in which we could store our jars of drying herbs and preparations and already we were gaining in our knowledge in their uses.

September 14 1620

My brother, John who was twenty one in March, was at last granted his land right of fifty acres and requested the same for Amy, her being eligible by age and length of time in the colonie and soon the two of them left the town and set up their home with their young sons on their farm they called Ipswiche. We didn't see them for many months over the summer, as they cleared the land and prepared the soil for plowing and then the planting. Labour was a difficulty, but father and Amy's parents and John added all their coins together and paid the passage of three indentured servants for five years and it was a start.

Philip, my other sibling, meanwhile does not appear to have any great interest in working the land although he says he will take his land allotment, as I must when my time comes, father and Cris likewise, for, if we do so we shall in time have a sizeable holding, while many of the new settlers are only allocated five acres. But to return to Philip, he has become associated with the newly appointed governor, as we are now a colonie of the crown. The governor's name is Sir George Yeardley and Philip's plan is to make himself indispensable to the man and his successors to secure his position in the office, clerking and offering advice as he is able.

But now there is news that will affect many of us and has set the towne alight in many ways and will hopefully keep the Reverend Mr Whickham and the midwives busy for long into the future, for a ship arrived this morning full of young maids. They were said to be uncorrupted and had come to make wives for the many single men of our growing community, and I hear through rumour of course, for neither father nor my brother were inclined to venture to the dock to make a selection, many of them were wed before coming away from the vessel. It was not a situation I would wish to find myself in and for that I was most grateful in that I was able to know and care for Cris before we wed. However, the marriages took place and we trust that this night will remain peaceful and the Indians will not determine to launch an attack, for they would face a goodly number of the men of the town without their muskets and their breeches, but perhaps that would be sufficient to repel an attack, as they would surely fall about in laughter.

I am unkind and it does not behove me to be so, but Mary and I had much humour at the thought when it came to our heads as we brought food to the table for supper. This caused much consternation to the men of the house who thought we were sick. However when we had control of ourselves we were beseeched to reveal the nature of our discourse. I confess the expressions on their faces lacking understanding of our humour, did send me into a giggling fit once more. Soon enough though we ceased our noise and consumed our supper with decorum befitting us, although even now as I write I can't fail to raise a smile to my lips when I imagine the scene.

September 30 1620

Mary is to teach me how to brew ale. We have all the necessary equipment for mother was knowledgeable of the process but as I told you at the start almost of our tale, when she passed so suddenly it was one of the occupations I had yet to understand. Mary, it was, approached father and asked now that the wheat was harvested, perhaps he could allow us a measure to use and seeing the benefit in brewing our own ale he readily agreed. Mary was busy out and about gathering the other ingredients necessary, trading and purchasing as she could and in due course she set out a large tray in our covered work area outside and spread the wheat ears to malt.

Brewing is a long drawn out process and Mary did most of the work while I watched and learnt and helped when the children allowed but eventually it was time for the tasting. She placed a small barrel on its side and filled it carefully, securing the tap and refilling a number of jugs for our immediate use. When father, Cris and Philip sat down to supper that evening, they gingerly began to sip the brew.

"You know how to brew a fine ale Mary" father said wiping his mouth as we all agreed with his verdict. "What will you surprise us with next?"
"I don't know to be sure" she smiled and do you know I think she blushed. I glanced at Cris over my glass but I don't think he realised at all, or if he did dismissed it, but I had a little grin to myself and hoped very much that father was beginning to notice another women at last.

March 1621

What a dreadful time it has been in the months of the winter, freezing cold so that the drips from our noses seem to turn to icicles before we can wipe them away and snow as deep as a man's thigh. Inside our houses with the exception of the draughts, they are warm enough, ours especially for we have expert craftsmen to build the structure and Mary and I were always on the lookout for cracks and gaps that required to be repaired and filled and of course there is an endless supply of timber for the fires. In fact in our house we were often as warm as toast with our large number and good accommodation but whenever we ventured outside which was every day for whatever the weather the animals required feed and the cow to be milked and the eggs to be found, we struggled in the elements.

Crispin and father cleared a path from the house to the store and the covered area though we worked not out there as you will imagine, but it was a task that required repeating most every day with nightly falls of snow. But the inconvenience of the snow was also in many ways most useful to us for we could preserve cut meat in the frozen atmosphere, which lasted well into early January until a hunting party ventured out into the woods around us.

As I said we were most fortunate for we had warmth in our house and sufficient food on the table because we judiciously made preparation in the fall. Several families did not make suitable provision and there were numerous deaths throughout the winter from lack of food but more especially from the cold. Such deaths were unnecessary for a man only had to go a short distance from his house to chop a tree or even pick up fallen branches and he would have sufficient fuel to warm his house through the cold of the winter, but sadly some men were not prepared to work to benefit themselves, let alone their wives and children, so it was not a surprise that folk succumbed to the colder climate than we had previously been used to in England. It didn't make the passing of individuals any easier to bear but it gave the Reverend Whickham much matter for his sermons.

Perhaps I should not be so critical as to mention that the cold of the church and the exceedingly long services, resulted in many folk, including ourselves, catching chills and colds from the temperature and others who passed them around. We were left quite debilitated for many days and only with the welcome sign of the spring and the warm heat of the sun in the sky did our maladies

April 1621

Philip arrived home from his employ with the governor with a tract extolling the virtues of growing flax to produce cloth for cash.

"I immediately thought of you and Mary and Lucy" he suggested brightly "it would be something to fill your days and bring another income into the house"
I looked at Mary uncertain if Philip was in humour or seriousness and I decided the latter.
"What do you think Mary and I do all day, sit around drinking the ale and playing games of chance with the cards?" I asked.
"Well I know you clean and cook and such. It was just a thought"
"Well it is a poor one" I retorted "If you didn't spend your days prancing about following the governor hither and thither and remained here and undertook real work, I might consider helping you when this babe is born" I added patting my already bulging belly.
"I work hard" Philip protested with some vehemence "It's different. I didn't intend to infer you did not work"
"Enough!" Father raised his voice "perhaps the idea has virtue for us all to work at" I looked across at my father in surprise. "I am serious, there is always work for carpenters and I believe a need for cloth and cash or exchange"
"But....."
"We could all work at it's growing and making the cloth in the evenings, as we do now with the provender, Philip likewise. Mayhap we could pay the passage for a pair of indentured servants if it becomes over burdensome"

"But where will we put them?" I asked "the house has no spare rooms for servants"
"I'm sure we could make arrangements. We should look further into this. It will be too late for this season" Cris spoke now in the discussion, in full agreement it seemed "but we can begin to clear the land and obtain our plants"
"You're in favour of this scheme as well?" I asked.
"Yes, we must have divers interests to provide income and occupation"
"I have an occupation having your babies" I declared.
"It's not what I mean and well you know it Swefling" Cris said a smile on his face despite his words.
"I suppose so" I conceded.
"If we are to work together" Mary smiled, one of us now "and with two extra workers, we'll hardly notice the extra tasks, you'll see"

July 28 1621

I feel tired today, in fact quite exhausted. The heat of the summer has been excessive with no air even off the river to cool us and it is on this most difficult of days my newest daughter Rowan Elizabeth decided to arrive. At one stage I felt to take myself during my labour to the river and throw myself into the slowly flowing water and cool down, but eventually, really in no time at all, she arrived and is welcomed dearly into our family. Her elder brother and sister were most intrigued with the squirming bundle but my son soon lost interest when his grandfather took him off on some adventure outside, although Swefling clung to me, but was quite happy once she realised she was able to cuddle up and feed as well as her new sister.

For once in my life, well it's happened every day I've

been delivered, so that's three times now, I am highly pampered and I cannot say how much I enjoy lying in bed and being idle. Although as Mary advised me on the first occasion when I told her how guilty I was feeling, that in giving birth I had undertaken the equivalent of a full days labour of any man. I had thought it unlikely but now I just doze or wake dependent on the needs of my new child and do not concern myself with feelings of guilt or otherwise.

Just before the midday meal Joane shyly came into the room with some flowers Mary had let her collect in the garden and she climbed on the bed for a cuddle. At eight years old now she is a delightful child and I love her as well as my own babies and treat her and Lucy exactly the same I believe, however she is sadly overshadowed by her elder sister who is so different and exceedingly difficult, not only to me but to everyone. She is ten and quite capable of helping around the house and garden and undertaking chores but repeatedly she endeavours deliberately it appears to fall foul of some mischance. Several times for instance when sent foraging for eggs for breakfast, she suddenly drops them or trips up and spills the fresh milk and I've seen her drop a pile of dishes on the stone floor and watch them smash to smithereens. Initially we believed these were just accidents but as oft times we witnessed these occurrences, it is now the concensus of opinion, they are deliberately intended and consequently she is rarely asked to undertake any chore where there might be spoilage for she can not be trusted one iota. Even her father is at a loss to know how to deal with his wayward daughter for she tries on many occasions to twirl him round her little finger, but he too has become very wise to her schemes and it causes no end of discord in our home.

But just now as I chatted to Joane, her sister was taking lessons with the Reverend Whickham who wishes to instruct the daughters of artisans, over ten years of age in the scriptures. Whether it will in time amend Lucy's way we know not, but there is a peace in the house on the mornings she is away.

"Did my mother like pretty flowers?" Joane asked out of the blue.
"I expect so Jo. We didn't have any on our ship when we came here, but she liked to watch the flying fishes in the water"
"Father told me about them" Joane said as she curled up on the bed beside Swefling, who was asleep now and Joane gently stroked her stepsisters hair and smiled at the infant.
"I saw them once" I told her, "my father said they were called dolphins. Like big grey fishes leaping out of the waves, just like they were flying"
"Do you miss your mother?" she asked suddenly.
"Not as much as first" I said, "but sometimes I sit and think about her"
"I don't remember my mother at all" she said "is it bad?"
"No! You were only a baby, I wouldn't remember if it was me, but you have all of us now to love and care for you, Mary as well"
"You're like my mother" she smiled "and Mary is like yours" which I thought was very wise of her "I like you and Mary to be my mother and grandmother"
"Then we are" I smiled, "Mary is very clever you know, she teaches me all sorts of things"
"Like making ale, grandfather likes the ale she makes. Will they wed?"
"Because he likes her ale. I don't think so"

"Why did you wed my father, so you could have babies?"
"I wed him because I liked him very much and now I love him"
"And he gives you babies"
"And he makes us laugh and works hard for us"
"We all work hard, except Lucy and the babies"
"Lucy will work soon. If not for us then for someone else, perhaps she'd like to do that"
"Lucy doesn't say nice things does she?" Joane asked.
"She's an unhappy little girl"
"But if she smiles she won't be unhappy"
"It's not easy to do that"
"But we're all happy"
"We try to be don't we. Are you tired Jo?" I asked as she yawned "close your eyes and have a little sleep on the bed. We all could"

And we did.

I became aware some while later we were no longer alone in the room and opened an eye to see Cris standing in the doorway watching us. He came in as I woke and crossed the room and kissed me.

"My favourite girls all asleep together" he beamed at me "How are you?"
"Enjoying the rest and the quiet. Is everything alright, you're usually so busy during the morning"
"The midday meal is on the table, Mary sent me to see if you were awake and I wanted to see you and our babies and" he said passing me a roll of parchment, tied together with green cord "Philip has come to deliver this"
I untied the papers and read my brother's neat hand and the governor's signature.
"Our headright land" I smiled "one hundred acres Cris,

we could farm if we chose to"
"We could, but not this day, you should rest and Mary wants to grow the flax in the acre to see how to do it, with instruction first"
"In a year or two then" I grinned "but we've got our land and that's the most important thing. Do we have a map to show where it is?"
"Father's taking a look. He has his land too, all next to each other, just up the track from John's near Middle Plantation"

November 1621

There has been much unrest in the towne over recent times for some of the new arrivals will not work and are forever lying about our streets in a drunken and lewd manner, women as well as men. I haven't observed for myself but father reported the noise almost drowned out the Assembly when they foregathered recently. He also reported the members debated at length on the virtues of clapping the offenders in irons to teach them a lesson. I said they should be prevented from obtaining whatever libation caused their situation and be made to work, which I do believe was father's point of view at the Assembly, but the decision was made to do nothing but warn them.

On the day before yesterday however, there was much rioting and bad behaviour in the old towne that spread from around the barracks past the alehouse and down to the dock. There was much fist fighting and punching and rolling in the dirt and once at the waters edge, much falling into the river, which had the benefit of cleansing the assailants, making them more sober and stopping the fighting, although as sailors were involved, some fighting continued in the river.

Father who again was relating the tale smiled broadly at the antics of others but I thought it not amusing.

"But whatsoever let to the altercation?" Mary asked.
"A woman I believe" father replied.
"It is always so" Cris agreed.
Mary and I just looked at each other in silence and waited for father to continue, practically ignoring Cris's comment even though he now grinned, probably fearful of Mary and I, I mused.
"It seems several men off the 'Rosebud' became over familiar with the wife of one of the drunken rabble near the ale house and a fight broke out"
"Oh dear what did the governor do?" I asked.
"The Governor? I don't know what he did, hid probably" father smiled "but the Captain of the Guard called out his men and that's how it ended up down by the dock for some of the rioters ran and the soldiers gave chase"
"What a rough towne this is becoming" I said "lewdness and fighting wherever you turn"
"Where?" Philip asked, always one for a smart retort.
"There'll be fighting about this table between you and I in a moment" I grinned.
"And lewdness Swefling?" Cris smiled, so I kicked him fiercely under the table.
"Brother in law" he spoke to Philip while feigning injury "your comment has resulted in my being pained by the foot of your sister and now I'll have to take my belt to her backside. She'll not forgive you"
"It's what she's long needed" Philip laughed "I always said father you were far to soft with my sister and now she's too opinioned for her own good"
"I was far to soft with you all" father laughed at Philip and

cuffed him around the ear "now enough of this banter, poor Mary and Jo and Little Cris are quite bewildered and concerned at this behaviour which is not conducive to eating and digestion nor appropriate for a God fearing family such as we"

"Yes father " Philip laughed not at all disheartened.

"Swefling apologise to your husband"

I was about to protest but changed my mind.

"I'm sorry sweetheart, my foot accidentally found its way to your leg and caused you so much pain and discomfort. Will you be able to work again?"

"I will make every attempt but if I'm unable to put food on the table, sadly everyone will blame you"

"I will" Lucy declared as she stood in the doorway watching us.

"We may always rely on Lucy to blame you for something Swef" father smiled, offering the girl the chair beside him, which she ignored.

"Well it saves us from doing it" Philip replied standing now as he finished and offered his chair to Lucy, which this time she accepted. "I'll return to the governor. Thank you for the meal Swef, Mary" and he was gone.

July 1622

Cris and father extended the area between the workshop and the house so we may work under cover, as much from the strong rays of the summer sun as the rain and cold in the winter. They provided an area for storage for the flax but perhaps more importantly for our vegetables and ale which are essential to our well being.

Throughout the summer they erected a cottage for our indentured servants who are to arrive from England, in September. I'm not certain how I feel about us having servants at all nor for them to live cheek by jowl with us for the time of their indenture, which father says will be four years. We would never expect them to toil any harder than ourselves and they will never want for a roof over their heads, food in their bellies and a fire in the hearth, but even so. I only hope they are personable folk who I may get on with well enough to be a good mistress to them. After the decision was made for us to send for our servants, Cris sent a communication to an acquaintance of his in England to locate two likely persons and we were in time advised a young married couple of about twenty two years each and going by the names of Edward and Kathren Ranger would join us. Everything now awaits their arrival, their house is complete and partly furnished and Mary and I had some discussions on how we would employ the female, but resigned ourselves to wait for her arrival to ascertain what she was competent to do.

In the meantime, while we wait there is a period of quiet in our lives before the harvest. Quiet, that is except for our endless chores and the fact that in addition to my three children of five, two and one years I am once again with child. I am pleased for once to be free from birthing or waddling around in the heat of the summer for I am barely four months gone but come the cold days of winter when the snow is everywhere I will deliver, but that is many months distant and in the meantime I may enjoy myself.

Mary and I spent our days in the fields, in the shade as much as we are able, where Cris and father had set up a lean to, under which the tools we needed were stored and where we worked. We have harvested the first crop of flax we have grown. The leaves turned yellow and the seed brown, and Mary, Joane and I have spent many backbreaking hours pulling the plants from the ground by their root and spreading them on the earth to dry. We hope the weather will be kind to us, and mostly it is although we experience thunderstorms often this month so we shall pray to the Good Lord our efforts will not be in vain. Mary and I have read and reread the instruction information Philip brought to us on growing and harvesting our crop and I feel competent enough.

The first step in the long process of manufacture was to regather the flax that had dried and tie it into bundles, which we carried to the lean to. Backwards and forwards we trudged, Mary, Joane and I and we really could have used Lucy's help but that was another matter.

Once we had a large pile of bundles and Mary and Joane continued to gather others, I sat in the shade and began to comb each and every one to remove the seeds and other matter that remained. At the end of each day whatever our tasks our arms and shoulders ached and we were grateful for the salves and grease we had produced earlier to help ease the cuts and scratches and our protesting muscles. Before we commenced our labours we also planned ahead for our larder so that at the end of the day, we did not have to set about cooking a meal for we had cold meats and pies, potatoes and onions and a variety of sauces and all manner of provender easy to set out on the table in addition to gallons of ale.

Returning to the process of the flax, when the bundles were free from seeds and other matter, the next step in converting the plant into a thread was to separate the long silky inner fibres from the harsh outer ones or straw. We were fortunate to have the James River at our doorstep of our acre to assist us and although it was not a fast moving stream being more of a wide expanse of deep water, it flowed at a reasonable pace. We tied our bundles of flax to a frame which Cris and father constructed, extended out into the river and once the bundles were submerged, the water began to soften the fibres. After a time we removed one of the bundles from the river and found the straw came away quite easily from the inner fibres, and so began a very wet part of the process. Mary, Joane and I carried the heavy, sodden bundles from the water and onto the ground near the lean to, becoming very wet ourselves much to the delight of my eldest children who thought it amusing to see us drenched through and had much fun joining us in the soaking, but it gave us a welcome moment of humour in our tasks. We untied the bundles and spread them out on the earth for a number days to dry, and whilst this occurred we were able to catch up on our other tasks at home, but of an evening when Cris and father tended the crops after their days work, we would accompany them as always and check the drying of our flax, turning the fibres to catch the next days sunshine.

And then our work was completed and the flax now it was completely dry was loaded onto the handcart and transported to the dry storage by the house where it would age for a number of weeks while it and more importantly I believed, we rested.

August 1622

The flax has been aging for a number of weeks now and we know that when we come to the next stage of the process we shall have help, for the ship that is bringing our servants has been sighted in the river, and by suppertime they should be arrived.

As the sun began to lose some of its heat Mary and I set the table outside for our meal on our return and in the company of our family, Lucy included we headed through the towne gate to the dock, where the Oceans Apart was just tying up.

In due course the gangplank was set down and eventually Cris and father went on board where they were lost from our view for a time. Mary and I sat on the handcart with the children chatting as we watched and waited for their return. Lucy wandered off and despite my warnings stood near the edge of the dock where she joined the company of some boys and girls horsing around. I was not the least bit surprised when all of a sudden we heard a splash and a cry of anguish and Lucy toppled into the water. Assuring myself my babies were safe with Mary, I hurried to where Lucy seemed none the worse for her escapade, laughing and splashing in the water as the other children looked on. Several of them and two men attempted to reach her outstretched hand but she was in no urgency to remove herself from the water.

"Lucy" I called to her "you'll catch a chill come out"
"Help me step mother" she called and foolishly I knelt down and reached out and when it was too late, I realised my error, for she eagerly grabbed my hand and with a sudden tug pulled me off the dock and into the water with her.

Once I recovered from the shock and surfaced, spitting out water and hopefully nothing else, I swam towards the dock, hampered by my skirts. Fortunately eager hands reached out to me when I was close enough and one of the young boys, who had been fooling about with Lucy, jumped in and helped me back to the dock. I noticed though, he made no further attempt to offer assistance to Lucy, as Cris, on his knees assisted in my recovery from the water.

"Father!" Lucy called with so much innocence in her voice I could not believe what I heard.
Cris helped me to my feet and when he saw I was safe, turned to his daughter.
"Get yourself out of the water and be home when I arrive. I will deal with you later" and with a protective arm about my shoulders led me away. As I was surrounded by my other would be rescuers, we heard loud screams of anger and rage from Lucy who was I saw, when I glanced back, clambering out, almost unaided from the water.

Cris was most concerned for my condition but in truth I was none the worse for my dipping, if very wet and feeling quite foolish at being tricked by my step daughter. Soon enough though we reached our family and although bedraggled and untidy, I was introduced to Edward and Kathren, our workers. He was such a young looking man, I thought younger than his twenty two years, but appeared an honest sort of chap and spoke with a soft country accent not dissimilar to the Suffolk sounds I knew so well. His wife Kathren about my own age had a pretty face surrounded by dark hair tied back with a ribbon and a comely figure and smiled in a friendly manner when I arrived.

Their few possessions were loaded onto the handcart and with the babies on Mary and my hips we walked along the street to our house, Cris and father chatted amicably to Edward and Mary, Joane and I to Kathren and by the time we arrived at home I was convinced we would all get on very well.

We ate together at the big table in the garden under the tree as we have done every evening since, and during the meal when Edward proceeded to thank us for their passage to bring them to America, I knew my earlier surmise had been correct and we were already like one big happy family.

Over the next day or so whenever we had a moment in our day, Mary and I sat with Kathren and talked and early on, with a quill and paper before me we got down to discovering her skills, for it seemed appropriate to detail tasks accordingly. For instance Mary I knew, could spin and we agreed she would undertake to turn the flax fibres into thread. I had been taking instruction on weaving from my neighbour but I was not able with it at all nor cared overmuch for the task and was quite relieved when Kathren revealed she had learnt the basics but would be willing to take further instruction. I am delighted to reveal she proved as competent as I was useless and I was more than happy to relinquish that area of responsibility to her.

We sat in the shade of the tree around the table during our discussions a pot of freshly brewed coffee with us. The coffee was in part an experiment of Mary and mine for we added chicory as I referred to before to our ground beans and we discovered we liked the flavour. Of course it made our expensive supply go much further and Kathren was much interested in our adaptation of food we grew and found in the forest.

"Do you like to cook?" I asked.
"Very much" she replied with a smile "Edward says I am

able to produce a banquet out of nothing but we were newly wed then, so perhaps that accounts for his view" she laughed.

"Perhaps you'd like to show us" I suggested "And gardening, do you like to grow things?" I asked to which she shook her head "brewing" a nod, "children?" mostly unfamiliar with them but she offered to take Lucy under her wing and see what she could do, which Mary and I believe with smiles on our faces, that if that was all she may achieve, that alone is worth her passage. In no time at all we have divided all our daily tasks up most satisfactorily between the three of us and we refilled our cups with coffee to which I added a small measure of Cris's brandy and we toasted our association.

September 1622

Mary, Kathren and I with help from Joane and to my surprise Lucy, have worked tirelessly these last number of weeks breaking down the straw and unusable material from the dry flax and loosening the fibres to reveal what we require. Mary and I work together undertaking the process above while Kathren, and Lucy spend their days beating the flax on a board with blunt knives, and Joane is willingly occupied caring for my three babies, although Crispin at five years old is becoming very much a handful for his sister.

Now we have completed the procedures referred to above, the fibre is drawn through a series of metal combs we have procured from the blacksmith on sight of the instructions, but I do believe he is familiar with the items for we aren't alone in manufacturing flax. The reason for the combing is to remove the last of the rubbish from the fibres and when this is completed we are left with a pile of bundles of fine, long, light grey fibres very much like human hair. In another part of the workplace there is another pile of shorter fibres, which by nature of their length and courseness mean they will not be made into cloth for sale nor wasted of course but used to make sacking or poor quality cloth.

Now the hard work is completed Mary spends long hours at the spinning wheel producing a fine thread, which we will hang in the sunlight for most of the rest of the month to bleach the grey thread to the creamy colour we are used to.

We are well into harvesting and the work continues but it isn't the hard process of obtaining the flax fibres for we all enjoy to some measure, being in the fields at the end of the day with our men folk gathering our crops for the winter.

During the day we continue our tasks about the house and garden but with Kathren's welcome labour I am able to take a little rest now and then as my pregnancy approaches its final months and for that I am grateful. Most afternoons I spend the time gathering fruit and nuts from the garden and herbs and other plants we've grown for medicinal needs and then we preserve them for the winter and because I can perch on the stool. I prepare salves and hang plants to dry. Mary and I are happy to leave much of the cooking and baking to Kathren who is as excellent a cook as she predicted and enlists the help quite often of a changed Lucy. What exists between the two of them I have no solution but if it works and peace reigns amongst us we can ask for no more.

October 16 1622

A number of days ago after supper, a strange situation arose, which caused me much disquiet and I was not recovered when an even greater circumstance occurred this very evening. Mary thought my reaction, my over reaction she told me to the first event was due in much part to my condition but amid my tears I couldn't see it to be so.

What happened was this. Lucy was being particularly awkward with me and turned to Kathren looking up to her with her big brown beguiling eyes

"Kathren will you be my mother. She hates me" she said staring at me "and I don't like her either"

There was silence momentarily around the table and I watched some peculiar reactions from my family. Father put his head down and concentrated on his dish of food, as if he was tending intricate work on his lathe and Kathren looked at Cris and held his glance overlong I thought before he too inspected his food.

"I'll think about it" Kathren replied nervously.
"Oh thank you Kathren" Lucy beamed somewhat triumphantly at me "You'll be a true mother to me"
"Enough!" Cris spoke looking up at his daughter "eat your supper Lucy or go to your bed"

I said nothing but caught Mary's glance and I knew she had observed what I had, but the matter passed and nothing more was said then nor have I mentioned it to Cris. It has been on my mind though I considered perhaps Mary is right and it is my condition, but this evening something even more disturbing occurred even though it is now resolved I trust.

After supper Mary and I cleared the supper dishes away for it is our part of the arrangement that Kathren cooks and we clear and Kathren went into her cottage for her shawl as the air had a chill in it now fall is with us and I took the dishes inside. I returned to the outside some time later to wash over the surface of the table and watched to my great surprise, Cris and Kathren came from her cottage, and she with a most peculiar smile on her face. Normally I would have been unconcerned but Edward was away, having left Jamestowne that very afternoon with a cart load of sacks of wheat heading to my brother at Ipswiche and thence to the miller who was established nearby, with a newly erected windmill to grind the corn, so I knew Kathren was alone.

I did not believe I was of a suspicious or jealous nature but I stared at Cris in some disbelief, but when he looked my way he simply grinned. I continued to glare at him in horror and fled into the house, bursting into our room sobbing bitterly. I heard the door open and close softly behind me, as I sat on the bed in much distress.

"What ails you Swefling?" Cris asked, reaching a hand to my shoulder.
"Don't touch me" I said twisting away "you and Kathren?" I looked up at him. "Have you taken her?" I asked voicing my thoughts "I thought you cared for me?"
"Swefling!" Cris said his voice most angry "Stop your words. You do not know what you are saying. I will not be so accused. It is entirely unlike what you think"
"I'm not an idiot Crispin, I saw you coming from her cottage and Edward is away. She's young and pretty and

I'm fat and ugly like this"
"Swefling" he said softly, sighing, his anger gone "I love you, you know that. I have never deceived you in that way or knowingly any other, nor will I"
"But I saw you"
"And you are beautiful" he declared as if I'd not spoken.
"But what were you doing in her cottage. I saw the two of you close together. She is our servant, you have no business being in her cottage"
"I don't have to explain myself to you, not every action"
"Crispin go away. Go to your fancy"
"Swefling" he laughed "you're my fancy, you know that"
"Then why go to her? My father knows something, I'll ask him"

Cris sat down on the bed and took hold of my hand even though as I tried to remove it, he held it fast.

"You trust me?"
"I thought I did" I looked at him and so wanted to again.
"I should have told you" he said and I felt my heart fall "but your father and I decided you didn't need to know"
I was totally confused now and had absolutely no idea what he was to say.
"Kathren is my daughter"

There was a silence in the room for several moments as I took in his words and then I laughed somewhat hysterically I suspect.

"What kind of fool do you think I am? It's impossible. She's too old to be your daughter. Try another story. No don't I've heard enough of your lies"
"It's true Swefling, I was fourteen years old when she was born"

"Fourteen! How ridiculous. You must think very little of me Cris to consider I'd believe such a tale. How can you possibly have a daughter the same age as me. Where's her mother? Not Rebecca of course, did you deceive her as well?"

"Kathren's mother is dead. She died when Kathren was born"

"So why is she here? Not by coincidence I'll be bound?"

"No, not by coincidence, your father and I asked her to come"

"You and my father asked her to come? What are two doing?"

"Dry your eyes Swef" Cris said "I should have told you before but I didn't want to burden you. Rest now you're looking very tired"

I dried my eyes and sat back on my pillows and lifted my feet onto the bed, I wasn't in a mood to be hoodwinked but I might be prepared to listen. Cris sat where I had been and picked up my feet in his hands and rested them on his lap.

"I don't know where to begin" he said seeming to be quite at a loss, but I couldn't help him nor wanted to, he had to explain on his own, for I didn't believe a word of what he had said so far, but …. Perhaps there was some doubt now in my mind.

"My mother" he began "and her sister made a decision that one day two of their children would be wed. My aunt only had one child Catherine and I was the youngest of my parents sons, so we were wed when we were thirteen"

"Good heavens!" I exclaimed, knowing such arrangements occurred in the families of the nobility, "so who were your parents to allow such a marriage between children?"

Cris hesitated again.

"My father was the Earl Athelington and Catherine's the Earl of Finchingfield"

"So you're an earl, not a carpenter at all? What other lies are there" I laughed disbelieving him still.

"None!" he laughed "And I am not an earl nor do I own title or land, I am the youngest of eight children by a good few years and I am content to be a simple carpenter"

"You and Kathren's mother were wed when you were thirteen years old" I asked with some incredulity even in these enlightened times. "Barely old enough"

He nodded, a smile on his face and perhaps relief.

"Maybe but marriage at such an age was permitted, legal then and quite soon Catherine was with child"

"You were thirteen when you consummated your marriage?"

I asked stating the obvious.

"Yes. When Kathren was born her mother died. I was send to France and my daughter handed to a family on the Finchingfield's estate"

"But why didn't her grandmother look after her? It was her fault her daughter had died"

"I don't know Swef, I tried to get answers from my mother, for Lady Finchingfield had died by then but she would not speak of the matter. When I returned Kathren came to visit with my mother, and she related the story and I met my daughter. I couldn't remain in my parent's house for I was bitter and angry with them for what they had done, so I went to live with my sister and her husband in the village you are named for. It's where I first met your parents"

"I see, so why didn't Kathren come to America with you and Rebecca and her daughter?"

"The woman who raised Kathren was sick and she wanted to be with her for her remaining days and then

she married Edward. He worked on my father's estate"
"Why didn't you tell me Cris. Everyone knew except me"
"I didn't want to upset you. I was wrong I see that now"
"You deceived me" I said "How many other wives and children do you have?"
"I have no others"
"But how can I trust you?" I asked feeling full of despair.
"I don't know Swef, but it's the way it is. We'll have to hope to manage as we are able"
"You can't just hope, don't you care?"
"Of course, but it's not as if it's between you and me, it happened many years since. I have to confess Swefling I'm ashamed. Ashamed to have a daughter the same age as my wife"
"But why should you be ashamed, you always wed young girls, you should expect children when you wed. Your first wife was thirteen you say, Rebecca was sixteen when she had Lucy, and when we wed I was barely seventeen"
"You make me sound a monster Swefling, taking child brides. I'm not at all"
"I know you're not" I looked at him regretting my words, feeling sad and wishing none of this upset had occurred for I felt sick too. "Cris, the other night when Lucy said she wanted Kathren to be her mother, why did father pretend he wasn't there? You and Kathren...... " I couldn't finish my question, the horror of where my thoughts were heading were too wicked and hateful for that.
"Kathren is Lucy's natural mother" he said with no emotion in his voice at all.
"Oh" I lay motionless on the bed fearful that my thoughts continued along the same awful path as before "who is her father?"
"Kathren would never say" He looked at me with a growing realisation of my thoughts "Oh No! No! Swefling" he sounded horrified "you surely didn't think?

No! You couldn't possibly … Oh Swefling how could you think so of me?"
"I don't know what to think" and I also didn't know why I felt so much despair, from what Cris had told me the explanations were easy and straightforward.
"Why did Lucy come with you then?" I asked.
"You don't believe me Swefling, it has no matter?"
"Does Lucy know?" I asked.
"Not to my knowledge"
"Oh that poor child, believing her mother is dead when she isn't at all. And my own father knew all this?"
"He knew, yes. I begged him not to tell you and he agreed"
I nodded now, having no more questions, in fact I had nothing to say at all.
"Swef?"
"I'm tired Cris" I said struggling to sit up "I need to sleep"
"I never meant to distress you, I just wanted to protect you, to keep you safe" he said as he stood and watched me remove my day clothes.
"I'm not a child to be protected"
"No, but you are my wife, it's my right and duty to protect you"
"Duty! Is that what this is, a duty?"
"Listen when I tell you" he said his voice raised now "my right as your husband I said, as well as my duty"
"Yes Cris" I replied meekly now, all the fight gone from me. I lay in our bed and pulled the cover over me, wanting Cris to lie beside me and hold me, and tell me this was a horrible dream, but I was too stubborn to ask him and Cris too uncertain of me to offer.
"You'd best go for now" I said contrary wise, feeling very sleepy. Cris looked down at me for a time, then turned on his heel and left.

I lay on my side facing the window but sleep wouldn't

come to me so I turned onto my back and ran my hand over my belly, thinking about my baby and wondering what would happen now. I must have dozed for when I opened my eyes I became aware that darkness had fallen and sitting in the candlelight was Mary.

"What are you doing here?" I asked.
"I brought you a drink to help you sleep you but you were already gone"
"No I wasn't" I argued rolling onto my side "I just had my eyes closed"
"Sometimes Swefling you are exceedingly awkward" she told me.
"Who are you to tell me?"
"I am your friend. Don't be angry with the world"
Her words meant in kindness, had a strange effect on me and I felt my tears begin to fall again.

"There's nothing to be distressed about" she said softly.
"But he deceived me" I wailed.
"It's not anything to be concerned over, telling you he had another wife who died the year you were born. How could it hurt you?"
"But he brought Kathren here, his daughter, that's why he should have told me. I believed she was a stranger but it is not so. Did you know?"
"Not until your father spoke of it after supper this evening"
"So they deceived us both"
"Don't take on so. You know now"
"But all the anger and upset with Lucy is so unnecessary if I'd known he was her grandfather, if she had known. Mary I'm her grandmother!" I gasped realising the situation "I'm the same age as her mother but I'm her grandmother"

I looked at Mary and she smiled at me.
"That is different" she agreed "But the fact that Kathren is his daughter has no effect on our lives, and imagine how pleased Cris must be to have his long missed daughter with him"

I was about to protest again but I realised I hadn't thought of that before.

"He must be pleased" I agreed wiping my eyes.
"You should tell him that at least" Mary told me.
"Where is he?"
"He was in the garden with your father. Now let me wipe your face. You don't want to see him like this do you?"
"Mary, you know what Lucy said about wanting Kathren to be her mother, will you be mine?"
I asked trying a smile now.
"I'm almost that already sweetheart" she smiled again "I love you just like a daughter"
"Thank you Mary, I love you too"
"Now enough of this or you'll have me bawling my eyes out. I'll tell Cris you're awake shall I?"

I nodded and lay back against my pillows.

...

"So!" Cris stood by the door "you've seen the sense now" which were not the words I expected to hear, nor the tone.
"I was going to say how pleased I am for you to have your daughter with you but if you're going to argue with me and be horrible I'll not bother"
"I thank you for the thought Swefling nonetheless, but a man should be seen to be master in his own house"

I was on the verge of reminding him this was my father's house but stopped myself just in time.

"Yes Cris. You are master. We always try to do as you ask when we are able and not disagree"

He moved to the bed and sat down looked at me and I noticed a hint of a grin playing on his lips.

"You swore to obey me when we wed" he reminded me "I know you didn't agree but you have to try harder. I always do my best for you and the children. I don't always succeed but I try. You could do the same, to agree, at least in public"
"I suppose so" I agreed and looked down at my hands twisting the fingers together, calmer now. "How is everyone?"
"Mary and father are gone to their rooms, Kathren is in the kitchen and Lucy has gone to her bed as happy as a lark that you and I are fighting" I smiled then.
"Well I shall have to try to change that. What I can't forgive you for" I said feeling much better "Is making me a grandmother at my tender years"

Cris stared at me in surprise and began laughing and moved closer to me, pulled me into his arms and began kissing me.

"I didn't say I had forgiven you for not telling me" I protested.
"Oh yes you have Swef, I can tell" he grinned holding me tightly "I should have told you, explained when Kathren and Edward said they'd come. I'll not keep secrets from you again"
"She's very pretty" I said changing the subject "I really

thought you and her...." I began.

"I never would be with anyone but you Swef, ever. I love you too much"

"Should I apologise to everyone do you suppose?"

"Not tonight, it's too late and I want to hold you all night long"

"But I cannot sleep leaving Kathren alone, not knowing if I hate her or not"

"She wouldn't. Anyway I wasn't planning on you sleeping all the while"

"Please Cris, let me do this, then I'll stay awake all night if you want me to"

Cris smiled and reached for my hand.

"Come speak with Kathren"

In the darkness of the parlour Kathren was sitting at the table holding a cup in her hands and staring out of the open door into the blackness of the night beyond.

"Kathren" Cris called breaking into her thoughts.

"Oh" she gasped seeing us both standing in the room and hurriedly stood herself and in some confusion.

"When Edward returns we should go elsewhere if you'll allow us, we'll pay you to free us from our indenture when we are able I promise"

"That won't be necessary" Cris told her.

"Kathren" I began unsteadily feeling very forlorn with my tear stained red rimmed eyes, dressed in my summer shift over my bulging belly and my hair awry, facing a neat and tidy, pretty fresh, faced woman, "Kathren, please stay. I didn't know. I should have trusted Cris, your father I mean" the words sounded strange to me "I'd like you to stay, to be with us for as long as you care to be"

She nodded and looked from me to Cris and back to me.

"I'd like that" she said" and as we looked at each other tears came to our eyes and we moved closer and held each other in a tight embrace.

October 31 1622

We have just returned from my brother's farm, which straddles the road to Middle Plantation, four miles from towne. We travelled in the wagon to help with the harvest, although I absented myself from the hard labour in the fields and cared for the children and helped in the house, making butter and preserves for the winter. It was a great change for us being with family in the countrie side, despite the hard work. Near the end of our stay Cris and I took an evening stroll beside Archer's Creek and spoke once more on the possibility of removing ourselves to our acres of land.

"We could all come, father and Mary as well" I suggested "put our land together, we'd have such a large farm, enough to support us all"
"We're settled where we are" Cris declared "in a number of years perhaps Swef, when the children are grown a bit and this one is with us, at least" he smiled patting my belly.
"You like living in town" I said "why is that?"
"It's safer for you and our children, for all of us"
"I suppose so" I was forced to agree "but you'll think of it?"
"Every year without fail, sweetheart"

...

We returned to Jamestowne surprisingly rejuvenated by our ten days absence and once more became involved with our work and tasks. Kathren spent much of the day at the loom in the covered area between our house, the workshop and her cottage, and produced some fine cloth, which for our very first attempt we were most pleased with. Lucy who preferred Kathren's company to all of ours, except Cris's, removed herself to the cottage in a small room set aside for her. Generally life was more peaceful than before, even though she was as difficult as always with me, but as she spent more time with Kathren our meetings were less frequent.

One afternoon, it came to some form of resolution, which lasted for a long time, when I asked Lucy to collect the eggs from the garden, which she had not done in the morning when they were usually searched out.

"Do it yourself" Lucy barked at me to the surprise of all around particularly Kathren who was sitting at the loom. I was about to insist but before I was able to speak, Kathren whirled around on her stool and stood before Lucy.
"You will not speak to anyone in that manner" she said fiercely, yet very calmly to Lucy, watched I saw from the doorway of the workshop, by Cris.
"Who are you to tell me what to do, you're just the hired help"
"Since you chose to live in my house" Kathren told her daughter "you will consider me your mother"
"My mother is dead!" Lucy screeched at Kathren "I hate you all"
"You do as I say or remove yourself from my house. Now collect the eggs and do not break a single one. Do you hear?"
Lucy stared in an utter rage from Kathren to Mary and then myself and saw no hint of support and then she spied Cris.
"Father!" she cried "she can't speak to me so. I don't have to do what she says"
"Do as your ….. as Kathren tells you" he said firmly

"without discussion" and he turned his back on her and returned to the workshop, leaving Lucy with no choice in the matter. She glared at us most fiercely and snatched the basket from my hand and stormed off to where the hens scratched their living. Kathren let out a deep sigh and smiled nervously at Mary and I.
"Very good" Mary nodded, turning back to her brewing.

December 25 1622

As we walked back to our house from church this Christmas morning I leant heavily on Cris's arm, feeling a deep pain, low in my belly that momentarily stopped me in my tracks. Cris looked at me as our family walked on a few steps.

"It's started?" he asked knowing it to be so. I nodded and began to walk again as the pain subsided but by the time we reached home I knew I'd have to take myself to our bed before very long. I spoke quietly to Mary and together we left the family in order to make preparations for my delivery.
"May I help?" Kathren asked joining us as I sat on the bed aware of another pain approaching but I giggled at a sudden realisation I had.
"What amuses you Swefling?" Mary asked, a smile on her face too.
"I have a thought Kathren, you're about to help deliver your own brother or sister"
"I'd not considered it" she giggled. "Isn't it most peculiar?"
"Mmmm" I muttered as the pain reached its height and eventually began to fade away once more. There was not a great deal to be doing just then so we returned to the family where I sat quietly and Kathren and Mary returned to the kitchen to prepare the meal. We were in

the middle of our repast though I was not eating for the pains were constant and I could no longer concentrate. I stood suddenly and pushed my chair back.

"I'll be alright" I said as they all looked at me.

"You just want to get out of going to church this evening" Philip ever the humourist declared.

"You could be right" I gasped and rested a hand heavily on Cris's shoulder. He and Mary and Kathren were on their feet and I was greatly assisted into our chamber before he was summarily dismissed from the room by Kathren. Not before time either I reflected, for I had no sooner laid on the bed, my petticoats flung to the floor when my newest child arrived in a great hurry. As Kathren opened the door to fetch water and clothes, Cris stood before her and I heard her happy yet tearful whisper to him.

"Father, I have a brother" I saw her hug him and he returned her pleasure with a kiss and I wondered what everyone except father and Edward would make of that, but the thought vanished as Cris came into the room to welcome his newest son.

"I thought we might name him James" I said when Cris, sitting on the bed beside me looked down at our baby, while Mary and Kathren completed their tasks.

"My father's name" he said smiling "yes it will be so James Thomas" and there were smiles in the room from Mary, but not from Kathren who seemed suddenly most upset and anxious and left the room with the basins and cloths without a word. Cris alone in the room did not notice but Mary and I put it from our minds for there was a knock at the door and Crispen, Swefling and Rowan, led by Joane and followed by father, came into the room.

"Where's Lucy and Kathren?" I asked father but he shook his head.

"Look children" Cris was smiling at the children "you have a new brother" and whilst he did not pick up James he was eager to show them "All my family are here together now in this house" he said when he sat down again, "I am most pleased"

March 1 1623

At last the ice, frost and snow is leaving and today we saw a weak sun from a pale blue sky for the first time in many day. The severe weather had befallen us in early January and we have barely left the house for almost two months. The food position was much improved particularly for ourselves but generally for most of the community, for the harvest had been good and more and more folk devoted time to growing plants that flourished in the rich soil of Virginia and laid aside the crops they had been more familiar with in England, that seemed to wither and die in this new land.

Wood for fires was readily available for everyone, all it required of course was someone with an axe, so no one went cold any more but sadly one household overbuilt their fire to keep their house warm. Whether it was a spark flying into the room or the chimney igniting whilst they slept, no one would ever know for certain, but before help could be rendered, the house was ablaze and the inhabitants, a family of nine, perished, except for Mr Doutham and his infant son. The remains of his wife, aged mother and five young children were laid to rest on a day when the snow swirled around and froze our noses and toes. The baby was cared for by a neighbour and his wife, who also offered accommodation to the widower, but a number of days afterwards, he wandered out into the forest and was never heard of again.

We were well used to death and dying in our

settlement, for illness and disease frequently visited our colonie and the cemetery was always in need of extension. There were accidents and misadventures too but it was hard to listen to the Reverend and accept the lessons of his long sermon, knowing the deaths were a result of a desire to do no more than keep warm, while we shivered and sneezed in the cold church.

...

Before the tragedy I refer to above, I was well recovered from the delivery of my child and soon up and about the house. Mary and I had a quiet conversation with regard to Kathren's reaction when Cris had announced the name of our son and we decided we would enquire if ought ailed her. Well Mary was to ask, but Kathren simply smiled and declared she was only surprised at the name, no more than that. I'm afraid we were not totally convinced with her words but thought not to pursue the matter for it was probably nothing and if it was, it really was not our business unless Kathren chose to discuss it with us.

June 1623

There are reports in the towne of a tragedy amongst the Indians and father, hearing such news from the Assembly of which he continues to serve, was loathed to reveal the same to us. We all knew approaches were being made to reach some form of peaceful existence, for although isolated attacks and incidents were few and far between they were worrisome and put us constantly on our guard. Eventually however father was persuaded to impart some measure of the information and I must say we feel in a more vulnerable circumstance than before.

What happened was this. Captain William Tucker from the garrison and Doctor John Potts, the secretary of the Assembly undertook negotiations with our Powhatan Indian neighbours. The talks were successfully concluded in a peace pact and whilst remaining in the Indian village a toast was suggested by the Captain and the Doctor to settle the arrangements. It transpires the drink offered to the Indians, was laced with poison by the doctor and many of the natives, trusting our leaders there present, died immediately. Reports are, father tells us, as many as two hundred men and women also perished. There followed a period of intense mayhem and carnage and at least another fifty more were slaughtered afterwards by the soldiery. It is a dreadful disturbance and now puts us all at grave risk from reprisals and attacks, which are bound to occur in retribution.

Since that day Cris and father prohibit our venturing from towne in our own company until Mary, Kathren, Lucy, Joane and I become suitably skilled in handling and discharging a firearm, which we are to carry about our person on all occasions outside the confines of the towne.

I attempted to protest at this measure and declared I would not go about with a pistol in my belt whereupon Cris told me in no uncertain terms that if that was my intention I would not be allowed to leave the towne under any circumstance. I was in no doubt he would indeed have prevented me by some means, of leaving and going about my business. From then on we always went armed and rarely took the children unless Cris or father or my brother Philip was with us. It certainly curtailed our freedom to work in our acre or collect plants and produce from the forest as you may imagine, but we are resigned to the circumstance and protected ourselves as we are able, should the need arise, but thankfully thus far that need has not come upon us.

April 1624

The Virginia Company that set up Jamestowne in 1607 and explored Virginia in the early days, have had their Charter withdrawn by King James and we have become a royal province. Exactly how we shall be affected by this change no one seems to understand, but what started out as a commercial enterprise is no longer and perhaps that is a good thing for we shall become part of England overseas.

One change we have already noticed is the influence of the Assembly over our lives in making laws and judgements by which we live. This is important particularly for those folk who come to Virginia to escape some of the restrictions in England and seek freedom. But theft is theft by any name and anywhere as the bible records. Nevertheless there are those who believe such laws do not apply to them and consequently continue their lawless ways without thought or concern of the consequences to themselves and others.

The Assembly, father tells us, will order the enlargement of the barracks and the cells therein to accommodate the increasing number of felons as the situation worsens. Although some members of the Assembly did suggest such undesirables are placed on the first available vessel heading for England to be dealt with by the King and his court. If we are to be controlled by the King let his Majestie resolve the difficulty. These last words my father spoke in our home, not, he advised within the hearing of the Assembly, for there were calls he said, that such sentiments were seditious and nigh on treasonable and the perpetrators of such notions should be the first to be deported.

One measure the Assembly have determined on, is to take a count of the number of English men and women, free settlers and servants alike and others currently residing in our province from overseas, but not the native persons. For what purpose we have no knowledge other than to tax us further Cris suggested. In due course people were set on in all nineteen settlements from Jamestowne, to the Hundreds, Middle Plantation to Elizabeth City, across the river and wherever there were settlers. The Assembly members for each settlement was responsible for collecting the names and ages of every individual, and father was assigned new Jamestowne and with Mary at his side to assist him, he visited every house and asked for the information required. For the most part he received willing cooperation and in due time a report came from the Assembly with the discoveries made.

It came as a surprise to us to discover that Elizabeth City at the edge of Virginia where the James and York Rivers meet in the Chesapeake Bay is larger than our own community with sixty more people. I wondered why that should be and father suggested perhaps because when folk arrive here in Jamestowne, which remains the only entry into Virginia, they wish to locate a place of their own and not remain in the first towne they come to, as we had done of course. It made me think once again how much I would like to remove ourselves to the land. I knew there would likely be more danger and there would not be the closeness of the river, beside which I delighted to stroll, but there would be so much land and space away from other folk and their business.

There was another even more interesting revelation in the census and that was the total number of individuals now residing in Virginia. Most arrived like us on a ship sailing across the vast ocean but there are many children born here now, the first generations and this is important. The total number of the population is 1032 of which 902 are men and of the one hundred and thirty females only sixty one are married women. It is an interesting piece of information and not totally unexpected of course, for whenever we wander outside, women are very sparsely seen.

"And just consider this" Cris grinned at us over our supper when father finished telling us "we have three of them in our own house alone. There must be many of our brothers who are not so fortunate"
"Or is it we who are unfortunate with the three?" my brother grinned at us, assuming he was being exceedingly humorous and clever.
But Mary, Kathren and I and even Lucy and Joane did not share his laughter.
"When you grow up" I smiled at him "and have a wife of your own, you'll understand just how wonderful we all are"
"Not me" he laughed, not one to be bettered.

October 1624

Cris and I have been exceedingly fortunate in the years since we wed in 1617 for he has gotten me with child four times and we now have four healthy, growing children to bear witness to our union: Crispin, Swefling, Rowan and James are delightful and dear children, and we offer our thanks to our Lord every day for giving them to us to love and protect and care for. However with much sadness I have to write that our good fortune has deserted us.

Our third son, who we named John Philip for my father and brothers was born on 10th of this month and four days later after a desperate struggle, he passed from this life and rests now with Jesus. There is much sadness in our house, my daughters Sweffie and Rowan cry bitterly at the loss of their eagerly awaited brother, my stepdaughters too, Joane of course and yes even Lucy, likewise. Mary, Kathren and I cry in the quiet moments we may, away from the children, but the men and boys do not wear their hearts on their sleeves as we women do and carry on without discussion or tears.

A number of days after the burial, I worked with Mary collecting the last of the nuts from the trees. It took us longer now for she collected and I sat with a pistol on my knees for Cris instructed us to be ever watchful of the enemy.

"Mary" I said "when we first met you told me of the herbs I could take to prevent babies. Do you know where we may find any?"
"You've decided"
"I have, I cannot carry a child for nine months for it to die as John"
"We have the herbs we require I believe in the garden and here about. I could make up a mixture for you and we will look in your grandmother's herbal book"
"Yes we shall do that if Cris agrees, four children is enough don't you believe"
"If you think so" she smiled "and there are Cris's other children, he has done much to populate Virginia" she laughed.

"Oh Mary. What a thing to say" I giggled realising it was the first time we had had any humour between us this month "You're right, eight children he's given his three wives and six surviving in Virginia. I hear tell in England some families have as many as fifteen babies"

"And the woman falls down dead soon after, but they don't work on the land as you do, so your four are plenty"

June 17 1625

I am desolate, bereft and in deep, deep despair for my much beloved husband, my dearest darling lover and my very best friend is with me no more. He lies on the bed we once shared with so much joy and pleasure, as if asleep. I sit in the chair and watch over him, and cannot believe it is so. I want so much to lie beside him and feel his hot kisses on my lips, his hands roaming over my body and his magnificent manhood thrusting deep inside me. I want to hear his laughter, his whispers, his kind words and to see him working at his lathe, his firm muscles rippling in the sunlight. But it will not be ever again for us, for he is dead.

The Indians [natives] rose up all over our colonie, in the morning of yesterday, attacking settlements here and there and any outlying undefended or protected areas. It was a total surprise for despite the awful situation almost two years ago which I wrote about, we firmly believed there has been a measure of peace between our communities. But it was not so. The very first we knew there was any notion of trouble was the firing of muskets some distance away and we thought it of little significance, for we often heard hunters in the forest. Cris and father were in our acre of land tending the crops on this Saturday, with my brother Philip and Edward, Kathren's husband and divers others.

Mary and Kathren were with the children in the vegetable patch in the garden and I was in the area between our house and the cottage and the workshop, when father arrived covered in blood.

"Papa" I cried never once before using in my life using the new term of endearment, "Oh Papa what has happened, are you hurt?" I asked going towards him. He stood to one side and I saw Philip and Edward carrying Cris between them, and knew the blood was from my husband.
"I'm unhurt Swefling" he said "Come to your husband. Take him to the workshop"
"Oh my Lord, please don't take him" I prayed at their side. "Oh dear God." I cried when I saw his left arm sliced almost from his body. "Into the house"
"The workshop" Papa said, and the two men hesitated briefly until they followed my father.

I held onto Cris and his eyes flickered briefly open but in their haste his poor injured body was jostled every which way and blood dripped on the ground, leaving a bright trail behind our procession. I stared at it in wonder before I turned as Philip and Edward lay him on the workbench.

"Why did you let this happen to him?" I asked the three men as I laid my hands on Cris. He opened his eyes as I took his good hand and smiled.
"Swef" he whispered my name.
"Cris, it's alright" I whispered seeing more clearly now the fearful injury to his shoulder. I pulled my apron off and folded it to make a pad to stop the flow of blood but he swooned in pain as I touched him. If only I could

stop the bleeding it would be alright but I couldn't apply enough pressure without causing him further pain. I became aware of movement about me, and looked up briefly to see Kathren join us. Edward put an arm about her to give comfort and strength, but who would hold me I wondered.

"I'll get the herbs to make you comfortable" I whispered again.

"Swef, don't leave" he whispered weakly now, as if it was a terrible effort, I could barely hear his words "it's time for me"

"No! I won't let you go I want you to stay with me" I cried.

"Kiss me Swef before I go" he said, his voice suddenly clear, his uninjured hand gripping mine fiercely with a strength that belied his wound.

"Take care of yourself and our babies" he said as I looked down at his face, pale now despite the colour of the sunburnt skin and his eyes began to lose focus. I leant forward and kissed his warm soft lips I loved and as I did, I felt his life slip away and when I raised my head I knew he was dead.

I found a work stool placed behind me and I sat down heavily as a silence fell amongst us. I don't know how long I sat looking at Cris not believing for one moment he was gone. It may have been just minutes or maybe hours I had not notion of anything until I felt my father's hand on my shoulder.

"Swefling, my dear" he said softly "it's time for the living" I turned and looked up at him and slowly left Cris's side. My father held me in his arms, as I sobbed and I became aware of another crying and turned to see Kathren in a similar state as myself. Father and Edward released us and my stepdaughter and I stood locked in a tight embrace until we were led away towards the house.

The children were inside the house with Mary, aware something fearful had passed, but just now not knowing what.

"Oh dear God" Mary spoke seeing the state of us as we entered.
"Where's my father?" Lucy demanded to know "what have you done to him?"
"You are a wicked girl to say such things" Mary told her as she ushered Kathren and I to the chairs at the table but Kathren held back.
"It's alright Mary, I'll deal with her directly" she said and ignored Lucy for the moment and finished the glass of brandy Edward had already poured for us.

I gathered the children close to us, all except Lucy who refused to be with us and reached out wanting to touch them all, before I spoke.

"Jesus came for father" I said as tears flooded into my eyes again, "We must be brave, he is no longer with us"
"Why did Jesus want him?" Swefling asked "He was our father"
"Because he was a good man and Jesus needed him"
"What rubbish" Lucy retorted.
"Be silent girl" my father spoke, in a voice I'd never heard before, that frightened the other's considerably. Kathren stood and took Edward's hand and crossed to Lucy.
"Come with me" she said.
"I want to stay here" Lucy declared but Kathren and Edward both took an arm each and dragged her, protesting still, out of the house and I presume to their cottage, but I took no more notice for my children and

Joane needed me.

"Might I call my father, Papa?" Rowan asked.

"He'd like that very well" I smiled despite myself at her words.

"Papa will see us if he is with Jesus. Jesus watches over us and so will our Papa"

"Of course he will" I agreed.

"Can we see him, Papa I mean?" Joane asked having been so quiet up to now. I took hold of her hand and realised how brave she was and how much pain she had suffered in the thirteen years of her life, Lucy also I thought, I must not forget that.

"Not just now, later perhaps" I looked beyond the children where Mary was cleaning the blood from my own father which despite his words about not being hurt had clearly sustained some injury but he was much recovered as she finished.

"We must fetch the remainder of the vegetables" Mary said to the children or there'll be nothing to eat for any of us. Come along"

Reluctantly as they were, with a little encouragement all four of my babies and Joane followed Mary out of the house. I sat back in the chair and looked at father and Philip and watched me in silence.

"We must get Cris into the house while the children are out" I said "I'll get the bed ready, he will lie there until the burial"

I sounded organised and practical I know but I wasn't at all for inside, my heart was breaking. I went into our chamber and stripped the new linen and threw it in a heap on the floor and pulled the birthing quilts from the storage box at the bottom of the bed. I worked automatically immersed in my grief and soon father and Philip carried Cris into the room and laid him on he bed and we stood looking down at him.

"I'll be alright" I said "you have things to be doing"
"Not today" Philip said "We could do with a drink though" and he left father and I in the quiet of the room, with Cris. I looked at my parent and nodded to him.
"I will be alright" I said again and slowly he looked from me to Cris and left me alone with him. I sat in the chair beside the bed and took hold of his hand, not looking at his injuries but his face, calm and peaceful now. For I time my mind was blank and I cannot recall my thoughts at all.

I didn't hear footsteps come into the room until I became aware of others about me and turned and saw Kathren watching me, with her arm on Lucy's shoulders.

"Kathren says I am to apologise for causing upset" she sniffed tears in her eyes "my father is dead isn't he?" she asked knowing it to be so.
"Yes Lucy, he is" I said softly and to my surprise she moved forward and wrapped her arms about me. Despite my surprise I did the same to her and Kathren joined us as Lucy cried and cried.
"What will happen to me and Jo?" she asked a short while later "we are orphans"
"You have a family here with us" I said looking from her to Kathren, "never doubt that Lucy"'
"Come now" Kathren said softly as Lucy looked across us to her father, "don't distress yourself"
"Did it hurt?" she asked holding onto Kathren.
"Don't think about it?"
"I'm not a child Kathren" she shouted at her "Oh father,

why did you leave me?" she wailed taking his uninjured hand in her own now "they'll turn me out into the street"

I looked at Kathren, who was suffering much at her own loss but I could not at that moment help her and was much relieved when the door opened and father stood in the threshold.

"Come Lucy, leave the women to their work"
"But…… " she began and for once in her life did as she was bidden.
When the door closed behind her I sat again looking at Kathren.
"Oh Kathren what will we do now?" I asked, "all hurting so much, how will we get through this?"
"We shall help each other" she said softly crossing the room to me and taking me in her arms "we all need each other just now, every one of us"

A little while later the door opened again and my other brother John and his wife Amy came in and closed the door.

"Oh thank God you're safe" I sighed as Kathren and I separated "what are you doing here?" I asked surprised and pleased to see them and worried they'd be on their farm, lying dead on the hard baked earth.
"We were here to collect supplies off the ship. Father told us Swefling. We're so sorry for your loss" John said.
I nodded.
"I have to clean Cris, he can't be buried in this state what would everyone think?"
"I'll help you" Amey offered and she, Kathren and I began to wash off the fast drying blood from Cris's face and arms while John went into the parlour. We were about to

remove Cris's blood stained clothes when we heard Mary and the children return to the room outside, and Mary alone came to join us.

"I'll do it" she said "you go to the children and there's food to be made ready. Everyone all right at your place?" she asked Amey.

"Mostly, thank God, though my brother Andrew received a severe gash in his thigh with an axe blade, but Mother believes he'll live. It's just so terrible"

"They were attacked in the towne?" I asked most puzzled.

"No, he was in the pasture nearby Cris" she replied "I'll stay" she said to Kathren and I, and we finally left the two women talking and cleansing and changing my husband.

How we got through yesterday I don't know. I was thankful to have my father and brothers close beside me and Mary and Kathren and Amey to help not only me and the children. When John and Amey left late in the afternoon they insisted on taking Swefling, Joane and Lucy with them to Amey's parents. Father also left to locate the priest who we suspected may be very busy. We didn't know how many from the town had perished, but there was all manner of rumours coming from neighbours about. Some said as many as fifty died from our towne alone.

When he returned father told me the burial was arranged for the following afternoon but we would have to dig the grave ourselves. Father organised Edward and Philip on that task the following morning, and began to wander away to his workshop to investigate timber for the coffin.

"Father, we have linen enough" I said.
"It's the best I may do and I need to be busy"

"Grandpa may I help?" my eldest Crispin asked.
"Come lad then, perhaps Philip you'll give a hand directly?"
"I need a drink" I said suddenly finding everything becoming too much for me and proceeded to open and close cupboards searching for the brandy, until Philip announced it was on the table. I looked up when I had a glass poured and saw them all staring at me in silence, Philip, Mary, Kathren, Edward, my sons and Rowan.
"What's the matter now?" I asked.
"Swef you don't drink" he reminded me.
"I'm having one now and I may have another" but once I'd taken the glass to my lips I knew I would not even finish the one.
"I'll get coffee brewing" Mary said "much better for us. Philip, Edward you go off now to father, we'll be fine on our own"

We sat at the table for a time with our coffee after I'd put Rowan and James down for a nap and we became enmeshed in our thoughts once more.

"What will I do without him Mary?" I asked "I cannot believe he has gone"
"You are young, you'll get by and plenty will be willing to help you especially with the land Archer's Creek"
"I ought to find Cris's will, he might not have left a thing to me and our children"
"Hardly likely Swefling" Kathren declared "Time enough to read it in a day or so. You should rest, you're looking quite peaky and I must check on the meal"
"I never told him" I whispered to Mary running my hand over my belly "I'm so pleased he wouldn't listen to me about not having more babies but I'm still not certain"
"Looks that way to me" she smiled "Cris's legacy. All his

children"

I nodded again, not voicing my awful thought that I'd give them all up to have him back. A bargain with the devil it would be and in my heart I knew I never would consider it, how could I anyway?

...

I insisted at bedtime I would sit in the chair in my room beside the body of Cris, despite everyone at great pains for me not to remain on my own.

"But I'm not on my own Papa" I said "Cris is with me"

Reluctantly I was left and my family wandered to their rooms, but in the early hours just before dawn, when the human spirit oft falls to its lowest point, my father came down the stairs and sat with me and my husband, and I was thankful for his company.

"I'm just a number of years older than Cris" father said "it's hard to believe Swef, my own daughter a widow to a man almost my age. He was a good friend to me. I liked him most well, as a son in law, and as a man" he said, as he held Cris's hand.
"You and Mother were good to Cris and Rebecca on the ship"
"Our voyage was the start of many good times. I could never have believed it would be so. I was so fearful. We have had much sadness but its part of life. I'd like you to call me Papa, Swef, it's a kindly word"
"It is isn't it. I'm pleased to do it" I sighed.
"Why don't you sleep for a time, I'll watch over you and your husband. I'd like to speak with Cris. Close your eyes

now" he suggested and although I protested I now felt much comforted with my father's presence and did drift off to a sleep of sorts.

I woke as the long streaks of the new day began to light up the sky and before long the bright sunshine of another summers day filtered into the room and I reached for my ink and quill and journal and as the birds began their joyous chorus I began to write.

July 23 1625

A day passed and then another and before we knew it a week was gone and then a month. It's been six weeks now since that dreadful day and in many households families are slowly resuming their lives after the loss of a dear one and so it was in ours. Throughout the days the children resumed their lessons and play but at bedtime as I listened to their prayers their Papa was always included and before they closed their eyes they'd talk about him. All except Lucy who had sunk back into her earlier melancholy, but as each day passed the next became easier and took us further away from him.

I was less able to accept Cris was gone and felt his absence continually. We had so few years together, just eight this year but we had four beautiful children alive and thriving, and for that I was grateful, for life was difficult enough bringing babies into the world, without the sadness of them dying. Cris and I had been fortunate in that regard and once more I was with child. I was delighted with the thought of the new life growing within me but at the same time devastated I would be alone when he or she was born and they would never know their dear father.

October 1625

The harvest is gathered and everywhere folk look tired after one of the most difficult of years since Jamestowne was founded eighteen years ago. It is a thriving community and people arrive to remain or pass through continually, as almost weekly it seems, a ship arrives with emigrants and supplies. The free newcomers, as we once were, eagerly take up their plots of land, despite the Indian attacks in June and continued minor skirmishes hither and thither.

At the end of September a change in our household arrangements occurred which at the time brought a much need peaceful atmosphere to the house for we acquired a position of employment for Lucy, now she was thirteen years of age. I wasn't certain if Cris would have approved but Kathren, who was after all her natural mother, determined she wished it. I agree Lucy certainly needed something to occupy her days, for her reluctance to work with us at our tasks was a battle we wished to relinquish. She was not best pleased with the arrangement as you will imagine but her role as housemaid in the reverend's residence, we believe will be a good opportunity for her and so it appeared to be, for when she returned to the room she shared with her sister each evening, we often heard her relating certain tales of her day and sometimes even laughter could be heard. But that also changed for as the weeks have passed, she returned to her room in Kathren's cottage and she seems satisfied with her new accommodation.

One day Kathren and I were in the cool area crushing the dried bundles of herbs and filling the pots for later use, discussing Cris as we often did.

"I had three years with my papa and I'm pleased to have known him, but how you must be feeling Swefling I cannot begin to imagine, for even in my deepest thoughts if Edward was taken suddenly I don't know how I would get through each day. Perhaps your children remember him and that helps"
"Perhaps it does Kathren I don't know at all. The daytime is easier for there is much to be doing, but the nights are long and lonely"

She nodded and I was sure she understood completely.

"I've seen you at the table sewing or reading or writing 'til the early hours or sitting on the bench outside the door looking up at the stars"
"It's the only way, to be so tired I can barely keep my eyes open, but even then I oft times lie awake for hours. It will pass I am told. How is Lucy these days, we barely see her in the house now?"
"As angry as ever with us all, her papa included, I mean her grandpa. I have thought to tell her, but I'm not clear any purpose would be served with her knowing. Working at the reverend's house helps I think and she's always tired at the end of then day and soon falls asleep"
"It seems a shame, Kathren, she is so young to be working" I said.
"It happened to us all" Kathren reminded me "none of us may be idle when we are capable of work"

December 1 1625

Five months, two weeks and three days have passed since my beloved has gone and I miss him as much as on the day he died and today I lost my unborn child in the seventh month of my pregnancy. I have been feeling unwell and thought I'd caught a chill although Mary suspected it was as much to do with the fact that my appetite had not returned and I have become quite thin, not the usual circumstance in my condition. Whatever the reasons, I was sent to my bed by Mary and Kathren, and made to rest. I woke from a nightmare doze with cramping pains in my belly and knew then exactly what was to occur. The pains were only marginally less than full labour, which surprised me, but the end was in no doubt. Mary and Kathren were so very kind and gentle as I cried endlessly during the delivery and Mary sat with me for some time afterwards, holding my hand while Kathren organised the children and the food and everything else that required attention.

"It is meant to be" I said to Mary most mournfully, having dried my tears and begun to think more reasonably, "Cris never knew. How could I bring a child into the world without a father"
"What nonsense Swefling" Mary told me "Many babies arrive in the world without a father, for a variety of reasons. You are weak just now but when you recover from this, you will eat properly once more and grow strong. We need you, we cannot cope alone"
"Oh Mary" I sighed knowing she meant well "I'll eat when I'm ready"
"I shall force feed you like a child if you don't" she smiled, "Now I've things to be doing, I'll leave you to sleep and bring you some supper directly"
"Yes Mary" I smiled at her, thankful for her care and attention.

Later in the evening when the children were in their

beds having come to say goodnight, I lay back against my pillows as the day came to an end and picked up my journal but I could not write at that time.

There is light now, of a new day and I pick up my quill for I had to recall the death of my child, another son, seven month, no hope to survive, nor baptised for he lived not a moment. But I find I have no interest in my writing, so I will say no more.

April 19 1628

Two years have passed without a word written, but today I took my journal from the drawer in my nightstand, where it had lain since I put it away the day after my child died. I feel now inclined to record my thoughts and relate the everyday events of our lives. It is almost three years since Cris left us and time has enabled us to grow a shell about us and keep us safe and protected from despairing thoughts of melancholy. Life goes on of course and not much has changed at all other than we are older.

Our son Crispin is ten years old this year, Swefling eight and they are exceedingly helpful about the house and the garden and industrious in learning their letters and numbers well. Rowan applies herself also but she is less interested and James not at all. Joane is working at the Governor's house and is becoming friendly with the young people about her which is excellent for her to broaden her outlook, Lucy has been quieter and a little less argumentative in the house, she continues to give us much anxiety. She has been seen on more than one occasion, surrounded by several young men at the same time. We would expect her to be taking an interest in the males of our community as she is now almost sixteen years of age, but we are concerned at her inappropriate behaviour with them reported from various sources. There have been two warnings issued to her by the assembly regarding her unseemly behaviour and argumentative nature. Kathren and I are at a loss to know how to deal with her, being mere females and Papa, Philip and Edward have no sway over her and none would take a belt to her backside. The only person she would have listened to is no longer with us, so we entrust her to God to watch over and keep her safe.

The work on our land is unceasing. Cows to milk, for butter and cheese and fatten for beef and leather, and growing our food, but on occasions there is enough now to sell at the weekly market in towne. We also have candles and soap we produce and often barter them for other items we require. Only recently we exchanged a dozen candles for enough fish to feed us all very well for supper, which was a grand variation in our diet, but mostly our business is for pots and pans, and needles for sewing that we are unable to produce ourselves.

Our garden thrives with turnips, carrots, potatoes and onions. The trees in the orchard are small in stature but are bearing fruit and we have ample supplies of apples and pears, cherries and peaches and beneath them we grow mint, garlic, sage and rosemary for our flavourings and with lavender and yarrow for our ailments, we are well provided for in all manner of situations.

I am pleased also to relate we have begun to sell our production of linen we make from the flax. We have improved our techniques although it remains laborious but with Philip's assistance in setting a fair price we are more than satisfied with the return. One drawback though with the growing of flax is similar to that of the tobacco plant I understand, for it takes much from the soil, so there is a great need to clear the land. We can't complain though because we've only changed once and now papa and Edward have added two more acres to the small plot, the intention is to rotate the crops, as was the case in England. So we grow flax in one field, wheat and beans and maize in another and let the other return to grass where our cows and horse graze for two years and then it is our intention to change around. How it will work in reality we have yet to discover but we have at least a plan.

Yet our lives are not all toil and endless days of work with no joy, for during the last year Governor Yeardley decreed we should have a celebratory day for the founding of our colonie on May 13 1607 twenty years since. There was much excitement beforehand and the day was a lot of fun. The housewives provided several dishes of pies or breads or sweet foods, there was ale and cider to refresh us, and much music for dancing and games for the children. We sang songs and blessings and gave thanks to our Lord, conducted by Reverend Whickham. Everyone agreed it was a most excellent occasion even those gentlemen who lay in a drunken stupor outside in the night air or were dragged home by their wives and soundly beaten about the head, I shouldn't wonder. We are now all busy preparing for a repeat celebration in a number of weeks and larders are piling high with provender and several animals being fatted for the roast.

In the recent past I have become quite popular amongst the single male members of the populace and I am reminded of the days when we first arrived and I was trailed everywhere by potential suitors. On the first occasion recently I was much upset for I did not welcome such attention, but papa laid his arm about my shoulders and told me a few home truths.

"You are an eligible widow Swefling. You are in possession of a hundred acres of prime, virgin land, a fine home, everyone knows you work hard, and" he hesitated briefly before continuing "and all may see you are a fertile woman and will give any man the children he desires. You'd be a very good catch"
"Papa!" I cried at his comments "I don't wish to be wed" then seeing the smile of humour on his face, for he meant his comments to be received in lightheartedness.
"Can't we nail a notice to the door to say I am not available?" I replied.
"Swefling, shame on you, denying the menfolk of our towne the occupation of vying for your charms, and your land. Is there none to take your interest?"
I looked at him and would have spoken firmly but he grinned at Mary who had joined us in the yard.
"Leave the girl be, John" she said sounding I thought quite familiar with my father.
"Swefling knows I'm a tease. I'll not let any man cross the threshold and fight his case for my daughter until she's ready. Now I have work that requires my attention. I cannot wile away the day in idleness as some folk I may mention"
"Be off with you" Mary laughed, going after him with the yard broom, she was leaning on.
"Men!" I exclaimed referring to no one in particular.

...

In the last number of years the population of our community has been growing most quickly as on almost every vessel that sails up the James River emigrants arrive to seek their fortune. Some are free settlers with a little capital and the wherewithal to acquire land, but are able in due time if their circumstances are such, to acquire their fifty acres of head right. An increasing number of folk though, arrive as indentured servants from England, who like Kathren and Edward in general terms, came when their passage was paid, and are subsequently tied to their benefactors for at least four years. Not all who arrive in this manner acquire their freedom for many are indentured to unscrupulous individuals who cheat their servants or sell on their unserved time to others. However, as labour is the commodity most in demand for Virginia to flourish, I suppose it is inevitable folk will arrive in this manner and take their chances of freedom, and generally speaking their circumstances are improved from those they left in England, and they do have at least an opportunity to better themselves if they are treated well by their masters.

You will recall I mentioned in 1619 I believe it was when the very first African's stepped ashore in Jamestowne. Those individuals became indentured servants to Mr Rolfe. Most have now served their time but papa says many remain on the plantation run by a manager following Mr Rolfe's demise, although several have, on gaining their freedom, obtained land and become farmers in their own right, which is an interesting situation and a good one as I am sure you will agree. In the intervening years many more African's have arrived and they too are set on as servants, but there is an increasing shift to extending their indentures so many may never obtain any freedom whatsoever.

One might wonder though the difference apart

from colour between the English and African servants and why I will accept the one and not the other. It has not a thing to do with the people from another part of the world I am unfamiliar with but rather the fact the English or the indentured servants from Europe arrive of their own free will. It is their own decision, whatever the reasons to cross the ocean, but I understand the Africans do not come because they wish to but because they have been captured, often by their own kind and sold to disreputable ship captains and brought to this side of the ocean. Papa says many vessels sail to the Spanish and Portuguese lands 1000's of miles to the south of us, beyond the island of the Carib and these poor souls are indeed slaves with no rights at all. Those who arrive in Virginia are therefore more fortunate in that according to our law they may obtain their freedom at the end of their indentures.

If such a free African arrived at my door at the end of his term, with his papers in order, seeking work, I would have no hesitation setting him on if I had need for a worker and I was assured he or she was familiar with the work.

Papa says it will never be allowed to occur, for most Africans would remain where they served or attempt to return to Africa.

"But how could they return papa? They would need to work freely for pay to make the passage"
"I believe you are correct Swefling" he conceded "they will never be able to return from whence they came, but soon they will not even be released from their indentures"
"Papa, folk can't do that surely?" I asked naively.
"White servants have been treated thus, you are aware

of it, the Africans will arrive as slaves before many years have passed to this colony"

"It's terrible. I thought Virginia was to be different, to give freedom to us all"

"No Swefling, that's not so at all. It was an investor's enterprise and for some of us it has succeeded, but it is different yet again in the colonies of the north in Maine and Plymouth, I believe. The folk are free right enough but they have rigid religious practices imposed on them. We simply are instructed to attend church twice on Sunday and read the bible but we are not forced to comply"

"There is so much confinement everywhere Papa, why is this so?" I asked

"Who knows, perhaps control means law and order for us all. If we had no control there would be anarchy and all would suffer"

"What a terrible world we live in"

"Our world here in America is better than we could ever have dreamt of in England. Do you recall the little cottage in Ipswiche, barely more than a hovel despite your Mama and you working long hours to make it habitable for us. Here we have a fine house, a few acres of land beside the river in Jamestowne and several hundred acres between us no more than five miles distant. We are in heaven Swefling, but what we don't have, any of us, are sufficient labourers to work the land. The only solution is by indentures and inevitably slaves"

I had no answer then to my father's words but he smiled. "Enough of this now, all this talk of work and you and I are taking our ease over a dish of coffee when we should be at our chores"

"Yes papa, you're right" I smiled then, and kissed him on his cheek as we turned to the tasks that awaited us.

September 1828

We are at my brother's plantation at Ipswiche helping as we always do with the harvest and enjoying the good air and openness away from Jamestowne and the swampy almost fetid area by the river. Amey's parents and brother Andrew are with us, as they had been on every year we gather together and whilst we work hard we also have much pleasure in good company.

This afternoon I sat with Amey, shelling peas for supper. There was a hush about the place in the heat of the afternoon but we were more than comfortable in the shade of the porch. I sat back in my chair and sighed, looking out over the land before us and watched Andrew from some distance coming across the meadow towards us. Well I watched and Amey watched me, I realised, as I glanced at her and felt myself suddenly and for no reason whatsoever that I knew of, quite hot and flushed.

"Andrew's leg doesn't hinder him at all now" Amey said apropos of nothing.
"No, I can see that" I agreed.
"We thought he would die when he was returned to Mama's house" she reminded me "what a dreadful day it was Swefling, for so many of us"
"Yes" I replied not wishing to be reminded of the past "he's never found a wife though"
"No, not enough single women for a cripple to be fortunate enough" she said a grin on her face.
"Amey! That is such an unflattering description of your brother, Andrew's not a cripple at all. He'd make a fine husband for someone" I said believing it to be so.
"Wouldn't he just" she giggled, I looked at her and realised where her very construed conversation was leading.

"Oh no! Amey. Don't be match making. Did Andrew ask you to do this?"
"He did not; but you can't deny it, it would be a fine match, and we'd all love to see the two of you happy"
"I'm happy" I declared "as any widow has a right to be"
"It's over three years now Swef, isn't it time ~~enough~~ to be done with mourning? Find yourself a new husband"
"Amey, I'm content as I am and don't you dare try to imply anything else" I tried to sound firm but I also caught her infectious smile.
"Well alright, but don't expect me to be quiet about things. I shall be watching the two of you. Now I think there are enough peas here for supper. I'll take them in and bring us a cordial" she said rising "Oh look here's Andrew" she remarked as if she had just noticed him "cordial Andrew?" she asked grinning at us both "Be nice to him" she whispered to me as he waved and came onto the porch.

April 1629

Although the Assembly has been disbanded when the Virginia Company lost it's charter a number of years ago and the King became our protector, the men who made up the legislature of our colonie continued to meet on a regular basis to ruminate the colonie's affairs. One day last week papa, who continued to represent the interests within our towne, returned home from their current deliberations with Philip, who served Governor John Harvey as his clerk. They were in deep, yet not over serious discussion, as they came to the back porch where Mary, Kathren and I were going about our business preparing supper. We poured them their customary tankard of ale as they sat and papa sighed, taking a long draught as he was want to do.

"What did you discuss today" I asked always keen to hear about the politics of the colonie.
"There are suggestions to build a palisade across to the York River" Papa said
"What right across? That's many miles" Mary asked most surprised.
"The thought is from the Queen's Creek to the creek near our land, Archer's Creek. Samuel Mathews and William Claiborne called it"
"A creek named for you and John, Papa?" I smiled "how marvellous"
"What would be the purpose?" Kathren asked, which was a far more sensible response.
"It is thought to make the land down the peninsular safe from Indian attack" Philip replied "and to build houses along the way and on the high ground a mile or so where the creek doubles back, near Middle Plantation"
"Who would do the work?" I asked.
"There's talk of offering fifty acres to anyone who will remove into the area and assist" Papa said.
"But we have many acres we don't farm already, why would we want more?"
"I didn't say we'd do it" papa smiled at me "but we've spoken of taking up residence on our land beside Archer's Creek, I wonder if the time is right now, so we may get a house built and establish ourselves away from towne"
"Edward may wish to, do you believe so Kathren?" I asked.
"We'd like land certainly, but I'd not wish to remove ourselves without you all, it would be exceedingly lonely"
"Perhaps you should all go" Philip suggested.
"Cris and I thought of it many times, that's why we have the land, but …… Papa what are you're thoughts?"
"There's more than enough work for us here and your

orchard is thriving now, it would be a disappointment to give it up. You should think on it Kathren, we could always clear a bit of land and put a cabin up for you, then when you're ready you'll have a place to go. Apply for your headright acres" Papa concluded.

"We're not entitled, we came as servants" she reminded us.

"I'll speak with Edward on the matter Kathren, but for now we should be heading to the field for the planting before supper" he announced rising and ready to be on our way.

March 30 1630

The sickness has reached our house. Four days since my sons succumbed within hours of each other and are very poorly. Crispin has sores all over his body and lies on his bed, delirious and fighting the infection. James though lies quietly as if his peace is made and he is ready to leave us. My girls are sick also but not suffering anywhere as much, whilst Joane and Lucy being older seem unaffected totally, as are most of the adults. Mary, Kathren and I do what we are able for the boys, giving them cooled boiled water when they are gasping with thirst and dabbing the sores with a cooling paste we made from mint and lavender which helps ease them for a time. All abroad the towne though children are dying and neighbour remains away from neighbour for fear of spreading the sickness and those poor souls who succumb are interred in lime and their possessions burnt by order of the Assembly. It is a terrible fate to befall our towne after the Indian (Native) attack that took so many lives of grown men and women: our population will be decimated of children and babies this time.

The vessel that brought this disease to our shore, the Abigail is gone, to where we don't know or care but we await anxiously the arrival of her sister ship the Seaflower with much needed supplies of the necessities we are unable to produce ourselves, but everyday we wait in vain and who can blame the captain for not putting into Jamestowne where death lurks around every corner. Papa says there were attempts to set fire to the Abigail with her passengers on board for it was they who brought the sickness with them, but common sense and a measure of humanity prevailed, thanks be to God, for there is sufficient death and dying in our community, without our adding to it in vengeance.

Some of the poor folk on the Abigail remain confined in an empty warehouse at the water's edge and what a plight it must be for them to lose their children and know they brought the disease with them and are responsible for so many more deaths. It is terrible.

And even as I sit and write I watch over my sons in their suffering and pray soon it will be over for them, either to recover or pass on. Perhaps we are all to blame. Have we been too busy with building our lives here and turned away from God and this is his vengeance on us. But why take the children? Why not those of us who have sinned? But we attend church each and every Sunday without failing and read the bible in our homes, a passage each evening at the day's end, after supper, and know ours is not a vengeful God.

Perhaps it is too late for any of us, for disaster has haunted this family almost from the day of our departure from England, when Rebecca gave birth to her child on the voyage and jumped to her death, holding her infant son, and then my dear Mama passing suddenly and without warning. But Cris and I had eight good years together before the Indian [Native] attack.

It is a life like many others, with heartaches and set backs, it is the way of the world, hard and tragic for most folk, scratching a living where they may, beholden to others for the bread they eat and the clothes on their back, even the wood for the hearth. But those of us who came to America hoped to break the shackles of such an existence and for many it has been successful, for us too, even in our darkest hour, for we have strong well build walls around us, a roof to keep us dry, food always on the table and a warm fire and soft beds to lie on. It is better materially than we could ever have achieved if we remained in England, but even so, I miss my husband desperately, even after these years of our parting. When I lie at night in my bed I hug my pillow to me, remembering him and seeing his beloved face before me, fading now as the years pass but loving him still. And what of my sons Cris and James? Will they survive? It seems unlikely, but my prayers are offered in the hope that God is listening. Has he turned his back on our community in our hour of need? I think not, he is perhaps, teaching us lessons, of what I can't imagine just now, but there will be something and changes to be made as we progress generation after [by] generation.

April 6 1630

My beloved sons Crispin and James were buried in wool with others two days since, the last of our towne to die, for since their passing no further cases of the sickness have arisen and those ailing are slowly recovering. Swefling and Rowan are already out and about, as are many folk relieved to be breathing the fresh air of the days of spring.

James went first, he was so quiet he simply drifted away as if on a cloud floating up to heaven where Jesus and his papa waited him with their arms open wide. He seemed to go willingly at his end with hardly a murmur, unlike his elder brother, who fought like a demon. I am able to raise a brief smile now he suffers no more. Yelling, and cursing even he was and fighting, letting us know he was with us still, even though we tried to calm him but his strength was sorely weakened and a number of hours after his brother, resisting still to the end, he gasped his last and lay still, eyes wide open and arms outstretched.

I thought of my two sons with affection and sadness of their young lives cut short. So different in nature but both so like their father. Good looking, handsome boys, even at twelve and eight, taller than average and the prospect of becoming big strong men. But it is not to be and Jesus has other uses for them, than to live long lives on earth with us.

Yesterday, a whole day after the burial, Mary and I gathered together the bedding of my dearest boys, and their clothes and few treasured possessions, to burn them in a fire behind the house at the edge of the field, as every family who had lost loved ones was instructed so to do.

"I can't burn this" I said to papa, in control of the fire, as I held the book of King Arthur and his Brave Knights that Cris delighted to read "I need something to remember them by"
"Swefling you have your memories. These are simply things, meaningless objects. You don't need to keep

them. You write how you feel, they'll never be forgotten, you wouldn't let it happen and neither will we"

I was about to protest but I felt Mary's hand on my arm and saw in her face, acceptance of Papa's words. My gaze returned to the book and I realised he was right and stood back as my sons grandfather added their personal items to the blaze and watched briefly as the flames drifted skywards.

"Go in Swef" papa said "I'll see to the burning"

...

Mary followed me inside and we went into the boys' room where we found Kathren scrubbing at the bare beds removing all trace of the infection. We should make use of the room I knew even though we had extended the house over the years when Mary joined us and the children arrived but I wasn't ready to let anyone sleep in there for now just in case, but as we washed and swept and cleaned I realised what a nice room it was, catching the early morning sunlight.

"I think I'd like to move in here" I said as we finished.
"You feel like shifting all the furniture?" Mary asked
"Mmmm, it wouldn't be too difficult and we could use the other room to sit in or something"
"We have plenty of space, perhaps your papa will want it?"
"We'll ask" I suggested "but wait for a week to let the air clear" for I was not that interested in moving until all trace of the disease was gone.

The more I considered the matter the more I came

to believe that to move out of the room Cris and I had shared would be good for me because I always felt some melancholy, as if his presence was there. He would always be in my thoughts and that's where I wanted to keep him, not in a bedroom. I wonder if papa would feel likewise if he returned to the room he had shared with mama many years before, but clearly he didn't for in the summer we changed rooms and he seemed as much pleased to be where he now slept as I in the room at the back that was entirely free from memories of my husband.

October 1 1630

Life can be most peculiar at times and so 1630 has proved to be for me. We have just today returned from our visit to my brother's farm, as you will recall we do every year at harvesting time. Ipswiche, is the name John gave his land, in recognition of the town we lived in Suffolk. It is a bustling place and although he employs free workers, and indentured servants, we go to assist with the harvesting and to have some relief from our own chores in towne. All of us, Amey's parents and her brother, Andrew included, travel together, walking for the most part for it is no more than four miles and as we remained ten nights it never is a hardship.

We worked hard in the fields throughout the day, ate well at a large rectangular table outside on the porch in the evenings and afterwards sat about telling tales, reminiscing now and then or on occasions singing tunes we'd all learnt over the years, and in the twilight of the evening before turning to our beds, I'd often take a walk in the cool air beside the creek named for our family. It was always a peaceful time listening to the call of the night jar or the owl and sometimes I'd hear an animal scurrying in the copse just beyond but they were the sounds of nature and not to be feared. It was silent too from human voices and that's also what I enjoyed, the solitude, being close enough to know they were near but alone on the land. However, one evening I was so startled by a voice close near me, I practically jumped out of my skin and straight into the creek.

"You should not wander about in the dark on your own Swefling" Andrew Butler, Amey's brother's dislocated voice and totally unexpected, came across the darkness.
"Oh you gave me such a fright" I gasped as I recovered, smiling at him as I turned and found him close beside me.
"It was not my thought to surprise you. Most folk hear my approach with this useless leg of mine"
"How is it?" I asked
"No trouble hardly at all" he grinned, "I'll never run and hop or jump again, but why would I want to" he laughed, quite undeterred by his disability.
"You always see the best in everything" I smiled, as we sat on the bench from which in the daylight looked away towards Jamestowne.
"I've had much practice over the years" he said "do you recall the day, not long after your Mama died and you walked with John beside the river?"
"Yes, you walked me home"
"I had a determination to enquire if you would consider being my sweetheart, but I couldn't raise my confidence, sitting on the seat underneath the window with your papa inside, as we were"
I smiled in the darkness, which had now fallen.
"I believe I would have said yes though"
"Would you? It pleases me to hear you say so after all these years, but the very next time I saw you, you were to

be wed to Crispin"
I nodded
"He saw us, saw you especially" I explained "he told me he believed if he didn't act quickly I'd be gone from him"
"Yes, I know, he told me also" he laughed "and I was just a boy of sixteen years, I could not fight a man for you"
"You wanted to?"
"Yes, and every day since. All my life I've cared for you, but I'm not even the man I was five years since"
"You are, your leg doesn't stop you working or enjoying life"
"No" but he seemed disinclined to take our conversation further and stood "come, we should return to the house before we catch a chill" and he offered his arm, which I took, for he was right there was a cooling of the night air about us.

Several evenings in succession Andrew joined me on my nightly strolls and I found I welcomed his company greatly. On the last evening before our departure the next day, we left for our walk soon after our meal was concluded, at Andrew's suggestion, much to the amusement of his sister and my family.

"I was wondering, Swefling" he began as we stood beside the creek looking out over the water in the fading light, "if you'd thought to take another husband"
"No, I hadn't thought of it" I said slowly "why do you ask?" I turned and looked at him wondering if he was about to make a proposal to me.
"No reason" he said, and I was suddenly quite disappointed. Then after a few moments, just before I was about to look away, he continued, "I was wondering if you might consider me, if you were thinking of being wed that is, but if you're not then I'll not ask you to

consider me"
I smiled at him in the darkness.
"I said I'd not thought of it, not that I wouldn't"
"So you might wed again?"
"If the right man should ask"
"How would he know he was the right man for you?"
"He'd have to ask"
"And what might your answer be?" he asked as we went round in circles, neither of us getting to the point.
"My answer might be yes, if the right man was to ask me"
"I see" he said slowly as we continued to look at each other and I confess even though it was dark I did try to convey that should he ask he would get a favourable response, but he was uncertain and didn't continue the conversation but offered his arm again. I hadn't thought to remarry, whoever did but of all the men I knew, which wasn't a vast number, despite my comments a year since of such overtures as I mentioned to you, Andrew would probably be the one I'd chose.
"I ...." I began as we walked on "I thought you were about to ask me to wed you"
"I was"
"But?"
"I decided you'd wouldn't"
"But I said I would" I protested.
"Did you?" he asked stopping again a smile on his face now.
"Try?" I suggested.
"Let's not do all that again" he sounded more confident now I thought "would you consider me for your husband Swefling?"
"Yes" I said now with no hesitation or teasing "yes I'd like to be your wife"

I felt Andrew's hand on the side of my face, as his lips

moved slowly to my own and we finally shared our first kiss.

"Are you certain?" he asked his hand on my arm now.
"Yes Andrew I'm certain" I smiled in the darkness as I leant against him, feeling his arms about me now, growing more confident as the moments passed.
"I am joyful"
"It won't be easy for you" I laughed "I have two daughters and two step daughters at home"
"I know, but your father and brother are there"
"So you've thought this over?" I asked slipping my arm about his waist.
"For many years" he confessed.
"So why now?"
"So many questions Swefling?" he sighed breathing in my ear "It seems the right time and if you're willing we'll have a child or two of our own"
"I hope so" I whispered kissing his cheek, then finding his mouth as he turned his head "Will we wed soon?"
"It would be my intention" he whispered ~~to me~~ holding me tightly "I'll not be disabled by my leg. I can work still and do most things a man should do. Love you and give you children. Well I believe I can, I mean I am able to do what I need to"
"Oh Andrew" I giggled "I never thought otherwise. We shall accept whatever we are given, but if we do it together, be married I mean" I giggled again my words becoming confused "it's good enough for me"

He kissed me again, this time with a promise of passion to follow in due time and seeming reluctant he released me slightly.

"Shall we go tell the family?"

"Yes, though I don't believe there will be much in the way of surprise" I grinned as we turned hand in hand now towards the lights of the house.

"You are looking most pleased with yourselves" Amey's words were the first spoken to us as we reached the porch, where everyone was sitting enjoying an evening drink.
"We're to be wed" Andrew told them, looking very pleased with himself.
"At last" my brother John, declared, and our family offered their congratulations to us.
"You can't wed him" Lucy announced sourly "You're married to my father"
"Your papa is dead" Andrew's mother told her, not meaning I was sure, to be harsh.
"No, he isn't it's a lie so she can lie with everyman in towne" Lucy argued as Kathren stood and reached for her arm intent on removing her from our midst, but papa spoke first.
"You will not speak to my daughter in such a spiteful manner. Apologise now or I will take a strap to your backside"
"No! I'll never apologise for it's so. She killed my papa so she could marry him" Lucy changed her story as Kathren and Edward now took an arm each. "She's a witch and a whore"
"Lucy you are so horried" Joane glared at her sister as moments after, Lucy freed one of her arms and knocked her Joane to the floor. But this time Philip took hold of her arm.
"Leave me! Leave me!" Lucy screamed "you always want to touch me" Philip released her immediately very much taken aback by her words, as Kathren raised her hand and slapped Lucy hard across the face.
"Be silent" she said very evenly but it was obvious she

was seething, "To your room now. I'm sorry for her behaviour" Kathren said sadly and she and Edward dragged Lucy away into the house.

"Come Joane" I said helping her to her feet "do not be distressed" and I put my arms about her shoulders and looked about the family. "I'm sorry, Andrew if you wish to change your mind, I will understand"

"I've made my decision" he said coming to my side.

"You will not apologise for that girl" his mother comforted me "she is surely touched in the head, but we shall not let her upset this joyous time" and she kissed me on both my cheeks "Welcome soon to our family Swefling. 'tis a pleasure to know you will keep Andrew at your side"

"I'll try my best" I grinned.

"Won't be difficult" the man in question responded.

October 14 1630

Two days ago Andrew Butler and I were married in the recently completed brick church, situated in the new part of Jamestowne and a lovely sunny, if cold day it was. The ceremony was witnessed by our family and friends, with the exception of Lucy who refused to watch the cripple and the whore, as she called us, commit such a heinous act in the eyes of God. As we returned for the wedding supper and celebrations she left the house and, ignoring her as best we were able, which wasn't too difficult under the circumstances, we prepared to enjoy the festivities. At a decent time in the evening those individuals who lived or stayed elsewhere, left the house, the girls went to their room and Papa stood to take his leave of us.

"I'm pleased to see you smile again Swefling" he said taking my hands in his, "I know you will be a good husband and wife to each other" and he kissed me on my cheek and patted Andrew on his shoulder "Take good care of my girl" he laughed.

"I will, have no doubt" Andrew replied and we watched Papa head for his bed. I began to tidy the parlour, which didn't need too much in the way of any attention, but I was wont for something to occupy myself.

"Swefling" Andrew called holding out his hand to me. I smiled at him and placed mine in his, "time for our bed" he whispered and led the way to our room at the back of the house, that I had moved into earlier in the year. We closed the door on the world outside and he took me in his arms and very soon we began happily and joyfully our married life together.

…

The following morning Andrew and Papa returned to their employment and Mary, Kathren and I to our chores and Joane to her occupation in the governor's household, caring for his children.

"Swefling" Joane began hesitantly "Kathren asked if Lucy slept in our house. She didn't return to her own bed last evening"
I nodded.
"Kathren and I will have a discussion"
"Lucy doesn't mean to be nasty" Joane began to defend her sister "I'm sure she doesn't. She gets very muddled"
"She's wicked" Mary said joining us.
"I don't think that's so" I started seeing both Mary and Joane looking towards the door.
"It's true" Lucy said sounding full of remorse and looking much the worse for wear "I'm sorry" she apologised.
"Where did you go?" I asked "were you safe?"

"Of course I was safe" she flared up "Who'd hurt me? I'm mad Lucy who lives with the cripple and the whore. Were you good to each other? Did the cripple manage?"
"How dare you be so awful" I said "your father would be so disappointed with you" I said wishing even now I didn't have to conceal the fact Cris was not her father.
"And with you I imagine Swefling" she laughed a strange little laugh as Kathren hearing our conversation and raised voices, joined us. "We both did alright last night then, you and me flat on our back, eh Mama? Was he good, your cripple?"

Joane stared open mouthed at her sister, her hand covering her mouth in horror. I have never struck out at a living creature in my entire life but I did then, and as Kathren had done at Ipswiche, I slapped Lucy a stinging blow across her face.

"You will not speak so in this house. If you are not able to curb your tongue, you must leave. I will not have you here"
"I live with Kathren" she declared but even as we watched her anger and wildness began to leave. "Mama" she said calmly, quietly, surprised and tearful "why did you do that?"
"You were in a trance" I said to which Mary standing beside me snorted with derision. Kathren who had watched this scene moved towards Lucy.
"Come have a soothing drink"
"I don't want your drink Kathren, I'm going to lie down" and Lucy wandered in the direction of Kathren's cottage.
"Oh Mama" Joane wailed "how could she say those things?"
"Your sister is sick in the head" Mary announced with some vehemence and sadly I do believe she was right.

"~~Off you~~ go to the governor's mansion Joane. You are not to worry" I smiled at her putting my arm on her shoulders. She nodded somewhat reluctantly.
"Yes Mama" she whispered and we hugged each other again before she left.

...

"The two of you will have to do something with the lass" Mary told Kathren and I as we worked at the laundry later in the day.
"But what?" Kathren asked "should I tell her?"
"I don't see how that will help. She'll hate you then for keeping such a secret" I said.
"You could look in your herbal book, there'll be curatives for troubled minds" Mary suggested "I'll ask around. If she's not controlled she will become worse. In the barracks I expect she was, no decent man will be with her. The menfolk had best watch out for themselves"
"Oh Mary don't say such things" I chided her.
"I'm only saying how I see things, but they should be warned, Edward likewise" she added to Kathren.

April 1631

It is six months since my last writing, not because I had nothing to say but because I had no paper on which to write my thoughts, for the sheets I kept so carefully, disappeared from the cupboard in the parlour where they were stored, waiting to be used. I have my suspicions the culprit is Lucy, but there has been no evidence, though I have taken to hiding my journal and other items I wished to keep safe, in secret places. It is not the way I wish to live at all and I can never speak of it to anyone for fear of making matters worse, but I feel Lucy is watching and prying constantly. Mary said, she believed Papa, being master in his own house, should take his belt to her naked backside if she misbehaved so again, but I knew he wouldn't for he had never to me and would not beat a volatile young lady who would instantly accuse him of all manner of things, added to which Kathren was her mother and ought to instigate such punishment.

Lucy aside, our lives were comfortable and easy through the months of the winter and time passed peacefully and without incident. We had plenty of food to eat, wood to burn in the fire to warm us, thick woollen clothes and Andrew and I had each other and I realised very soon in our married life how much I loved him. It didn't mean I loved Cris any less, it was just he was gone from me and Andrew was now my husband and we enjoyed being married very much in all ways both in the privacy of our bedroom and in our relationships in public and with our family and friends.

And now our joy is complete and Andrew agrees with me, for I told him only this very morning, as we woke and lay in our bed at the start of the day, as the sun beamed through the window, that in September time I thought we would have an addition to our family.

"You mean a lodger" he teased me.
"No a tiny human being, growing in here" I said patting my belly.
Andrew rolled onto his side and hugged me.
"It's a strange feeling Swef" he said "to know I'm partly responsible for the creation of a new life. I'll be a good father too, just like our own papa's, but if it's like Lucy, you may take her back"
"Oh indeed I will, I would not wish for another like her, poor girl" I grinned, where in truth, as far as Lucy was

concerned I never felt like doing, but I wasn't going to be down hearted for a time.
"What shall we have?" he asked.
"I don't believe we may choose" I laughed "but a son or a daughter for sure"
"A son would be fine. He'd grow big and strong and work hard and someone I'd be proud of, but a daughter would be beautiful and clever but then I'd have to protect her from all the beaus who'd come calling. Oh dear!" he sighed.
"Oh dear indeed" I agreed "what a dilemma"
"I shall ponder carefully on being a good father" he smiled kissing me. "Oh Swef, we're to have a baby of our own already"

I've never seen a man so overjoyed and pleased and proud of himself and wanting to announce his virility to the known world, and it was delightful.

September 13 1631

I am overjoyed, pleased, proud and not a little tired for early this morning I was safely delivered of a fine, healthy son, and we shall call him Richard Andrew after his grandfather and father. I cried when Andrew saw him for the first time and gently touched his first born as he lay in his cradle.

"He won't bite" I said a tease in my voice. Andrew looked up at me and smiled.
"Look at his tiny nose and ears Swef, and such little fingers"
"Have you never seen a new born child before?" I asked.
"Not in my life. Might I hold him?"
"Of course sweetheart, he's your son"

"How do I do it?"

So I told him and very soon Andrew, with growing confidence had Richard nestling on one arm, holding his little finger with the other, when the door opened.

"Look papa" he smiled at my father "look what Swefling has given us"
"You too I trust" papa grinned, inspecting his newest grandchild, before crossing to me and giving me a kiss. "and how are you my girl?"
"I'm fine papa, we're all fine. Are we still to go to the farm"
"You will need to rest"
"I will ride in the wagon with the baby within the week. We may go Andrew mayn't we?" I asked.
The two men exchanged glances and both nodded.
"In a week or so" Andrew agreed knowing I wouldn't be put off.

But for now I was happy to lie back in our bed enjoying briefly my break from the chores for surely as summer followed spring, in a day or so I would be up and about tending to my family and the chores helping to keep us happy and well fed. I wouldn't probably be helping with the harvesting this year but I could just as easy prepare the food for the workers and feed my son of course and spend time with all my children and Andrew, so like everyone else I'd be very busy and it was no different for me than any other woman in my position. Sometimes though, when I was very tired I'd ponder about my parents and think of the other life my mother had given up to be with papa. Once again I reflected how much she must have loved him, and every time I thought of it, I smiled recalling how young they'd always seen to me, barely more than children themselves when John,

Philip and I arrived in successive years at the turn of the century.

October 17 1632

A year has passed in peace and calmness and we all remain healthy and full of life. Richard is a delightful child loved by all of us and with a sunny nature that no one could possibly ignore. And now, as of yesterday he has a brother to keep him company, for our second son has arrived and is to be named John Philip, for my Papa and brothers. Like his own brother Richard, he has a mass of dark hair and deep dark brown eyes and feeds well at my breast and sleeps greatly, which is most convenient and I love him to bits.

September 28 1633

We arrived at my brother's farm today, following a great debate on whether to leave the relative safe confines of Jamestowne for there have been many reports of isolated attacks on travellers, perpetrated by the Indians, throughout the whole colonie of Virginia and we were much afeared. For a number of years there has been some peace between us and Powhatan's people, but I suppose there are always rogue elements in every society, I know there are in ours. Andrew, Papa, Philip and Edward reasoned though, there were enough of us who could handle a musket capably to fight off the indians if we were unfortunate to be attacked and we set out, watchful, our eyes searching all about for danger, and ensuring for once the children all rode in the wagon. But it is clear to determine, we are safe and secure following our journey.

Neither Lucy nor Joane accompanied us this year, Joane because she is living in the governor's house now as her employment necessitates and also because she is sweet on one of the grooms. She is such a delightful girl, a woman now already of seventeen years. I was married to her father at that same age and the thought brought home to me how quickly the years pass us by with barely a murmur.

Lucy no long lives with us either, that is I mean with Kathren, for she has long since removed herself from the main house. It was of her own choosing and we knew that for a time she found a room with one of the soldiers from the barracks, although some folk advised me, there were usually several young men there at any time. I do not comprehend how she is the way she is, wild and uncontrolled and seemingly with no moral standards at all. My heart bleeds for Kathren for I can't imagine how she could have produced such a wayward daughter, for Kathren is as calm and placid, honest and straightforward as Cris ever was. Perhaps the difficulty for Lucy stems from the upheaval of her early life, for she believes still she is the daughter of Cris and Rebecca and she had, I must never forget witnessed Rebecca's death, if not at first hand certainly close to. She also could not ignore the fact that Cris and I became wed within the year, and thus perhaps we are all to blame for her nature.

But despite all this, whenever Lucy wasn't raging and being immoral, I liked her well, for she could be most pleasant. Those occasions though were becoming more [less] and more infrequent [most] for her turns, when she became quite hateful, were increasing and I never wanted to see her again. Of course I felt bad myself thinking such thoughts about a poor woman who was not well. But the pattern of our poor discourse continues.

Our son Richard is two and became most excited with our adventure and crawled over the wagon, from Mary to me and back again, throughout the journey, exploring and waving to his own papa who walked along with mine. With us, we brought our second son John who is to be one year old next month, October 16 and every bit as mischievous as his elder brother and the two of them are as slippery as eels but such is the nature of babies that before we know what is happening they will no longer depend on us but be off into the world leading lives of their own. In the meantime we arrived full of expectation for the company of family, some hard days helping with the harvesting in the sun, but much relaxation at the end of each day.

October 1633

I have had no opportunity to record our sojourn with my brother, for the ending was too painful and is not yet resolved, but I feel the need to set down my words now.

One afternoon in the second week of our visit when the work was nearing completion, Swefling who is now thirteen went on a horseback ride on the property, quite close to the house I must stress, with her cousin Sarah, my brother, John's daughter. I tried to dissuade them from their excursion for although we have heard of no recent incidents concerning the Natives, it didn't mean they weren't still about. We have found to our cost, our lack of vigilance is seriously wanting.

The time was long past when the girls should have returned but there was no sign of them at all and we were more than anxious. Andrew and John, Philip and Edward rode along the same pathways Swefling and Sarah had taken early in the afternoon but on their return to us had just one extra rider with them.

"Where's Swefling?" I cried feeling a panic rising within me.
"She's gone" Andrew said, climbing from his horse and taking hold of me.
"What do you mean gone?" I asked struggling free from his arms. "Sarah's here, where's Swefling?"
"The Indians took her" Sarah cried as she was held safely by her parents.
"Why didn't you stop them?" I asked foolishly and so I was informed.
"I couldn't" she wailed from her mother's arms "they came and grabbed her pony and she was off before I could do a thing"
"Why didn't you return immediately" I asked
"I was trying to find her. I know in which direction they left"
"We must go after them and fetch her back. We shall leave now before it's too late"
"Swefling we will" Andrew said and already fresh horses were brought from the stables.
"I will ride to towne and get the soldiery" papa suggested.
"Oh hurry" I cried now seeing what I considered to be no urgency amongst the men, but soon enough with food and liquid in their saddle bags Andrew and John, Philip and several of the farm workers prepared to depart, leaving Richard Butler and Edward for our protection.
"Don't worry Swef" Andrew said before he climbed aboard his horse "we'll find her"
"How can I not worry?" I asked "and you're leaving too"
"Best be on our way" John said looking at the sun

beginning to drift slowly downwards in the sky.
"Take care of yourselves and bring my baby home" I cried in tears and let Andrew's hand go and gathered Rowan, Richard and John about me as we watched the men ride away without a backward glance, down the road in the direction they had not long since returned.

...

The waiting was dreadful, hour after endless hour, and as the twilight came and the night fell about us there was still no news. Papa returned in the company of six soldiers from the towne and Edward who had ridden out earlier explained in detail the place from where Swefling had been taken and they too rode out following the tracks of our family.

I refused to go to my bed but had the needs of my infant son John to occupy me for a short time. When he was fed and asleep, I joined papa on the porch staring out over the land towards the creek.

"Why papa? Why would they take her?" I asked "she wouldn't hurt a fly"
"I don't know Swefling. Who can say?"
"And why didn't they take Sarah as well?"
Papa reached for my hand and held it tightly in his, stroking my arm.
"They'll find her. I know they will"
"But what if they don't? Hardly anyone who's been abducted has returned"
"Your daughter is a strong girl Swefling, like you. She'll find an escape if she's able"
I looked at him knowing he was trying to help, but even so his words had a hollow ring to them.

Throughout the night we sat on the porch, joined from time to time by others unable to sleep, but papa and I kept our vigil, hardly speaking as I grew more and more despondent, convinced now my daughter would not be found and returned to us. As the first streaks of dawn appeared in the eastern sky I rose from the chair and stared out over the land once more. I heard a baby crying in the distance and knew I had to go and feed my son.

"I'll keep watch" papa said. I nodded to him and went inside feeling weary and very ragged and tired now, but I could not sleep while my child was missing. I picked John up from his cradle and settled myself on the bed and opened my shift and let him feed. and in the quietness of the room I felt my eyelids become very heavy and begin to droop. I fought to remain awake whilst I held my son, and when he was almost finished the door opened slowly and Rowan peeped her head around the door.
"Swefling is not in her bed Mama" she whispered closing the door and standing by the bedside.
"Papa Andrew has not returned with her" I replied "but they will I'm sure" I was grateful for the company of my twelve year old daughter, and patted the bed beside me.
"come sit with me Rowan" I suggested and she clambered up beside me and lay very close.
"What will they do with Sweffie? The Indians I mean"
"I don't know sweetheart, we have to pray Papa will find her. Let's not think of anything else"
"I miss her"
"I know you do. We must say our prayers for her safe return and the searchers too"
"Papa Andrew is a good man to us isn't he? He is a papa to Swef and I"
"Of course he is"

"I can't remember what my real papa looked like. Will God forgive me?"

"Rowan you remember when he made you smile and cuddled you, that's what's important. It doesn't matter that you can't recall his face, you were only four when he died"

"Sweffie doesn't remember either she said. We know he had dark hair and he was tall, taller than papa Andrew"

"That's enough to remember" I smiled.

"Mama, is it true that my papa was not Lucy's father?" she asked all of a sudden.

"Where on earth did you hear that?" I asked not answering her.

"Sweffie overheard you and Mary and Kathren talking one day"

"I see"

"It is so. Who was her father?"

"I don't know at all"

"But Kathren is her mama? And she was papa's daughter. Kathren is my sister"

"Yes Rowan, but it is not something to be discussing. It is Kathren's secret"

"I'll not say Mama, I promise I just wanted to know"

I looked at her knowing she would not break her word but was curious she chose this time to ask such questions, perhaps she wanted to have everything sorted out in her mind, with her sister missing.

I looked from her to John who had finished his feeding, then back to Rowan and smiled at my children.

"Come, let us start the day and see if your sister will return to us"

...

For three days we waited for our searchers to return and when they did, they returned alone. I was staring out across the fields towards the forest beyond, when I heard the clatter of horses hooves in the yard and hurried around the side of the house to find our party of riders looking most weary and dejected, dismounting their horses.

"Why have you returned without her?" I asked Andrew and my brothers.
"The soldiers are continuing the search" Andrew said, reaching an arm out to me, but I moved away. "There was no trace Swefling, we rode as far as Hopkins Plantation on the Richmond Road but no one has seen anything of her"
"You should have stayed 'til you found her" I told him.
"Swef" he said firmly "I know it's hard for you to wait but I'm sure the soldiers will find her"
"How can you know, you can't. She's gone, dead most probably and I'll never know. They'll surely kill her"
"There's no reason" my brother John declared "Why would they take her and then kill her. If they were to do it, they would have done so on the road and we would have found her"
"John's right" Philip agreed "the fact we haven't found her means she's alive"
But I was not convinced and shook my head.
"She's dead. I know it" I said flatly and turned and walked away.

November 1633

A month has passed and no one has seen or heard a word of Swefling. The soldiers returned after an absence of ten days with likewise no news at all and I am forced to carry on with my life, for my other children need me. Not only that I realised last week I was with child again and I am in despair for I cannot replace my lost child with another. I have always been so delighted to discover my condition in the past but on this occasion, tears come to my eyes and I continually mop them. I was in such a state just yesterday when Andrew came upon me.

"Please Swefling, shed no more tears, there's hope" he said, repeating the comment he had used almost every day this last month.

I nodded and reached for him, comforted briefly for his strong arms about me, but I did something I have not done since Cris died and I cried and cried bitterly as he held me. As my sobs ceased I wiped my eyes again and he kissed my wet cheek.

"Each day will be easier" he consoled me.
"It's not only Sweffie" I sniffed "I'm with child"
"Oh Swef" he said, a smile on his face clearly pleased at the news. "She'll be back before it's born, you'll see" he encouraged me but I shook my head.
"Don't Andrew, please. I have to believe she's gone. I can't live in hope, wondering all the time"
"But even so" he began "don't close your mind to it"
"Alright" I agreed sighing, not wanting to speak of my loss, our loss, for Swefling was lost to all of us.

April 1634

I couldn't face writing throughout the winter. It was very cold with much snow and when it wasn't snowing it rained and the wind blew constantly. The days were dull and dark and we hurried to our fires as soon as we were able. My thoughts were muddled from thinking Swefling was dead to if she was alive how could she possibly survive in the dreadful winter and either way I was melancholy and low in spirits.

Matters were made worse, if that was at all possible on one occasion, when the children and I walked with Andrew to his parent's house and came across Lucy, on the arms of two young men, both of whom appeared exceedingly intoxicated.

"Not so high and mighty now, step mother" she called to me "your precious Swefling taken. The Indians will use her well, a pretty little virgin" she laughed bitterly at me and the other folk who overheard her. "Nothing to say then, Swefling"
"Not to you" I replied angrily feeling myself react to her words. Andrew drew us away but the meeting unsettled me and Rowan especially, and it took us some while to get over our ill chanced meeting.
"She's simply evil" Andrew's mama Bettris, remarked when we later spoke of the incident "She'll get her comeuppance one of these days, you mark my words"
"I cannot understand why she is so. Joane is as sweet as Lucy is unkind. Joane came to us as soon as we'd returned and was told the news. She's always been like a daughter to me"
"And you've been as her mother since was but a year old" I was reminded.

"She's to be wed" I said, pleased to be able for once to impart good news "to the governor's groom Joseph Jones"
"I know his mother, a widow. Will they live with her?"
"For a time" I said "It'll be good to have something to look forward to"
"You have the baby, Swefling" Bettris said clearly surprised at my words.
"I know" I smiled now stroking my belly "I feel so guilty. I should be happy and I am really, a new life, but it reminds me of my other baby"
"What nonsense Swefling, there's no connection" she said firmly to me, which was exactly what Mary repeated almost daily "enjoy your new babe. It's not it's fault Swefling is gone, so don't put blame on the babe"
I looked at her steadily knowing of course she was right and acknowledged it was so.
"Good now I'll expect you to talk to baby all the time 'til he arrives" and finally I smiled at her.
"That's better, now what else is new in new town?"

May 17 1634

We have a new son. A fine boy was born yesterday as dawn broke. Mary wrapped my new child in a clean cloth and handed him to Andrew who used to such occurrences now took his son eagerly, smiling through his tears at the tiny bundle in his arms.

"We shall call him Gabriel Crispin, Swef, what do you think?"
"Gabriel Crispin" I repeated "It's a good name, our own angel Gabriel"
"You are a romantic as ever my sweet" he glanced at me, the smile not leaving his face for a moment, as he reached across and planted a kiss on my forehead. "I'll leave you

with our son and announce the news to the family, they will be overjoyed"

And they were, and a week later, we took Gabriel to the church where he was baptised, and for the first time since the fall, there was much happiness in our household, despite our constant thoughts and prayers for Swefling.

July 21 1634

Joane was wed today to her young man and a fine couple they are. The church was crowded with family and friends and to everyone's surprise, governor Sir John Harvey, the most unpopular of men at this time, took his place in his usual seat to witness the ceremony. There were many comments overheard as to the reason for his attendance, but he was Joane and Joseph's employer and from that perspective he had a right to be there. Whatever the circumstance, thankfully it did not affect the day, unlike another marriage not so many weeks previously when there had been much altercation against the governor.

Joane asked papa to escort her along the aisle to Joseph and very proud he was to do so. He appeared happy as the afternoon passed and later stood with Mary awaiting the arrival of the guests at our house. It was then as I watched, I had more than an inclination there was a growing affection between them.

"Has papa spoken to you about Mary?" I asked Andrew moments later, following my observation.
"Many times" he agreed.
"No! I mean about caring for her" Andrew looked at me and grinned as he realised the inference behind my

words.

"Why would your father speak with me about caring for her" he declared avoiding my eyes.

"Well you work together"

"You are becoming a meddlesome matchmaker, my sweet" he laughed "and I would not break a confidence even if he did speak of her, as well you know"

"Oh Andrew, tell me, I know you know"

"Swefling" he laughed again, linking my arm through his "whatever your papa chooses to do or say are his concern, not his daughter's. Enough now, enjoy the day, it's a rare treat to have our family and friends together in joyful celebrations"

Reluctantly I had to agree with him and allowed him to lead me towards his own mama and papa "but I'll find out" I added getting the last word.

August 1634

All is revealed with my father and Mary and quite by accident as it happens. Last night was hot and stifling, the air still, the children restless and fretful, although we slept well enough under one thin sheet when they allowed us. I rose early in the morning to visit the necessary and make an early start on preparing breakfast, in the coolness of the hours before the sun rose. I quietly closed the door to our bedroom where Andrew lay just waking while Gabriel slept on and came face to face with Mary doing likewise at the door to papa's room. She gasped as she saw me and immediately her face became flushed, for I do believe she was blushing as she stood before me in a thin wrap over her shift.

"You're up and about early Swefling" she said to me in a

highly embarrassed fashion.
"Yes, I couldn't sleep in the heat. Is my papa alright?"
"Yes, I mean he's......" she was most flustered for a woman of her age, which I believed to be close to my father's fifty years, at being discovered.
"I think I know what you mean" I smiled "I have suspected the two of you since Joane's wedding"
"You have? Oh deary me" Mary said.
"I think it is good, you being company for each other"
"You do?"
"Indeed I do. But why are you sneaking about the house? I will speak to my father about that" I giggled, as we made our way across the room.
"Oh Swefling, please no, your papa, he would be ......"
"Embarrassed?" I asked "I expect he would be. I will think of something. Would you like some coffee, I'm just going to put some on"
"I should get my day clothes" Mary said "but directly I would"

I smiled to myself as she wandered up the stairs and I to the kitchen to build up the fire and put the water on for the coffee. After, I opened the door and sat on the step, forgetting my chores for the moment, enjoying the warmth of sunshine on my face, when I heard footsteps and a voice behind me spoke.

"And Mama said she was to make your papa his breakfast" Andrew was telling Gabriel "we have to watch her all the while son"
I stood up and kissed them both as Andrew placed our grizzling son in my arms.
"Are you hungry sweetheart?" I asked Gabriel.
"Papa is too" Andrew advised me.
"Papa will have to wait 'til I've fed his son. Coffee should

be ready I expect and Mary will be down directly. She'll fix it"
"You've seen her?"
I smiled and whispered softly to him.
"Yes coming out of papa's room"
"He's sick?" he asked in a tone of voice that told me he knew it wasn't so. I looked up from Gabriel who was quiet now he was at my breast.
"You know as well as I do Andrew Butler, my papa is in the peak of good health and …… whatever else it might be" I giggled.
"Perhaps you're right" he agreed knowing it was so much safer for him to agree than continue his role of innocence. "Just leave them to themselves Swef. It's none of our business how they spend their nights and with whom"
"Oh, I was going to ask why he let Mary wander about the house to her room in her shift"
"Don't you dare" he grinned at me, sitting on the step beside me, his arms about my shoulders, the fingers of his other hand softly stroking our son's cheek, before gently caressing my breast. I turned to him and smiled.
"I will not" I agreed as he kissed me. "I love you Andrew" I whispered apropos of nothing and he kissed me again. Suddenly we heard a giggle and felt little hands on our heads and turned to find our three year old Richard, two year old John and their big thirteen year old sister, Rowan standing behind us.
"Come and sit on my lap" Andrew said to the boys as Rowan knelt on the floor her arms about our necks. "What a lovely family we are" he said when we were all together.
"And Swefling" Rowan reminded him "my sister will come back to us one day"
"Of course" Andrew beamed at her "We pray for that, do we not sweetheart, each and every day?" he said to me.

"Yes we do" I agreed which wasn't altogether so for me, but perhaps our thoughts were correct "should we go to John's this year?"
"Why ever not?" Andrew asked. "We must. Swef knows we always go there, if she came back and found us absent she'd believe we'd forgotten her"
"We'll never do that" I said, pleased I could hear Mary descending the stairs and turned the conversation away from our loss, as she, as I predicted, began to prepare breakfast.

September 1634

Our last night at my brother's farm arrived and we sat on the porch satisfied with the harvest gathered and safely stored away, the crops for shipment ready to go to market and profit and the food for the winter in the barns.

"How fast the year has passed since Swefling was taken" I said "and our lives have gone on without her, when she should have been here with us"
"Life continues always" Papa told us "whatever comes to pass, it's the only way the human spirit will survive"
"And you have Gabriel now" Rowan joined in
"We didn't have him to replace your sister" I replied more stridently than I intended "Oh Rowan, I'm sorry, come here" I said holding out my arms to her, "I didn't mean to upset you, none of you can ever be replaced by another baby. You're all too precious for that" she looked at me for a moment longer than necessary and came into my arms and I held her for her time.
"I am pleased you say so Mama" she said sitting beside me.

Despite the reminders for all of us that returning to the farm brought into fine focus, I believe it was the right thing to do and was another step along the path to recover from the loss of Swefling, and we returned to Jamestowne to prepare for the months of winter and prayed they would be less severe than on previous occasions, for it much controlled our lives.

July 1635

What a busy time we are experiencing just now. I am in the fifth month of my pregnancy, much to Andrew's delight and myself marginally less so, so soon after Gabriel's arrival but as we always say, such is life. But just now we are celebrating a step grandson, for Joane gave birth a month since to a lively and noisy son. She was a picture of health throughout her pregnancy and I knew her husband's mother with whom they live took great care of her. Joane is a natural mother and has taken to caring for her baby, who they named Joseph Crispin, with a passion I can only barely recall.

Lucy meanwhile, we rarely see but hear much of her exploits, which are becoming most serious, degrading and commonplace. Such are her activities, she is the centre of discussion, for many in our community have words to say regarding her behaviour and unseemly language. Sadly for Lucy, we do suspect it won't be overlong before the governor is forced to take action himself against her. How Crispin must be turning in his grave, blaming himself for leaving his daughter with such an offspring.

...

Two weeks ago, we were taking a stroll beside the James River from our acres of land towards home when we stopped and watched a vessel sail towards the town. The boys loved to see the ships and now he was becoming older, Richard asked endless questions of where they came were from and who was on them and thus numerous tales and stories were invented by Andrew and papa to occupy the mind of our son. We stood long enough to watch the ship tie up at the dock before we proceeded towards our home. We were not long returned and settled on the porch in the shade with a glass of ale, when there was a sudden and unexpected loud knocking at the door.

"Are we expecting anyone?" Papa asked as he rose to investigate our caller, making such a commotion to disturb our peaceful afternoon.

We shook our heads as the knocking came again, and we turned and peered inside as Papa opened the door.

"You appear in urgent need to speak to someone of this house, young man" he addressed a tall fellow dressed, we could see even from our distant vantage point, in the finest of cloth and cut of clothes, we'd only dreamt of over the years.
"John Archer. I seek my Uncle, John Archer and my Aunt Ales" the young man spoke, as we, more closely inspected him and much admired his handsome appearance and fine way of speaking.
"I'm John Archer, who might you be to call me Uncle John?"
"I'm William Cobbold, same as my father, brother of my Aunt Ales. Is she about?" he asked looking towards us on the porch.
"William Cobbold?" my father asked, a smile coming to

his face "William Cobbold! Come in! Come in!"
"Swefling" papa smiled at us when he led the young man onto the porch "do you recall your cousin?"
"I believe I do" I agreed standing to greet the man "You've grown some"
"I trust so ma'am I was just six years when I saw you leave on the ship" he laughed "how is my aunt?"
"My wife died a year after our arrival" papa replied "but enough of the past, let me introduce you to my family, there are several of us now"

We were most surprised to meet the young man, for folk did not visit unannounced, especially from across the ocean and no letter had arrived beforehand from England.

"I departed before I could advise you" he confessed as he sat with us a short while later, a glass of ale in his hand.
"My father died unexpectedly and my grandfather advised me I would take his place and be educated in my role as head of the family. I'm not ready for that, if at all"
"Your grandfather was e're a forceful man" Papa acknowledged.
"Grandmother spoke often how his bitterness and anger caused your wife, Aunt Ales to be disowned when she went against his wishes"
"How is your grandmother?" Papa asked.
"She remains a formidable lady, ancient now, 74 years she tells me but good for a few more yet"
"Does grandmother know you're here?" I asked feeling her loss for her grandson, as I did still for my daughter.
"Oh yes" he laughed "I came at grandmother's suggestion. I have letters for you. Well for Aunt Ales"
"I could never write to tell Eleanor" Papa confessed "that was wrong of me"

"She did wonder how you faired. Arrangements are made and I shall write to her at her sister's home in Otley and advise her I am arrived and found you all in the rudest of health. She will be delighted and relieved"

"And you will be welcome to remain with us" I smiled "and I will write, Papa if I may?"

"Indeed, our letters are long since overdue. What plans do you have William?" Papa asked as Mary and I began to busy ourselves with the evening meal.

"I arrived with others of my acquaintance. My companion, William Tye says he is known to you"

"I recall the name, most certainly" Papa said smiling and nodding. "And what will you do in Virginia?"

"I have a grant of one hundred and fifty acres" William explained "grandmother arranged the matter previously for my 21st birthday anniversary, 'always good to have land', she said 'but England is all taken, though I'll receive Cobbold Hall in due course unless I am disowned by my absence. I do miss her but I will not return for I mean to make my life in Virginia"

"You will not claim your inheritance?" Andrew asked and I heard the sound of a bottle touching glasses once more as they conversed.

"I have little need for a title in America and the farms in England are well managed. I will make arrangements, perhaps in due course, there is sure to be a cousin somewhere willing to take over, but whilst grandfather remains alive and in charge I will not bother myself over it. No, I mean to farm, tobacco and sugar cane are very profitable I understand?"

"Indeed so" Papa replied "there is a dire need for workers for such crops, folk here about own slaves, we don't hold with that. My son, your cousin John, he runs a small farm, a place called Ipswiche, he gets by without. It is not easy, though he grows corn and such like. There are free

blacks and servants of course, and we all help as we are able. We go September. It was when we were there two years since, Swefling's daughter was taken by the Indians"
"Swefling's daughter" William was clearly confused "I thought you and she were wed?"
"Oh yes" Andrew laughed "we are, she was married before but Crispin Martin, her then husband, was killed in an Indian attack, the same one when I lost the good use of my leg"
"I hear tell it remains a dangerous place and there are fierce wild animals roaming free"
"It's been mostly quiet for a time" Papa said smiling, "but life should be full of ups and downs. We'll take a visit with you lad and inspect your land, when we go to Ipswiche if 'tis nearby"

September 1635

Papa, Andrew, William and my brothers John and Philip who was now a member of the assembly, I forgot to say, returned early this afternoon to where we stayed at Ipswiche, from their visit to William's hundred and fifty acres and seemed well pleased with what they had found. William's land lay about a mile or so distant along the road to Middle Plantation, where the settlement was apparently thriving. Along one length of the property was Archer's Creek, which ambled from Middle Plantation to the James River and bypassed also my brother's property. The land is heavily forested which will require much effort to clear for planting but there is some open space beside the creek.

"There's a parcel next to it on the other side of the creek that's unclaimed" William told Mary and I and it seemed to me some discussions had already been made.

"Is that so?" I asked.

"The governor would listen favourably to any requests" Philip said "he is anxious for land grants to be taken up"

"Perhaps we should make an application" Andrew said much to my surprise.

"Why do you want to leave Jamestowne? I thought you liked it here?"

"Of course but land it good currency"

"Sensible" Papa encouraged him "see how John has prospered adding another parcel of land only this year. And what of you Philip, you'll not have any land?"

"I have some acreage father, over Henrico way, lying untouched as yet, but I'm content to be involved in the governance of our community just now"

"I'm proud to see my family so prosperous and making good lives in this land" Papa said suddenly serious "your mother and I were afeared for you when we came to America but you were all grown and about to make your mark and what better place than here"

"And we thank you papa" Philip smiled, laying his arm affectionately around papa's shoulders. "You gave us the best start and now we have a cousin to join us. We should raise a toast to our success in America" And we did.

…

"Do you intend to live on your land?" papa asked William later over our large family supper.

"I hope to yes, not that I wish to leave you all so soon but work has to start clearing the land and building a cabin before the winter sets in. I believe they can be very fierce"

"It is so on occasions" Papa agreed "we will assist with the building. Andrew and I and there's folk with others skills around"

"You'll remain here 'til it's ready" Amey suggested.
"You are all most kind" William said.
"We're family" I said "it is how we are"
"Grandmother will be overjoyed" William beamed.
"Perhaps she'll want to join us" I suggested.
"She may very well, she's a determined lady that's for certain" William smiled.

November 15 1635

Cousin William left the confines of our house a week or so after our return from Ipswiche. He was accompanied by a number of men who sailed from England with him and didn't have the wherewithal to acquire their own acres, and kin of his by the name of William Tye, who Papa was acquainted with but who had acres of his own. They began the arduous task of preparing their land for planting and have already made a start on clearing trees. Before much time is passed, the frame of a house will be erected under papa's instructions and skill, and as winter comes plans are well set for some comfort and security.

Andrew arrived home this morning looking well pleased with himself and took me by the arm and gave me a kiss.

"Where have you been to make you smile so?" I asked returning the greeting.
"With Philip and the governor" he said proudly taking a scroll of parchment from the table where he had moments ago placed it. "We have our land Swef" and he untied the red cord wrapped around the scroll and opened the papers, laying them flat on the table. The first sheet was the grant for Andrew's fifty headright acres, written I saw, in my brother's fine hand and signed elaborately by the

governor. The second was a neatly written confirmation of the acres Cris and I acquired on our own arrival. Those we had received for bringing Kathren and Edward to Jamestowne was added to Andrew's, together with papa's fifty, giving a total of three hundred acres. The third sheet was a drawing. It showed William's land, now known as Cobbolds, and across from Archer's Creek extending a way across the road, was another plot, with the name of Butlers.

"My! Oh My, Andrew" I declared, pleased and proud my husband was prepared to look into the future for our welfare. And yet I was fearful we should leave the relative safety of the towne for the wilds of Virginia, even a few miles distant. "Do you intend us to live there?" I asked.

"Maybe, when our babies are grown a little" he grinned "I thought on the land opposite, across the road, we could have cottages erected for our workers"

"Like a village?"

"Yes indeed. You are pleased with this Swef?" he asked suddenly as if my opinion was necessary.

"Yes" I confirmed regardless "What will you do with it until we are ready?"

"I thought William could use it, not to grow tobacco, I hear it destroys the soil and there are not nearly enough workers, but he could grow other crops, have cattle and hogs. We will visit in the spring time and in time I will build us a fine house"

"What of the carpentry work here in towne?"

"We can do that alongside mayhap. We have much work and now there is coinage coming into the colonie, we are able to set workers on and give them pay. It's all changing you know. More and more people are arriving. Philip says there are over 10,000 of us in Virginia now"

"10,000 people" I gasped "Jamestowne is very busy and crowded isn't it, but if we leave, Papa and Mary could

have this house to themselves"
"Papa thinks to come with us" Andrew said which surprised me "all of us will leave, Mary too" he grinned.
"She is one of the family" I giggled "I don't know why they are so secretive still, don't they think we know?"
"It's because they're no wed"
"What foolish nonsense" I said "It doesn't matter to us"
"Other folk would object if they knew"
"Well perhaps they ought to be married"
"Who should be married?" a voice behind me spoke. I turned my countenance surely a bright shade of red and faced my father.
"No one" I said hastily.
"Swefling was saying you and Mary could be wed" Andrew said as I kicked him lightly on his weak leg.
"I told you Swefling I'll never wed again and what I chose to do is no concern of yours or anyone else for that matter"
"Yes Papa, I apologise for my unseemly words, I simply thought if you and Mary were wed you would not have to be secret lovers" As the words left my lips, I gasped in horror wishing the ground would open up and swallow me. "Oh Papa. I am so sorry. It was wrong of me to speak so"
"Indeed so, Swefling. Enough now" but to my relief he didn't sound overly affronted and left the room heading for the workshop, with what I thought was the beginnings of a smile on his face.
"Now see what you've done" I glared fiercely at Andrew before a smile spread over my face "well, we shall see what effect that has on the pair of them"
"Yes Sweffie, so we may" he grinned at me, giving me a hug, before he too went about his work.

And to my great delight, my words did have a very

good effect for although my father was determined not to wed and I suspected Mary likewise, it was clear now to all of us at home, the affection they felt for each other. Consequently, the secrecy of visiting each others rooms ceased soon after, when Mary removed her few possessions into papa's room and declared to me one morning when we were cleaning, she had no further need of her room.

May 1 1636

One of the first ships of the year arrived today from England. It brought with it as always, more settlers to our fair land, together with supplies of foods, weapons and such, a large trunk of possessions for William and letters for William, Papa and myself from my grandmother Eleanor Cobbold nee Otley, to the countie of Suffolk.

I have never before in my life received a letter and I turned it over and over in my hands numerous times, looking at the spidery writing and marvelling that such a small, insignificant piece of parchment had found it's way from England, across all the thousands of miles of the oceans and now rested safely in my own hands. I looked up, aware Papa and Andrew were watching me and slowly I unfastened my grandmother's personal seal depicting a swan and unfolded the paper.

"Read it to us Mama" Rowan begged me. I looked up again and smiled at their eager faces and began.

December 21 1635

Cobbold Hall ,Swefling, Suffolk

My dearest granddaughter Swefling,

How strange it is to write these words, for I cannot imagine you a grown woman with a husband and children of your own, but I remember the rare occasions I was permitted to visit your mama as you were growing and I know you will be a fine woman.

I had no hesitation in encouraging your cousin William to join you in Virginia, even though I heard nothing from your family. We hear Virginia is a land abundant with forest, rivers and food and free from the constraints of politiks, which are turning for the worse. There is much unrest between his Majestie and his parliament.

And how fair you Swefling? Your cousin says you have a fine home and work hard to make a good life, when at the end of the day you gather together. I am pleased your brothers do well, that could never have been imagined had you remained in England. Your father made a good decision to take your mother and you from these shores, but I am sad never to see my sweet daughter Ales in this life once more.

Not so yourself my dear, for it is my intention to take a ship across the ocean and live out my days with you.

My husband does not yet know of my decision for my life has not been his business for more years than I care to recall. His mind is now gone and he is a shell of the man I wed so many years since and he will not long be for this life I believe. I do not intend to be a burden on you Swefling, for I shall travel with my maid and many trunks of goods and chattels to make my stay as comfortable as I may.

"Oh my goodness" I exclaimed looking up at my family

watching me as I read.

"Continue Swefling" Papa urged.

When we shall arrive I do not comprehend, but we have plans to take a ship in the spring when the sailing weather is reasonable and clement and we may find a suitable vessel.

This has been much about myself, Swefling, but when I arrive perhaps you will be able to devote some of your precious time to informing me of your life and your hopes and dreams so I may be in a position to know you better. I was very pleased to receive your letter telling me of your children and your dear husband and look forward to meeting you all.

With much affection to you all my dear
Eleanor Otley Cobbold

"What a tremendous adventure" Andrew exclaimed "such an old lady to be sailing the seas"
"Will she arrive soon?" Rowan asked.
"We do not know" I smiled, feeling suddenly quite tearful for no reason I could comprehend.
"We shall have to make arrangements. There will be changes too" Papa declared laughing "if she is to bring a shipload of possessions, they will never fit in the governor's house let alone ours"
"What will we do?" I asked realising our home was not suitable for the daughter and wife of member of the English aristocracy.
"I will speak with Philip" Andrew said, "perhaps the governor will be able to offer accommodation until such alternative is available"

"There is much to be done to make ready and be prepared" I said, finding myself suddenly very nervous.
"Now Swefling" Papa, always a practical man, reproached me. "Eleanor is your grandmother and she will accept us as she finds us in Jamestowne. We do not have the finery of Cobbold Hall and she is aware of that"
"Yes Papa, but….."
"Swefling, listen for once to your papa" Andrew told me, very sensibly before becoming much his usual self with his teasing "but a real lady in the house, now that will be a treat"

I moved to cuff his ear but he was quicker than I and the laughter released my immediate concerns of the imminent arrival of our relative.

June 1636

The summer has arrived and the weather is perfect, warm sun and cooling breezes off the river and everything is bright and healthy.

We have heard nothing further from grandmother regarding her arrival and we are still in some debate over her accommodation.

"We could extend the house again" Andrew suggested to papa as we sat in the shade at the back of the house under the apple tree that had served us well over the years, with fruit and shade.
"I was thinking" Papa said slowing drinking his ale "about the land"

Andrew and I looked at him wondering what he was about to suggest.

"It is closer to Middle Plantation than here, there would be plenty of carpentry work, we could remove ourselves, build a large house for us all and work the land"

"It's a fine idea John" Andrew said "but do you wish to give up your own home and business, you've already allocated your land to us"

"I gave up what I had before, when we came here. I'll do it again. And I do mean to leave Jamestowne" Papa was insistent. "Mary and I, we will no be wed as you know, but folk are cruel and the lass deserves to be away from gossips and meddlers"

"Is it Lucy?" I asked.

"It is not for me to say for sure Swefling, but her name has been mentioned on occasions"

"Kathren or I will speak with her" I said.

"You will not" Andrew declared "you will become distressed and I will not have that either. I believe we should consider this suggestion, we should make another inspection to see the lie of the land and visit William and John" He smiled as he finished, "Yes, I like the notion greatly"

"But we cannot all go just now" I reminded them "grandmother might arrive"

"Andrew and I will leave in a day or so Swefling" Papa declared "for no more than a week, you will be fine without us about for the time we are away and Edward will remain to protect you"

"We shall manage it is so" I said not wanting them to be away. I never did but I too was warming to the idea of living on the land and knew it was necessary to investigate the matter further.

July 1 1636

Andrew and papa have returned to us looking exceedingly well pleased with themselves and spent some long time discussing business that didn't concern Mary, Kathren and I but they are able to tell us we will remove ourselves to our land in due course. Already the plans for our new house are beginning to take shape it would appear and we are anxious to see them and where it will be situated. First though a workshop is to be completed, for it is there that Andrew and Papa will work and conduct future business.

"The land is closer to Middle Plantation than we believed" Andrew said over supper, "less than a half a mile, and just over a mile to John's. It's a good position"
"And there's plenty of work as I suspected" Papa said.
"And the house, will it be large enough for us all, when grandmother arrives?" I asked
"It won't be commenced 'til next year, so she'll have to make do with this for a time" Papa smiled, "and if we are able to separate her from her possessions John will clear one of his barns to store them until they are required"
"And planting the land?" I asked "When will that be done?"
"In due course Swefling" Andrew said "there's much work we have to do, but William's already cleared his land for winter planting and there're meadows for cows and swine, so we won't go hungry. And you'll start your garden again and there'll be fish in the river and so much space all around. It will be good for us" he smiled clearly pleased with the decision made.
"Are you happy Papa?" I asked certain it was so. He nodded.
"Jamestowne has been good for us these twenty years but

now it's time to put down more permanent roots. It's safe enough. The Indians are more peaceable and there's to be a small garrison in Middle Plantation. I am satisfied it is right to do this"

"You made a visit to Middle Plantation?" Mary asked.

"We did and discovered there to be sufficient work for carpenters, should we need to occupy ourselves in the employment of others, and some society. Rowan, you will enjoy the move, Jamestowne is crowded and poor compared to Middle Plantation"

"But my friends are here Grandfather"

"You will acquire new friends and perhaps in time find employment"

July 1636

Mary, Kathren, Rowan and I have been so busy cleaning the house, making it spick and span waiting for my grandmother to arrive. We had a brief note from her, which arrived a week since to advise she would sail on The Rosebud due to leave Ipswiche in the first week of May and we estimate that by the middle of this month she could be with us.

We have a room arranged for her in the house but Philip has spoken with the governor who advises a suite of large rooms would be made available for our relative and her maid and their possessions should the wish be so. I would suspect my grandmother would not welcome the noise and high spirits of our three sons now five, four and two years and thus I am prepared for the eventuality. So all is arranged and ready and we wait her arrival, many times taking the river path when news of an approaching vessel sailing up the river comes to us, but every occasion thus far, we return home, having enjoyed our walk but without the anticipation and expectation of greeting grandmother.

July 19 1636

All changed last week when Rowan came hurrying home, not for once solely for the mid day meal.

"She's coming mama, The Rosebud, she's in the river. Shall we go?"
"Yes" I smiled, as excited as my daughter "come boys" and I gathered my sons about me and began to wipe their faces and tidy their hair, to their great annoyance, while Rowan hurried to the workshop to tell Andrew and Papa.

By the time we reached the dock The Rosebud was already tied up and the gangplank in place. We looked along the side of the vessel and didn't have far to see an upright old lady in fine clothes, leaning on the rail.

"Grandmother" I called and waved frantically, watching the younger woman at her side whisper in her ear. She looked about her until her gaze fell on us and gave a gracious wave of her gloved hand.
"Who's that" Gabriel asked as Andrew held him up to see.
"Your great grandma, come across the sea from England" Andrew told our boys.
"She's old" Richard announced.
"Yes she is, very old" I agreed with him as we watched, as on the arm of the captain, Lady Eleanor Cobbold processed her most stately arrival down the gangplank to where we waited. I stole a glance at Andrew and saw his face full of smiles as he winked at me.
"Grandmother" I said "you have not changed hardly at all"

"Of course I have silly girl" she smiled taking my hands, as much for support I suspected than anything else, as she leant forward and I kissed her on both cheeks. "And where's your father?"

Papa stood before her.

"Welcome Lady Eleanor" he said.

"Well John, your girl looks fit, where are those boys of yours and my grandson Will?"

"John and William are at their farms and Philip is around somewhere" and just at that moment the governor's buggy arrived with Philip in charge. He hopped down and came across to us.

"Well then grandma" he said most at ease with her "you've come"

"So it would seem" she smiled glancing at the buggy "you've done well, a vehicle of your own"

"Oh no" he laughed "the property of the governor, he suggested you might not wish to walk to the house and provided the vehicle for your convenience"

"A most thoughtful man" she said "Indeed I would care to sit. You do not have your vehicle with you John?" she asked my father as she leant on his arm as he escorted her to the conveyance.

"We have no requirement for a buggy Lady Eleanor" he replied, assisting her aboard, as her maid, a very pretty woman, fussed about her.

"Marian do not bother so, this is America. It is different. I told you so time and time again"

"Yes m'lady"

"So Swefling, this fine young man will be your husband" she smiled, more at ease I thought now she was sitting.

"I am pleased to say Swefling is my wife and these are our boys Richard, John and Gabriel, all pleased to make your acquaintance"

"I'm sure" Grandmother smiled briefly, clearly not

enamoured with young children.
"And this is my daughter Rowan" I smiled my arm about her shoulders urging her forward"
"She has the look of you Swefling. Your father died girl, didn't he?"
"Yes madam" she said bobbing a little curtsey just as she'd practiced.
"I'm your great grandmother child, you will call me so" she said "and none of the curtseying nonsense. And your sister, is there news?"
"No ma' ... grandmother. Not a word"
Grandmother nodded and looked about her, at some of the other folk watching our meetings.
"We should be at your home John, I care not one jot for conversing in the street with all and sundry staring. Accompany me, Rowan" she said to my daughter, as Philip climbed aboard and took the reins and we slowly followed behind through the old towne gate to our house.

...

When we arrived at the house grandmother was already sitting in the parlour making herself comfortable with Rowan nervously assisting her.

"You have a fine home Swefling, a trifle small, but we shall manage until my chattels are delivered from the ship"
"We have a room ready for you" I said opening the door to the room Papa had just vacated and taken his and Mary's belongings up the stairs once again.
"Very adequate" she smiled "I will have to learn about being in America" she declared.
"The governor has offered rooms in his mansion" I said, "there will be space for your things"
"Trying to get rid of me so soon before I have time to

wash my face?"
"Oh no grandmother" I replied horrified she should even consider such a notion "we would wish for you to remain with us but you might believe it too noisy and crowded"
"We shall discover, we shall discover. Mayhap it is time for refreshment"
"Of course" I said still nervous and offered coffee.
"I was referring to real refreshment. Marian! Where is that girl? The Geneva if you please"
"Yes m'lady" she said as she pulled a bottle of the alcoholic libation from the large port manteau Philip had recently conveyed from the buggy into the house.
"Glasses, Swefling if you please" grandmother was far more able than I supposed and soon had us standing to attention filled glasses in our hands, except Rowan, much to her disappointment.
"To new adventures" grandmother declared and downed her drink straight away.
"I'd like to rest now Swefling. When do you serve the mid day meal?"
"Whenever you care to eat grandmother" I said, although it was not far from being ready when we had left the house to meet her.
"Nonsense, these men of yours have work to do, I will feed at the same time is that clear? I want nothing to be different. Tell Marian and she will fetch me" and she stood and reached her arm towards mine and I led her, followed by Marian across the room to her bedchamber. At the doorway, she paused and turned, smiling at everyone.
"I may be old and my bones weak, but I retain exceedingly good hearing. I shall not miss a word should you decide to discuss my arrival"
"Yes grandmother" everyone replied laughing, and I led her into the room. Marian closed the door behind us and grandmother sat on the chair looking about her.

"What a pretty room Swefling. Your family have made me most welcome. I thank you all, but now I need to sleep. Marian will join you directly"
"I'm pleased you have come to us grandmother" I said holding her hand.

She patted my own and smiled.

"Be off with you Swefling"

August 1636

We discovered to our delight that grandmother was quite happy and content to remain with us, provided we were all not around together, mealtimes notwithstanding. The boys were too much for her on occasions with their constant chatter and clambering over us, but when we explained especially to Richard and John that grandmother was not used to young children, they were remarkably good.

John and Amey, their children and cousin William, arrived together and after a brief introduction to the children, grandmother was left alone with two of her grandsons and on another occasion when Joane and Joseph came to visit, a similar situation arose.

"So many children" she said one afternoon when just she and I sat in the shade under the apple tree "and everyone so much younger than I"
"It is a place for young people" I agreed "hard work clearing the land and planting, needs such folk"
"But you like it here Swefling?"
"I do grandmother, I am pleased papa and mama brought us here. It was most brave of them"

"They were brave to go against your grandfather. So young themselves, barely sixteen my Ales when they wed. My husband had such high hopes for our daughter. He'd arranged a marriage for her with the Lord Worcestor's son, since they were children, but she met your father and she could not be turned from him and she was lost to us. But your father is a good man, from a good family, I discovered subsequently. He never told her I believe, the mystery and intrigue. Content to be a carpenter, as was your husband, Crispin"

She looked at me as if expecting some response but I'd never heard of any tales of papa's family, he refused always to be drawn.

"Papa considered mama and us his family, said he didn't need any other"

"Very sensible, and you Swefling you are happy and content I see"

"I am, Andrew is a fine man. He does not allow his poorly leg to hinder his work or anything, over much"

"How did it occur?"

So I told grandmother about that dreadful day eleven years ago, and the tale led me to the day more recently to when my Swefling was kidnapped.

"Never give up hope Swefling. I never did, I believed one day I would see you again. I had hope that my Ales would be here, but I have found my grandchildren and to be with you is as good a place as any as I could wish for to end my life on God's earth"

...

Several days later, with grandmother's goods and chattels, apart from some of her clothes, safely stored temporarily in a warehouse by the river, she received a brief note from the governor.

"Read it me Swefling. Marian mostly does but she is touring the towne and the countrie side with your brother" she smiled, a twinkle in her eye.

I unfolded the note and read slowly to her:

My dear Lady Cobbold,

It is with much delight we welcome your gracious personage to our humble town and trust you may afford us the honour in attendance of a quiet, midday repast with my lady wife and several towne leaders on Wednesday next, at 12 of the clock.

My clerk, your grandson will call for you in the Conveyance and will accompany you throughout your visit should you wish it.

With kind regards,
John West
Governor of the Virginian Colonie of America

"A diverting excursion. What do you say Swefling?"
"You should attend" I said knowing it to be so "Shall I write the reply?"
"Marian will do it later, my dear. Now tell me more about your life here. I like the way you are so close to your first husband's daughters Kathren and Joane, tell me about them"

September 1 1636

Grandmother had a most delightful time at the governor's residence for the dinner, she was most pleased to advise me on her return. There were all manner of foods and flavours she had never before encountered in her long life, oysters and turkey, squash and melon and she returned late in the afternoon 'fit to bursting' she declared.

Lady West took her on a tour of the grounds and thence to the rooms in the mansion that were offered upon grandmother's arrival in the colonie, and where the furniture and possessions could be housed.

"I am tempted Swefling, for I like my things about me, but then I recall they are only things and I am happy to remain here for a time with you"
"Whatever you decide grandma, we love having you here. Sometimes I just cannot believe you undertook the journey to join us. You really are a remarkable lady"
"Thank you my dear, but when William died, after I'd writ you, I knew my decision was the right one, I did not wish to be rattling around the hall on my own. Cold and draughty it was and my grandchildren all here. I said to Marian when I first considered and made the decision, I will cross the ocean or die in the attempt and as you may see I am safe and sound"
"Will you travel with us to John's farm? We go every year at the end of September"
"It sounds most pleasant, will a carriage be arranged?"
"We take a wagon of course but…."
"If it can be made comfortable that will be just right. I am in America, I keep reminding myself and I must adapt to this new world. Andrew was telling me you have land

next to William's, why do you not farm?"
"We are taking steps. Papa is building a workshop and a house. We shall depart in due course. He would wish to leave Jamestowne with haste"
"Folk can be exceedingly meddlesome" she said clearly understanding the situation "narrow minded malicious busybodies" she added with some vehemence "Your step daughter, Lucy is somewhat inclined to that nature I understand"
"How did you discover?"
"Not much I miss Swefling and I listen. She has an unkind spirit. Be mindful of her. She is not to be trusted"
"Indeed so, grandmother"

Grandmother nodded her approval and continued.

"She is just as likely to stab you in the back as look at you"

September 30 1636

Joy abounds in our household, wonderful, happy, laughing times, for our dearly beloved Swefling is returned to us.

We were at John's plantation helping with the harvest. Close to the end of our sojourn, Papa accompanied grandmother and her companion, Marion on a visit, the mile or so to William's beautiful house. Now it was complete and the first harvest gathered it was a time to give thanks for our bounty and we were to join them directly. Before that event was occasioned our daughter was found.

My brothers' and our family were taking our ease over midday dinner on the porch out of the heat of the hot September sun, when a rider came galloping at great speed towards the house, and one of the housemaids came upon us, an urgent expression on her face.

"Mistress Butler, excuse me you are urgently required at Mr William Cobbold's farm"
"Is it my grandmother? Is she hurt?" I asked rising from the table.
"Oh no Ma'am" she smiled "the messenger says no one is ailing"
I looked at Andrew, who was already standing, wondering what could possibly be the urgency.
"We shall go straight away" he said.
"I'll get the horses saddled" and John was already on his way as we hurried after him.
"What has occurred?" I asked the messenger as we rode along at a good speed, but he could not or would not reveal the mystery and I could not for the life of me imagine what was so pressing to request our immediate presence.

At the house, we dismounted and our horses were led away as William standing on the front porch, hurried down the steps to our side and took my hands in his, kissing me on my cheeks several times full of great joy, before he spoke.

"Come cousin" he beamed at me, a broader smile on his face I'd never seen previously in my life. He led us into the parlour and I stood rock still at the doorway, for my grandmother sat on the settle, holding the hands of a young girl, barely clothed, in Indian apparel.
"Swefling" I breathed, tears of joy flooding into my eyes, "Oh my dear child" I cried, rushing into the room as the young female slowly stood before me.

"Mama" she said, her words sounding uncertain, nervous even, and she was clearly surprised when I put my arms about her and held her close, crying all the while. I felt Andrew's hand on my shoulder and drew slightly away and let him welcome her back to us.

"Oh Swefling, you're home at last" I sighed as her tears began to fall now and she sobbed and sobbed, as we held her.

"I didn't know if you'd want me back" she explained when our tears were dry and we sat together and grandmother insisted we all had a glass of Geneva, of which, she always took a supply wherever she went visiting.

"You are our daughter" Andrew said "of course we want you returned to us, why would you think otherwise?"

"I've lived as an Indian [Native] for three years"

"But you're here now" I said stroking her back "Was it bad Swef? Did they mistreat you?"

She shook her head and showed some considerable surprise as my question.

"No, they didn't mistreat me at all" she said slowly "I was Achak's wife, my husband's grandmother was kind and protected me. When he died it was time to leave, she said and brought me here. She left me at the roadside by the oak tree. I believed this was Uncle John's place"

"Oh Swefling" I whispered.

"I missed you so much Mama" she said her eyes glistening through the tears, "but grandmother Amounte [Onute] cared for me as her own. They are a kindly people"

"But they kidnapped you?"

"It was the young men. Amounte's [Onute] grandson Achak was one of them, she whipped him"

"But they didn't let you go?"

"We were a long way distant [many miles] from here and she grew to like me and her grandson was…… we liked each other"

"You were his wife?" Andrew thought out loud "Swefling

you were a child"
"I was thirteen or fourteen then papa. Not so young. Many girls are wed at such an age" I had to agree for my thoughts briefly went to Cris and his first wife Catherine, both thirteen.
"It's over now Swef, and you're with us, it will soon be forgotten"
"I do not wish to forget Mama. I will not see grandmother Amounte again".
"But your ~~real~~ _birth_ great grandmother is with you" I said, "and you have a new brother and a cousin here to greet you"

Swefling looked at her great grandmother, who sat the other side of her watching but not saying a word, simply nodding her head.

"I believe my great granddaughter should rest. This is very exciting and most strange for her, I have no doubt"
"Thank you" she said "I'm sorry mama. It is strange to be returned but you and papa are the same and I am at ease" but despite her words her tears began to fall again.
"Go with grandmother" I whispered giving her up again, against my deep feelings, but I knew she was back with us. "Papa and grandpa and I will be here when you're rested" As she stood I held onto her hand. "I love you Swefling" I whispered, "my daughter" and she hugged me and Andrew and papa and turned away to her grandmother who led her from the room, followed close on their heels by William.

The three of us stood in the room looking at each other.

"She's different" I said.
"Of course she is" Papa smiled reaching out and touching

my arm "she's a young woman now, sixteen years Swef"
"And she's been through much, don't forget" Andrew reminded me.
"How can I?" I asked "but she's distant"
"Give her time Swef, she left the Indian woman but this morning and if she cared for her as Swef says it will be hard to leave her and that life behind too"
I nodded and began to brighten listening to their words.
"But she's come back to us" I said, "She's come back"

…

We stayed at William's house for the remainder of the afternoon, sending a message to Ipswiche that all was very well and we'd return in due course. We sat on the porch with William and Papa, while Sweffie rested and they explained how they discovered our lost daughter.

"She was sitting on the grass under the large oak tree in the drive" William told us "We came across her just as we were showing grandmother about"
"She was so nervous poor lamb" Papa said "said she was looking for Ipswiche, but I recognised her straight away, there was no doubt in my mind"
"Nor hers" William agreed "but she was scared"
"Like a frightened deer she was. Didn't want William and I about her just then, so grandmother took charge and brought her willingly into the house and be comforted"
"Thank goodness you were here" I signed "she might have wandered away if not"
"She was most confused" Papa said "but she's better even now. Your grandmother will be the best for her now, being a stranger"

I looked at the three men watching me.

"But she's my daughter, I should be able to help her"
"This is about Sweffie" Papa told me gently "we have to do what she wants, to help her recover from her ordeal"
"We have her back" Andrew said "It has to be sufficient for now"

...

Later in the afternoon grandmother joined us briefly and I looked up as she came into the room, concerned Swefling was alone, but her smile was reassuring.

"Swefling will you join us?" Grandmother asked "Perhaps some supper William" I stood and hurried to my grandmother.
"Is she well? Is Swefling alright?"
"Rested. Come and speak with your daughter. She wishes to see you"

Swefling was sitting on a chair beside the window in the bedchamber, looking as grandmother had said, refreshed. Her hair was brushed and she was wearing a skirt, shift and bodice borrowed, I was advised, from William's housekeeper. It was ill fitting over her slender frame but Swefling looked more like my daughter than the Indian of before.

"These clothes feel strange" she said running a hand over the cloth and smoothing the fabric over her knee. "I'm still a maid, mama"
"You don't have to tell me anything" I said.
"I do" she insisted "three year's I've been away. I need to tell you. I thought of you and papa every day and I tried to pray to let me return, especially in the early days but then as time and the seasons passed, I believed I could never find my way back, for I had no notion where home was.

I lived with grandmother Onuto when we stopped travelling and remained in the village for much of the time. Achak, he was her grandson, was my husband. He was my age, a boy. He was my husband but….. we laid together often but….. and then in the second spring after I was taken, because I was not with child he was sent away with others on the Huskanaw, to be made into men and become the elders of the tribe. He was returned badly hurt. He was so poorly mama everyone knew he would not survive and it was so"

Swefling's eyes filled with tears and I wanted to comfort her but I realised she needed perhaps to do this on her own and then I could help her.

"I cared for him, he was kind and silly sometimes and angry and upset because……. But he was dead and when his bones were bleached white with the rain and the wind and the sun, grandmother and I brought him to the hut and in the morning grandmother and I left and we came here. And now grandmother, Onuto she too is gone to the ancestors"

Grandmother Eleanor and I sat quietly as Swefling finished her tale, brief just now, but a start was made to relate those events that led her back to us. She sat for a while staring out of the window and in the silence of the room we heard the low murmur of the voices of the men elsewhere in the house and the sounds of nature outside the open window. The birds in the trees and a late bee buzzing around as it collected pollen from the flowers that bloomed under the window, was reassuring and gave Swefling the awareness that whatever heartache and distress she suffered, life would continue for her.

"Grandmother Onuto was different after Achak was

returned to us, as if something within her died also. She asked several times if I was with child, but I told her as I told you, I am a maid still and there was much disappointment in her face. Achak was the last of their line, the important family of the tribe and I was the one to help continue it but it was not to be. Grandmother and I continued to live together ~~and I helped her now~~, but she had lost her wish to live. She told me we were to depart on a journey. I thought she meant all of us, but she meant just her and I. We left with our bundles one evening, undetected by the tribe and I knew she was bringing me home" Tears came again to Swefling's eyes as she spoke of the old woman. "She was a sweet kind person, but she knew her time was close. It was an arduous trek for her, but this morning we came upon the Lake Mataoke and I knew I was nearly with my English family. It was confusing. I wanted to be here but I did not want to leave grandmother Amounte. I tried to persuade her to stay but she wouldn't be turned. She left me on the track and disappeared into the forest, but when she was gone I realised it wasn't Uncle John's place but I was here and couldn't walk another step. So I sat under the tree and waited for someone to come along. It was then grandpa came upon me, with grandmother and cousin William"
"Oh Swefling" I sighed speaking now at the end of her tale, relieved beyond measure she was unhurt in her body and had found some kindness "would you like papa and grandpa to search for grandmother Amounte?"

She looked at me with surprise.

"You'd do that?"
"Of course, she protected you and you care for her"
"She'll not be found, the ancestors were coming for her, but it makes my heart glad Mama, you would think of it.

I am pleased to be with you"

I nodded, unable to speak for I was full of emotion.

"We should eat" grandmother Eleanor said, rising from her chair "come" and she led the way from the room. At the doorway Swefling stopped and turned to me.

"Are you happy with Andrew, Mama?" You'd not long been together when I left and I was still a child"

I smiled at her thoughtfulness in her time of distress.

"I am Swefling, I never thought, after your dear papa died, I'd ever want to be someone else's wife but Andrew is a good man and I love him dearly"

"I'm glad. I can see it between you. It's like being on the outside. I see all manner of things I never would have before. Grandpa is content too and grandmother Eleanor, I like her and cousin William"

"We are a happy family and overjoyed everyone will be at your return"

"They don't know yet?"

"No just us"

She nodded pleased I believe, as we joined Andrew, Papa, William and Marian at the table.

...

Swefling wasn't ready to face her brothers and sister and our kin that evening and with grandmother Eleanor remaining at Cobbolds with her, Andrew, papa and I made a reluctant return to Ipswiche, with a promise to return the following morning with Rowan.

We were greeted with great speculation and excitement, as the reason for our sudden call to our cousin's property was revealed and our family were, not at all to our surprise, totally unprepared for our wonderful news.

Rowan broke down sobbing and as I held her, I felt my own tears once more, but in time she was calmed and her smile was all Andrew and I needed to see, to know her tears were those of joy and relief for her sister's return.

"Swef asks you come and visit with her on the morrow" I smiled at my second daughter "will you?"
"Oh Mama, can't we go now?" she asked.
"On the morrow" Andrew laughed gently "you'll need your rest tonight, Swefling has much to tell you of her adventures amongst the Indians"
"But she's well?"
"Perfectly well" I told her, stroking the hair of my fifteen year old, "she's very emotional ~~and quite thi~~n but she's with us and wants to see you"

November 15 1636

We were returned to Jamestowne, Papa, Andrew, Mary and the boys, to our house. We were reluctant to leave but there was work to be done and we could not remain at Ipswiche forever.

Swefling and Rowan ~~however~~ remained at Cobbold's with their great grandmother and Marian, her companion and cousin William, who took to having four females residing in his house, with great fortitude and some measure of teasing from the other menfolk of the family. We missed seeing them all very much but it was so different now we knew Swefling was safe and knowing she and Rowan spent endless hours together in conversation. They had always been close but now there was a special something to their relationship that only they held, as Swefling spoke of things to her sister, she could not or perhaps never would, speak of to us.

The weather had begun to change as fall turned into winter, when Swefling and Rowan joined us in our house in Jamestowne, and grandmother and Marian to their accommodation in the governor's residence. There was, however, a restlessness about the girls, as if in the months since Swefling's return, the two were no longer my young daughters but young women, on the verge of going out into the world, without their Mama and step father.

We heard many expressions of joy from our community at Swefling's return but others less accommodating, speculating on her condition at the hands of the Indians. She also became the subject of attention of many of the less savoury young men of the towne, particularly those in the barracks and acquainted with Lucy. Joane on the other hand, came to visit a week or so after their return and they removed themselves for a time into Kathren's cottage where the four sisters had a joyous reunion, and we heard much laughter and giggling erupting from the building, to our great delight.

February 1637

We have a new child born five days since and we are delighted to welcome our daughter. Andrew loves all of our children and welcomed each and every one of them with great joy and celebration but to have a daughter, he is totally besotted and beside himself, holding her at every opportunity and quite reluctant to hand her to me even when she demands to be fed.

"You'd feed her yourself if you were able" I told him.
"I do believe I would" he smiled "and wouldn't that be an interesting circumstance" he beamed at our daughter "she's so beautiful Swef, just like you. I must be the most fortunate man in the world"
"Of course you are, but you have to hand her to me before she screams the house down about our ears. How you can bear to listen to the noise is beyond me"
"She'll be demanding to be allowed out of the house with boys soon enough. I mean to enjoy her company while I'm able"
"Have you spoken to the priest about her baptism?"
"Not yet, we've not finally decided on her name"
"I thought we said Ales Eleanor?"
"Perhaps we could add my own mama's name" he suggested.
"Bettris is a good name" I smiled "so are you to be Bettris Ales or Bettris Eleanor?" I asked our daughter who now nestled in my arms sucking at my breast.
"Bettris Eleanor" Andrew spoke for her "we'll save Ales for our next" he grinned.
"Andrew, might I remind you this is my eight child I am holding"
"And you do it very well Swefling" he laughed so full of good humour "especially the making, well the four I've helped you with, I cannot say how you were before"
"Indeed you cannot and this is hardly the conversation for a little one to be listening to" I smiled looking down at the newly named Bettris Eleanor.
"She needs to know her parents care for each other well"

I looked at him for a while, smiling and loving him very much.

"Do you know that day Swefling came back to us she asked me if I was happy with you" I said "it was the first thing she wanted to know about all of us"
"And you told her what exactly?"
"I said I love you dearly and she told me she was glad"
"And it's why I'm so fortunate, a loving wife, four children of my own and two, no four, step daughters, we mustn't forget Kathren and Joane"
"You're a sweet and wonderful man Andrew, and I love you" I told him again.

May 19 1637

We knew it would happen, for the gossip and meddlesome nature of some of the townsfolk finally drove our Swefling away and just today Andrew and I have returned from Ipswiche, where my two daughters have removed themselves permanently. Poor Swefling declared she had never heard such condemning words ever, about anyone, in the three years of her living with the Indians, as she had suffered in the short time since her return to Jamestowne in November and vowed she would never return.

It saddens me, so great was her desire to leave, but I would never wish to dissuade her. It was worse than unsettling, that so called civilised folk should so use a young woman, but they had, much as was so formerly, with the malicious referrals to Mary. And so three days hence Andrew and I had taken the wagon conveying our daughters and their possessions to my brother's property and saw them safely settled in.

Before we returned to Jamestowne, Andrew and I

paid a visit to William and in the course of the afternoon took a stroll to our own property across the creek. We walked from the road where William had cleared some of the land and plowed the acres for vegetables and we looked through the maze of trees to an open meadow about fifty yards from where we stood and from where we could just make out the blue sky reflected in the rippling waters of the creek that separated our two properties. Andrew took my hand suddenly and headed off towards the area where spring flowers waved their heads in the breeze amid the tall grasses.

"I've a mind to remove us here Swefling, soon, this year perhaps. The workshop is complete and your papa and Mary would welcome it. What do you think?"
I smiled twirling around looking at the land about us.
"This is a fine place for our house" I said taking his hand again "near the water, solid ground and our land all around"
"You like the idea?" he asked clearly delighted.
"I do" I said reaching out and holding his face in my hands as I kissed him and one thing led to another and we were lying in the grass, our clothes awry when we heard our names being called.

We looked about and waved to William, standing at the edge of the meadow by the trees and as he approached, we quickly tidied ourselves and sat enjoying the sunshine as he joined us.

"Have you decided?" he asked and I realised Andrew had already spoken to him.
"Yes" he confirmed "this is a good place for our house. We shall make start papa and I, in a month or so"
"The sawmill in Middle Plantation will prepare the timber

when it's felled, as they did mine and there's labour at Cobbolds" William seemed genuinely pleased for us.
"You have everything arranged" I smiled at the two of them.
"We've spoken of this often enough Swef" Andrew said "now the boys are no longer babies, it will be easier for us all"
"You are such a thoughtful man" I smiled and leant over and kissed him.
"You've no thoughts to take a wife?" Andrew asked our cousin who watched us.
"I have no time just now" he laughed.
"I thought grandmother's Marian was on your mind" I teased.
"Maybe at first, but Philip is making serious overtures"
"Is he now? He's kept that quite. It's about time he was wed, he'll be an old man before long"
"I hope not Swef" Andrew declared laughing at my comment. "he's just my age" "Yes, I know sweetheart, but I love you nonetheless"

September 30 1637

Here we are at Ipswiche once again where our family are gathered and all is well. Swefling is blooming now, a year since her return and seems well recovered from her ordeal, although we had no real knowledge of the details but when we saw her she smiled greatly. Amey confirmed there appeared to be no lasting difficulties for Swefling and she spent her days helping with the children and, Amey confided in Andrew and I, most secretively I thought, often visiting her cousin William at Cobbolds. Andrew and I grinned at each other and I hoped it was so for Swefling was of an age and William was a very personable young man, just ten years her senior. We had yet to see the two of them together to witness his response to her company, but we planned to call once more before we returned to Jamestowne.

We rode out towards our land to inspect the progress of the building of our new house. It was taking time but we were in no great rush until next year, for I was with child again and expected our new arrival in the early spring and we did not wish to remove ourselves before the arrival. The house stood at an angle to the creek and would have the advantage of the early morning and evening sun but there would be a wide porch all around, giving shelter and necessary protection from the elements. The building looked of immense size I thought, when we stood within the frame but I was told once we were installed we would soon fill it. William who was in charge of the build, by virtue of the fact he was here, told us now the harvest was complete, work on the unskilled tasks could continue while the weather held.

"I can hardly wait now" I said to Andrew as we wandered around on our own "I just love all this space"
"Papa wants to come early next year, he said he and Mary could manage with a bit of a roof over their heads"
"Oh? Now why would he want to rush off like that I wonder?" I smiled "Is he finding the children too noisy?"
"I don't believe it is that Swef" Andrew said quite seriously, "Lucy is gossiping once more and making all manner of accusations. It's time for us all to leave"
"What sort of accusations?" I asked.
"The usual nonsense" he said not looking at me.
"I thought she was over all her anger, it's been quiet for almost a year"

Andrew looked at me.

"Hasn't it?"

"No, but enough of this on such a fine day, Swefling. I should not have mentioned it. Now tell me where you are to have your garden and then we'll go to Cobbolds and take a look at Sweffie and William and see what's going on there" he smiled, dismissing our earlier conversation.

April 1638

Spring has arrived full of hope and expectation, the leaves bursting on the trees, the spring blossoms bringing colour everywhere and the sun warm on our backs as we plant our seeds for our crops. And there are changes occurring all about us, Papa and Mary removed themselves to Ipswiche, in March as the weather began to improve and everyday we were told, papa rode to Butlers to oversee the work on the house, which was taking shape very well now. Often Mary travelled with him and worked in the garden, planting as we'd planned and organising everything and everyone.

I missed her terribly for apart from her help in the house, which was legendary, over the twenty years since her arrival amongst us I had grown to see her as my mama and I felt quite alone for her company during the daytime. But I was not alone for Kathren, although she lived in the cottage beside our house and not with us, was as a sister to me. We had long since of course dispensed with the idea of our relationship being stepmother and step daughter, even while Cris was alive, for that was a ridiculous state of affairs, our being of a similar age. As a consequence Kathren and I worked well together, but even so we couldn't cope without Mary, so we set on a young woman, especially to help care for the children and other household tasks, for there was much to be done with the washing and cleaning, brewing of ale, together with the outside tasks, and in time Margaret became a great asset to our household.

Several afternoons each week, once I was confident Margaret was able and would stand no nonsense from Richard and John, who both had a naughty streak in them, and one which Gabriel was fast learning, I took myself off to the governor's mansion to visit grandmother Eleanor who was well settled in residence, and often 'held court', so my brother Philip oft advised me.

This afternoon I took a slow stroll in the sunshine to the old town, a basket of flowers on my arm for grandmother's rooms, when I came across Philip walking arm in arm with Marian, grandmother's companion.

"Swefling" he called as I approached "you are to visit grandmother?"
"Yes, I hope she might take a stroll in the gardens, it is such a pleasant day"
"Indeed it is" Marian agreed, "we asked her to join us, but she said she was waiting for you to arrive.
"I'd best not tarry"
"We shall detain you a moment longer" Philip smiled, looking at Marian "We know grandmother will speak of it, but we wanted to tell you ourselves, we are to be wed. Marian and I" he added as if I couldn't tell to whom he was referring.
"That's very good news. We wondered when you would" I smiled holding both their hands in mine.
"We didn't know ourselves until recently" Marian laughed.
"We did, last September I believe it was. William mentioned the two of you"

"Well I never" Philip grinned "we'd hardly spoken a number of words alone with each other at that time"
"I'm very pleased for you both whenever it came about. When will the marriage be?"
"We haven't made arrangements as yet but later in the year" Philip said "and now you'd best be on your way or we'll all be in grandmother's bad books"

…

I found grandmother sitting at the window overlooking the garden, when I approached and gave her a kiss on her cheek.

"Philip told you" she said.
"Yes isn't it good news? Are you pleased?"
"Of course, but I'll have to find another companion"
"She'll not leave you"
"She can't care for me when she has her babies Swefling, use your head"
"Yes grandmother. Is she with child already?" I asked innocently.
"Sometimes you are very silly. They are sensible and grown up. They will wait"
"Yes grandmother. I'm sure you're right"
"You're with child again" she said to me "Do you not have sufficient already?"
"Grandmother! If you are going to be argumentative all afternoon, I will leave now"
"No, do not leave Swefling. I do need to speak with you. You cannot keep having babies all your life Swefling, you will be worn out"
"How….. how can I not. I love my husband" I said feeling a flush come over my face.
"There are herbs, as well you know. Now enough of

that, are those flowers for me? Arrange them in the vase Swefling"

Grandmother watched as I added water to one of her favourite vases and placed the flowers inside, admiring the freshness and colour of the blooms.

"Arrange them, do not stuff them in. Goodness what is the matter with you today?"

I looked at her steadily, feeling a rising annoyance, despite her age but grandmother stared right back at me.

"Outside" she said suddenly "we shall go outside" and she stood and linked her arm through mine and with her cane to steady herself on the other side, we made our slow way into the garden and in time fetched up by the shady seating under a maple tree. We sat in silence for a few moments, then grandmother took my hand.
"There have been accusations made Swefling. The governor is to investigate and hold a public enquiry"
"Oh?" I asked surprised grandmother would mention such gossip for there were always stories and tales in the towne.
"Don't treat it so lightly. It concerns my family"
"Lucy!" I said very certain it would be.
"Yes. She is with child, did you know?"
"No I didn't. Who's the father?"
"I believe she does not know, but she has accused Andrew"
"Andrew? Andrew who?" I asked naively "No! Not my Andrew. How ridiculous! How can you believe it?"
"I do not but it is what she says. You held her down while he did it"
I opened and closed my mouth unable to say a word.
"Swefling, she has accused your papa too, of taking her

when she was a child, and John and Philip"
"Oh grandmother, it's foolish nonsense. Everyone knows she practically lives in the barracks, she's worse than a whore" I whispered the last part "I've heard such sordid tales"
"Be that as it may, the list of charges continues. She accuses your papa and Andrew of murdering her papa and you of killing your sons by him"
I stood up then and put my hands to my ears.
"Stop it! Stop it" I cried "why are you doing this? It's lies, all lies. You know it to be so. You know!"

And I began to hurry away and ran straight into the governor. He gently took hold of my hands in his.

"Calm yourself Mistress Butler, calm yourself"
I tried to escape his grasp but he held me fast.
"How can I calm myself? It's lies that grandmother speaks of. None of it is true! None of it!"
"I believe you Mistress Butler. The difficulty is that Miss Martin has laid these charges"
"But she's made accusations against us for years, everyone knows that"
"Indeed, and I am forced to conduct the enquiry because of that"
"But Governor, they are lies. You know it to be so, my brother is in your employ. You trust him"
"I am unable to pass judgement Mistress Butler until I hear the evidence, but I am aware of the …… the untruths that have been pronounced. I am positive all will be resolved satisfactorily. Now here is your grandmother. You should sit and calm yourself dear lady"
"Sit Swefling" grandmother instructed me "it serves no purpose running off and crying, we must determine a plan"

"We just have to tell the truth" I countered.
"She is a tricky woman. Insanely jealous of you"
"But I have nothing for her to be jealous of" I protested.
"Not now but you took her father from her"
"I did not"
"She believes otherwise"
"But…. "
"No, listen to me girl, this is what we're to do. Governor, I believe you should not be party to our conversation" Grandmother advised the man, who bowed to us and made his departure.
"When is the hearing?"
"In two weeks"
"Two weeks! Why did no one tell me before?"
"Philip thought it best not to concern you until nearer to the time"
"But I just saw him and he was happy and smiling with Marian"
"He was diverting you"
"Who will be called?"
"Lucy will be called to give an account of her accusations and the detail of the occurrences. But it will be mostly you Swefling, and your Papa and Philip. I should tell you one last thing. She's accused you of being a witch"

Grandmother's words shook me to my core, for of all the accusations this was likely to be the worst, for we all knew that even as we spoke, those similarly accused were being hounded to their deaths throughout the colonies in the north.

"Oh dear God" I said sitting down once more beside my grandmother.

…

I wandered home in a daze acknowledging the friends and acquaintances who spoke to me, passing the time of day, but I could barely reply and was certainly not in a frame of mind for any conversation. Instead of going straight away into the house though I went into the workshop where I knew Andrew would be working. He looked up from his lathe when he saw me, a broad smile on his face and he kissed me, seeing my melancholy expression.

"You look glum; had a disagreement with grandmother?"
I shook my head and blurted out in an instant, all the horror of the afternoon, as he took me in his arms and stroked my hair.
"She'll not get away with it Swef, everyone knows you've done everything to help her"
"But she's accused you of fathering her child, how can you prove you're not?"
"You know it's not so"
"Of course I do, but it's not me that has to be persuaded and she's said papa took her when she was a child, and John and Philip. Why? Why would she do this?"
"I don't know Swef, but we'll fight her. She cannot be allowed to lie and defame our family"

May 17 1638

The Virginia Assembly building was crowded with what to my mind, resembled a mob or at least a crowd come to watch a play at a theatre. Many of the townesfolk we were friendly with were there and for the most part sat with some reserve waiting for the proceedings to commence, but there was a large section of the audience who were in attendance for the spectacle and expectation of sordid tales of torrid goings on, in our house.

In the weeks prior to the hearing, Lucy's blood kin, Kathren and Joane, had given us much welcome support and words of encouragement when concern and worry began to descend about me. Kathren, who as far as anyone else was concerned was Lucy's sister, also declared she would reveal Lucy's background and origins if necessary, but we prayed it would not be. John and Amey arrived from Ipswiche with Papa and Mary, and I was much relieved at their presence, but I was dismayed they brought Rowan with them, for I believed she should not witness such humiliation, as we were likely to experience. At least Swefling declared she would remain away and for that I was relieved.

We sat together at one side, I between Andrew and grandmother holding their hands tightly for support and looked about us briefly. Lucy, I saw sat alone except for two young men beside her. She looked most large in her pregnancy, clearly nearing her time, as of course was, but she appeared unconcerned and looked around the room with a huge smile on her face.

Governor West entered the room looking resplendent in his fine clothes and took his place in his chair on the dais overlooking the rest of us. The babbles of voices quietened a little but he rapped the gavel and silence prevailed within the room.

"We are gathered to conduct an enquiry into the charges laid by Lucy Martin against her step mother Mistress Swefling Butler, Masters Andrew Butler, John Archer Senior, John Archer Junior and Philip Archer and divers others who may be accused as the proceedings develop" he addressed the room. "Miss Martin" he looked now as Lucy "Stand if you please. You have laid these most serious of accusations against these good folk, we would be pleased for you to tell us why you believe they be true. Would you prefer to sit?"

"No! Why would I, I'm only with child, it's happened before"

"To you, do you refer?" the governor asked amid titters from some of the crowd.

"Indeed not sir, I was a maid until he had me" she declared pointing at Andrew, but I believed that to be a lie.

"Mr Butler you mean?"

"Pah! Mr! The witch's familiar and they've been familiar, stuffed you as well again stepmother, two of us at the same time" she laughed as did the crowd.

I made to rise to protest at her words but Andrew and grandmother held me down

"Sit still" hissed grandmother furiously.

"Tell us from the beginning about Mistress Butler"

"Oh, she wasn't Mistress Butler then, just a plain Miss Archer, with a daft name, sailing on the Agnes Rose"

"When was this?"

"1616 I believe"

"And you were how old then Miss Martin?"

"I would be three years, Governor"

"And you knew Mistress Butler, Miss Archer, was plain, when you were three?" The congregation roared with laughter at the suggestion.

"I mean her name. She was always trying to make herself known to my father, even when my mother was alive. She pushed her overboard, you know and my infant brother, just days old he was"

I heard certain section of the crowd gasp at her words and they were quite damaging even if completely untrue.

"Your brother was born on the voyage?"

"Yes, her mother, interfering bitch, was with my mother when he was born. She probably did something to him as well. I was kept away. Then high and mighty Mistress Archer interfered again"

"Mistress Archer? You mean Mistress Butler's mother and Lady Cobbold's daughter?" the governor asked, knowing full well.

"Yes Mistress Archer forced my own mother to remove into their cabin"

"She had a cabin?"

"I just said so didn't I? The Archers had a cabin, all five of them in a tiny space. You will imagine what they did in there with the door shut"

"Your mother was moved into the cabin with the Archer family" the governor drew Lucy back to her tale.

"Jesu" Lucy blasphemed at the governor "It was a small cabin, Mama, Joane and me and the baby in the bed, her in the other" she pointed to me.

"And when did Mistress Butler begin her liaison with your father?"

"I don't know exactly but he was there and when mama fell asleep, I expect she did then"

"You didn't see this yourself?"

"Of course not I was asleep" There was much laughter again and I began to feel slightly sorry for Lucy, for I realised they were laughing at her, not so much at the tale she was telling.

"I see. So what happened next?"

"A few nights later, mama and the baby were gone and I woke her up and told her. She said Joane and I were to stay in the cabin and she'd bring my mama back to me, but she didn't, she pushed her over the side"

"Did you see that?"

"No I was in the cabin, but I know it happened that way"

The governor nodded at Lucy, then in the silence that followed looked down at the paper on his desk and began sifting through them for a time, before taking a book in his hands and opening it at a marked page.

"Miss Martin, when vessels arrive in Jamestowne, particularly in the early days, they were required to report the death of any individual during the voyage and Captain Williams of the Agnes Rose, made a copy of the ships log which was lodged with the assembly. I'll read it to you"

And we heard of course the true account of the events of Rebecca's death we all knew to be so. There was silence when he finished and he looked pittingly at Lucy.

"Do you have anything to say?"
"What about, he lied. It's not what happened and anyway the very next day, I saw her with my father, standing beside him at the front of the ship"
"What were they doing?"
"Talking"
"You saw that, you saw your father talking with Mistress Butler. Was anyone else there?"
"Her parents?"
"I see so Mistress Butler was propositioning your recently widowed father, with her own parents standing by?"
"Yes, I told you they were a very lewd family"
"And at three years old you knew all about lewdness, Miss Martin?"
"I know what I saw"
The governor sighed and turned to his papers once more before continuing.
"Miss Martin tell us about when you arrived in

Jamestowne"

Lucy sat for a moment or two as if she was collecting her thoughts before she began.

"We all moved into a house together. Miss Archer, as she was, Joane and I had one room upstairs, her brothers the other with my father and the parents down the stairs"
"And when were you first taken by the accused?"
"Which one?"
"Whoever was first"
"It was almost straight away. The brothers dragged me from my bed into their room and the father joined in and all three were at me"
"At the same time?" the governor asked, which was not an appropriate question I thought especially as there was much laughter in the room already.
"Don't be silly governor, one at a time" she laughed herself then.
"So you find it amusing?"
"Oh no Sir" she became serious once more "They did it lots of times"
"And where was your father?"
"I don't know with her I suppose"
"The three you accused, they didn't touch your sister Joane or Miss Butler?"
"Well no Sir they weren't as pretty as me"
"And you were three years old?"
"No I was four by then"
"I see. You have a good memory. Why didn't you tell anyone this was happening to you?"
"I didn't know anyone"
"Not even the priest?"
"No one I just told you. Don't you listen?" There was gasps of astonishment at Lucy's words to the governor,

who was being very patient with her.

"I suggest this is all in your mind Miss Martin"

"No it's not it's all true, you're a liar"

"Just like Captain Williams of the Agnes Rose I suppose"

"Yes Sir I suppose so"

"Let's move on. You say Mistress Butler stole your father, bewitched him you say"

"She's a witch yes. Not long after we arrived her mother died. They killed her I know so Mr Archer could have me, and she became very friendly with my papa. He was very sad and missed my mama and he was a weak innocent man. I saw them once in the kitchen. She was making pastry"

"Oh God no" I whispered to myself, but Andrew heard me and squeezed my hand for he knew of the events, for I had told him.

"My father came into the room. I was hiding on the stairs"

"Why were you hiding?"

"Just was. My father told her he thought to take another wife and asked her and she said yes and then he stood behind her and raised her skirts and had her, while she made the bread for supper"

I bowed my head, in embarrassment hearing the titters of the crowd at Lucy's words.

"Look up Swefling" Grandmother hissed under her breath "Be proud of yourself girl"

"You said pastry" Governor West reminded Lucy.

"Bread, pastry what does it matter?"

"It matters. But to continue, how did Mistress Butler bewitch your father, if he had already proposed marriage?"

"She always wiggled her arse at him and stood close"

"Your father always moved away of course?"

"Of course not, he was a weak man"

"I see and you were four years old when you knew this?"

"Yes Sir"

"Good enough, and your father and Mistress Butler were married and had four children"
"No five, one died just after he was born. She killed him I expect. I loved them all, they were my brothers and sisters"
"And Mr Archer and his son's, what happened to them?"
"John Archer married Amey Butler and she persuaded him to give me up and he got his acres and they moved away"
"When you were four or five?"
"Five I believe, but Philip and Mr Archer came to my room still. They shared the one next to mine. I saw them together as well" There were gasps from the crowd disbelieving the tales now it was obvious to hear.
"But you shared the room with your sister and step sisters. Didn't they wake when the men came for you?"
"No. Never once"
"The Indian attack of '25, you were twelve I believe, what do you know of it?"
"My father was bought back and taken to the workshop, but she wouldn't let me see him, nor Kathren. I thought she was my friend but she was just like the others"
"Kathren Ranger?"
"Yes, their servant, she was after my father too, they shared him"

I watched out of the corner of my eye as Kathren slowly got to her feet, despite Edward's attempts to prevent her.

"I wish to speak" she said in almost a whisper.
"In due time Mistress Ranger if you please"
"I prefer now governor, I'm sorry, but Lucy needs to know something"
"Go ahead if you must"

Kathren turned to face Lucy showing no sign of the obvious emotion she must be feeling, for she spoke softly and without malice.

"I will not allow you to malign our family further, Lucy. They have cared for you all your life and you mistreat them. I should have told you many years since and I wish I had not to do so in public, but you must be made aware Crispin Martin was not your father" There was a hushed silence in the room an air of expectancy waiting for Kathren to continue which was so very incredibly brave and difficult for her. "Nor was Rebecca, his wife, your mother. Crispin Martin was my father. I am your mother, and I am ashamed of you"

Kathren sat down and as Edward put his arm about her, cheers and applause broke out around the room amongst some of the crowd, but why, I had no idea. Eventually Governor West obtained quiet and all eyes turned to Lucy again who began to giggle, then laugh until she was almost hysterical but no one went to her side. Eventually she simmered down and stared at Kathren with as much hatred as she'd ever looked at me.

"You lie! You're a witch too. He was my father. He was my father" she screamed "You are not my mother!"
"Miss Martin enough" the governor roared and to our surprise Lucy turned and faced him. "Do you wish to continue?"
"Of course I do" and she continued as if Kathren had not spoken or made any revelation whatsoever. "She went into the workshop. I heard her scream and I ran out of the house and heard her cry to her father that he'd killed her husband"

"Mistress Butler you mean? What did she say exactly?"
"Of course Mistress Butler, you're not listening to me" she glared at the man who was being most fair to her for her outbursts and rudeness I thought. "She said, Papa you've killed my husband"
"Did she say how?"
"With a musket"
"And you saw the musket wound?"
"Yes Sir, in his belly"
"And how do you account for the axe wound to his shoulder?"
"I don't know, I didn't see an axe wound, you're trying to trick me again" she giggled.
"Yes I must be, perhaps because I'm a liar like the Captain and Mistress Ranger"
"Must be so Sir" she agreed smiling prettily.
The governor looked away from Lucy and at the huge clock ticking away just beyond his table and clearly made a decision.
"It is the hour to stop for provender and ale. We shall resume at two of the clock Miss Martin and you will continue your tale"
"I want to do so now?" she argued.
"A weak man such as I requires sustenance Miss Martin. Until two of the clock"

...

We remained in our seats watching the crowd leave the proceedings, until grandmother stood and turned to our family and friends.

"I have fare arranged in my rooms. Come" And taking my arm in hers, she led us from the assembly building to the governor's mansion and her accommodation.

I removed myself from her company and turned to Kathren, who followed with us.

"Kathren, I am so sorry" I whispered to her, tears in my eyes as I laid my hand on her arm. "It should not have come to this. I should have done something"

"No, Swefling" she said softly, "none of us could have done anything to avoid this" and we stood in the room and hugged each other. "I am glad to have said it but it will make no difference. It is not the time to speak of this but when you remove yourselves to Butlers, Edward and I will come with you. We have decided, but I ought to go to Lucy now, not be here" and she began to move away.

"Kathren" I called after her but my earlier words sounded inadequate to my own ears, for my step daughter, who was surely feeling grave emotional upset and I could not continue as I held onto her arm.

"Come Swef, sweetheart" Andrew said and he and Edward came upon us and I felt his hand on my back as we drew apart "time to get refreshment" and they led us towards the tables, laden with all manner of fare for our consumption. Kathren remained in our company throughout the break, but I'm sure, like me she wondered for the wellbeing of Lucy.

There was much reviewing as the morning's proceedings as we ate, but I grew weary of the comments and wandered out of the open door into the gardens and ambled amongst the flowers, waving gently in the soft breeze that passed by. I heard the familiar shuffling footsteps on the path behind me, but didn't look up as Andrew drew close and wrapped his arms about me.

"Love you Swef" he whispered softly, as if we were in a room of a 1000 people and did not wish to be overheard. "Thank you for believing in me" I said. He turned me round in his arms and smiled.

"Do not thank me Swef, you are my beloved wife, the mother of my children. We stand together, you and I to face the world and whatever it throws at us"

"Yes, we do!" I smiled then and kissed him briefly.

"Is that all?" he asked, pulling me as close as possible with my large pregnant belly between us and kissed me very passionately, as I clung to him. "So" he said as he released me and he led me back towards the room "I wonder what stories will be told this afternoon?"

"Do not jest Andrew" I said "We are all accused and poor Kathren, how must she be feeling, I simply cannot imagine"

"No one is taking Lucy serious. She is making an utter fool of herself"

"I know, that's what's so awful. She's sick in her head. Poor, poor Lucy"

"And she's out to do you harm Swefling, don't forget that"

...

We resumed our seats just before two of the clock and as the hour struck the governor came into the room and took his place and immediately got down to business. Lucy I noticed seemed very agitated and I wondered what had occurred over the break to make her so, for she had been quite calm in the morning, even after Kathren's words. Lucy looked about her and her glance rested in my direction and she glared at me most fiercely.

"I'll get you" she mouthed, then laughed bitterly.

"Miss Martin" the governor began with no preamble. "Mistress Butler's sons with your husband died in 1630, during the infection from the vessel Abigail but you say that is not so, that Mistress Butler killed them?"
"Yes, she killed them because they were my father's sons and she was carrying on with her familiar, when my father was still warm"
"Mistress Ranger says Mistress Butler's first husband was not your father"
"She lied"
"And Mistress Butlers sons, she had with Crispin Martin, they died five years after their father"
"You are not listening to me. She killed them when she wanted to wed him"
"How?"
"She infected them. Listen will you?"
"I'll remind you again Miss Martin, I am in charge of this enquiry and you will address me in the correct fashion"
"You should not upset me"
"Are you upset?"
"Yes!" she yelled.
"Tell me why, Mistress Butler didn't kill her daughters?"
"They wouldn't let her, the men, they had the girls. You know the one who was an Indian and the other"
"And yourself? Tell us Miss Martin do you enjoy men?"

I heard Lucy giggle quite hysterically and felt so sad for her I stood up.

"Leave her alone governor, please don't make fun of her" and I sat down promptly feeling very foolish.
"Thank you for your concern over Miss Martin, Mistress Butler. I am sure she thanks you"
"Indeed I do" Lucy agreed instantly "thank you stepmother. I've a confession to make. It wasn't you who

killed your boys, it was me. My dear sweet brothers such lovely little cocks they had, but they didn't know what to do with them"

"Enough!" roared the governor, so loudly and angrily it caused Lucy to cower in her seat.

"I made it up. I didn't touch them" she declared.

"Miss Butler, who is the father of your child?"

"Not you governor" she giggled braver again "Mr Butler's 'twil be. He's had us both and him a cripple, hasn't harmed his performing" There was silence in the room waiting for Lucy's next fantasy "or is it old Mr Archer or Philip, your clerk. Do you know Sir, I don't know, maybe it's one of these lovely boys" she grinned at the two lads beside her, who were even, as she continued, becoming less and less amused by the woman between them. "maybe anyone in this room, maybe.... "

"Lucy be quiet" Joane called out "You've caused enough trouble and discord all your life, don't make it any worse for yourself" and red faced she sat down, amid to our surprise a round of applause and cheers from the audience.

Lucy just laughed and laughed, sounding hysterical and she continued, as the governor hammered his gavel on the table repeatedly, amid the noise and mayhem, until at last some order was resumed. He sat quietly studying the papers before him and the notes his clerk, not Philip of course, passed up, then he looked directly to Lucy, who had resumed her seat and he addressed her most formally.

"Stand if you will Madam. Lucy Martin" He spoke again when she stood before him, his anger abated but a serious expression on his face "Not one of your accusations have been found valid and no one has any case to answer, except unfortunately, yourself. You have maliciously accused others of misdeeds and deviant acts against your person, you have lied and misled us and we are greatly fearful for your own safety and that of your child. You cannot be allowed to remain at liberty" He paused, as we took in his words and listened with bated breath as he continued. "You will remain in the care of the constable in Jamestowne until the birth of your child. The infant will be taken from you and you will live out your days in the House of Correction in Yorktown until you have learnt the error of your ways"

There was silence in the room as the governor finished his judgement. Then a low scream erupted from Lucy, as she sank into her chair, a scream of a wounded animal, a fighting mother for her child and it became a screech like none of us had every heard before.

"It's your fault" she screamed at me "You did this to me, all your planning and scheming. You're a witch. I hate you! I hate you!" Her voice became quite low again, almost a hoarse whisper "but I promise you Swefling Butler you and your descendents will rue this day you crossed me!"

As she spoke her final words Lucy collapsed and fell back in her chair and remained trance like until she was removed from the room, and I suspected, taken to a cell in the barracks.

...

I felt drained as we left the Assembly building and although many folk congratulated us on our success, I was not in any frame of mind to speak with them.

"I'm going for a walk beside the river" I announced.

"I'll come with you" Andrew said. I reached for his arm.
"Let me on my own for a time Andrew, come for me in an hour"
"Be careful" he said full of concern.
"I will, I promise" and I smiled at him as I turned away. I didn't walk far, just to the fallen tree, that for many years had been used as a resting place for the townsfolk to rest on whilst they watched the activity on the river.

All was quiet now as the afternoon sun moved around the sky and my thoughts inevitably turned to Lucy and Kathren, and I wondered if I should be with Cris's daughter, who must surely be suffering as much, if not more than I. As I looked out over the calming waters though, I found myself offering a silent prayer begging for forgiveness.

"Dear Holy Father, Please forgive me for all the wrongs I did to Lucy, to make her the way she is. I thought I was a good enough stepmother. I know I treated her and Joane the same, even when I knew the circumstances of her birth, after Kathren and Edward arrived. I didn't take Cris from her did I, nor him from Rebecca? I never thought of him at all in those terms, not until he asked me to wed, in fact God, you'll remember I was excited at walking home with Andrew.

Was it my misjudgement that caused this, by agreeing to marry Crispin? Certainly I would have saved those I hold dear, from all the anguish and accusations and suspicion they've suffered at the hands of Lucy. And poor Lucy, Lord, take care of her troubled mind, speak with her, I beg of you, calm her, for she is to be a mother herself soon. It will hurt her more than words can say to have her child taken from her. Hasn't she suffered enough?

Forgive me Lord for beginning you on a course of action that might not be in your plan but Lucy was once a dear stepdaughter to me and I loved her. I feel compassion and sadness, at such a waste of life but it is yours to give and yours to take away.

Dear God hear my prayer. Amen"

I sat for many moments, when I'd finished and slowly as the time passed I began to feel eased. A breeze blew off the water and ruffled my hair and as I moved to tidy it, I saw out of the corner of my eye, Andrew ambling along, his injured leg still a disability, but no more than a familiar hindrance. I waved and smiled at him as he approached.

"Just right" I said when he sat on the tree trunk beside me and wrapped his arm on my shoulders.
"Alright?"
"Yes, very good, now you're here"
We sat for a time in companionable silence watching the ripples of the river, until he shifted his position slightly.
"I believe it's time to remove ourselves to our land, Swefling"
"Yes, I am ready. I will speak with grandmother and see what she wants to do"
"I have already, she says yes. She will come before the winter"
"Good. Well, we should go, I suppose. I am quite hungry and there will be plans to be made"

July 1638

To my surprise it has taken much longer than we expected to remove ourselves from Jamestowne to our land, for apart from our packing, there were those of our family who needed much comforting, particularly following the enquiry. I spent many hours with Joane who was most distressed at the fate of Lucy, who she continued to consider her sister, although following her subsequent conversation with Kathren, she was aware of the full truth of the matter. Joane reluctantly agreed to care for Lucy's child despite believing it should remain with Lucy, but other's more influential in dealing with such matters decreed it should not be, so we did as we were able, to help.

As June arrived and I drew close to my delivery time, I became tired but most afternoons was able, thankfully, to take myself to my bed to rest and was therefore much relieved when on 28th of the month our daughter Ales Elizabeth was born, easily and without any difficulties, in the early hours of the morning. The following week she was baptised at Jamestowne parish church, without my elder girls and Papa and Mary in attendance, for they were busy on our properties making ready for our arrival and I was most anxious now to join them. As we returned to our house from the baptism, we came upon one of the women from the fort sitting on the bench, under the window, a most concerned and anxious expression on her face.

"Mistress Butler" she addressed me, yet drawing Kathren and Joane into the conversation, "'tis young Lucy Martin, she is lying in but 'tis a difficult birthing. She asks for ye all to attend if ye have the will"

I looked at Kathren, and Joane and thence to Andrew, who with a nod of his head took Ales, and Joane's eldest daughter and Margaret took care of Bettris and the boys and we left as fast as we were able, which for me was not overly so, it being barely a week since the birth of my own child.

We discovered Lucy in the house of one of the women of the fort and thankfully not in her cell, where her female relatives had visited several times in the days since she had been incarcerated. Kathren and Joane crossed to her and took hold of Lucy's hands. She opened her eyes, clearly in considerable pain as we had been led to expect, for she was thus far unable to deliver her child.

"There must be something you may do" I said to the midwife, as I remained by the door not wishing to distress Lucy any further than she was already, but the woman sadly just shook her head.
"Twil not be long, poor lass" As I stood feeling such sadness and compassion and hopelessness for Cris's granddaughter, she noticed me watching her and tried a smile.
"I'm sorry Mama Swefling" she whispered.
"I know" I replied and tears came to my eyes as Kathren urged me beside her and I sat on the bed no longer able to stand.

As the afternoon turned into evening Lucy's pain increased and we wiped her face and tried to calm her with soft words and the sweet perfume of lavender but with hardly a whimper from such a loud and angry woman, Lucy passed from us and at last into peace. The Reverend, who was summoned as the end drew near, spoke with Lucy as she passed and knelt with us afterwards. We offered up our prayers for her salvation and peace now her earthly life was done.

It was dark when Kathren, Joane and I walked slowly to our home, stopping several times as I felt weak and wet where my breasts, long overdue for my babe at them, leaked and were heavy and painful.

"Mama Swefling" Joane began when we sat in the parlour and my screaming baby was being satisfied and we sipped reviving sweet tea, while the menfolk sojourned outside with the children. "Joseph and I have decided to come to Butlers with you. Perhaps we could have a little house somewhere near?"
"It will be so good to be together. Get Joseph to speak with Andrew" I nodded looking at Kathren.
"We should be close" Kathren declared "Edward and I are to have a house and garden across the road and it is right my sister will be beside us" she smiled taking Joane's hand in hers.

August 19 1638

I woke this morning in my bed to find the sun beaming through the window onto my pillow. It was the first morning in our new home and I stretched, reaching for Andrew, surprised the bed was empty. I turned and saw him at the other window with Ales in his arms talking to her, showing her our land, his little finger in her mouth. I sat up and moved the pillows making myself comfortable, as he turned and saw me.

"Look Ales, mama's awake and ready to feed you, there's a lucky girl. I'll have to wait for my breakfast"

And he laid her in my arms and watched us, as she began to suckle.

"Well Swefling" he said sitting on the bed beside us, "here we are at last in our place. Our very own - Butlers" he sounded so pleased and proud and perhaps relieved "who'd have thought we'd have all this when we left England with nothing at all but a sense of adventure and a will to better ourselves?   We have much hard work before us, but it is our land we shall work on. We have enough of our house completed to protect us from the elements while the small harvest is gathered and next year we shall set on workers. Not slaves, I will not have slaves on the property, but there will always be new settlers who cannot obtain their own land, who will be willing to work for payment"

"And animals, we'll have animals, Andrew"

"Of course, cows and chickens and sheep, maybe for their wool and meat. You can spin and weave?"

"You know I cannot, but Mary and Kathren are able. It will be so wonderful, now we have the space and our family about us"

"And close to Middle Plantation to trade goods in the market"

Andrew stood and moved to the window once more, that overlooked the land I intended to turn into a garden of sorts, with grass and flowers, not the fruit and herbs which Mary had already planted and were thriving elsewhere as I write.

"We shall take a walk about our land today Swef, to the four corners"

"You mean a hike" I grinned "perhaps a picnic, just the two of us"

"If you're intent on taking food perhaps we should go on

horseback"
"Not laziness already Andrew?" I laughed.
"No, but it's a sensible notion. We do not know what lies beyond the trees do we?"

January 6 1639

We have just passed the most wonderful of Christmas celebrations with our family at our properties of Butlers and Cobbolds and such a gathering we have never seen before. The houses were full of gaity and laughter even though our building is incomplete with the final touches we wish for, but sufficient to keep us warm and cosy from the coldness outside. On December 25, wrapped in our warmest clothing though, we trailed along the Jamestowne Road, the short distance next door to cousin William's property for the afternoon and evening and we raised many toasts to our new venture on the land granted to us.

Decisions have been made over the winter and it has been decided that some of the land across the track, Andrew says it is about ten acres, will be made over for any workers we may have, but more importantly initially, for the properties for Kathren and Joane to be erected, for whilst it is good to live together, they also wish for their own homes and small plots of land to cultivate as they wish and as soon as the weather improves the ground breaking will begin for their houses and the completion of our own property.

It is such an exciting time, more so I believe than the day we stepped off the Agnes Rose in 1616, for now, whilst it is true we are older, we do not have the fear or concern of what this life in Virginia will be like for we have experienced it for twenty two years. Our removal to the countrie holds no worries for us as before, for we are settled and have a wide family and circle of friends about us and the danger and threat from the native people is less than before and we are more protected.

And now 12th night is passed we shall look forward to the end of the year and the arrival of spring bringing the warm weather and pleasant days spent outside.

April 6 1639

We have been so busy these past weeks on our land preparing the soil. Andrew and William spent weeks clearing the trees and the undergrowth, burning that which could not be dug with a spade and then using the plow pulled by one of the oxen, which made the heavy work of pulling and pushing the implement somewhat easier. The soil was turned and the loam broken down further until the men declared it was ready for planting.

We all became involved in the planting of the crops and Swefling has introduced us to some of the farming ways of the Indians she lived with. We have planted the seeds of tall maize as before but with beans in the same hole, in order for the sturdy corn stalks to support the wavering and trailing beans, instead of them running over the ground. We have sectioned off one corner of the field from the rest to make an experiment, and one day we sent Richard and John fishing. They thought it great fun to be away from their chores but they were in fact working, for their catch of small fishes were placed one by one in each hole with the seeds. We do not disbelieve Swefling, but we mean to see for ourselves that the plants really do grow more productively. We are most hopeful of the harvest for if we are able to increase the yield of our crops with little extra effort, and obtain a better harvest, the time saved will be well directed elsewhere and will mean improved food for us all.

Mary and I have also been working hard on planting the flax on our new land, although I am not convinced it is a viable crop, for the labour required is excessive and the work exceedingly hard and onerous as I have already testified to you but we are determined to make our farm as productive as it may be.

When all this hard fieldwork is completed each day, we spend what hours remain until darkness falls, working in our garden, planting all the crops for our kitchens as we did in Jamestowne and we have to find time to tend to our animals for they cannot be neglected for one moment. Of course you must not believe that Mary and I toil on the land alone while Andrew and Papa build our houses for it is not so. Kathren and Joane and their husbands: and Swef, Rowan and cousin William and the children and his employees all work together with us for all our mutual benefit.

Our one release from usual chores is that cousin William's housekeeper, Mistress Potts and her girls are charged with preparing all the food for our needs at this busy time, which is a welcome release for us. Thus each evening when we sit around a large table on William's porch taking our ease at the end of the day, all our aches and pains seem to vanish as we enjoy food provided for us and drink the newly brewed ale and there is always a great sense of achievement and much laughter.

As a chill comes over the spring night we stare at

the stars shining down on us and make our way indoors, still happy from our time together. We depart for our beds and as soon as our goodnights are called and our heads touch our soft pillows, most likely than not we fall asleep instantly, resting peacefully until the early morning when our work commences once again.

The pages following are all that remain of my dear Mama's journal that were salvaged from the garden after my careless mishap.

Swefling Ales Martin Cobbold 1668

the gardens were neat and tidy, ready and waiting for the guests coming from all over the countie, from Middle Plantation, Jamestowne and down the road at Ipswiche and divers other plantations and homesteads. In the kitchen the pies and tarts were ready, the meat turning on the spit and barrels of ale and bottles of rum and grandmother's favourite, Geneva standing to attention, and one or two already reduced from full. I surveyed the preparedness with satisfaction and went to the shaded porch, where the family were gathering. Grandmother Eleanor was holding court, as so often on these fine occasions, attired in her finest gown and bedecked with pearls and jewels, as befitting the daughter of a Lord and widow of another, but far too fussy and complicated in the heat of this June day in Virginia for other than a ninety one year old set in her ways.

"I am hardly able to believe the fact" she was telling Governor Wyatt and his wife "that my great granddaughter is to be wed and I am here to witness it. How can it be so? The years have passed so quick. Why I recall when I was just the same age, I'd hardly left my father's house and ventured out of the countie"
"Times change so quickly Eleanor" Lady Wyatt was saying "and this is a new world, there's so much for the young people to be doing and so much freedom"
"It is so" grandmother agreed "I am pleased not to have such freedoms, I would be lost and bewildered in no time and no doubt find myself wed to the first man that stopped by, whatever his standing or prospects"

I chuckled as I listened to the two women reflecting on the changes in our lives, for I had to agree with much of what they spoke.

"You find our observations amusing Swefling?" grandmother asked attempting to put a stern expression on her face and failing miserably.

"Oh no grandmother, I was considering you being bewildered"

"I was young and innocent once upon a time, Swefling" she muttered, her expression changing into a grin now. "You look exceedingly attractive, mother of the bride. I wager that husband of yours hasn't noticed"

"He has" I smiled at her "He said he thought he'd marry me all over again"

"I always knew he was a sensible man" grandmother laughed "and where's the blushing bride? Shouldn't she be showing herself?"

"She's almost ready, and very nervous. Rowan is attempting to calm her"

"What's there to be nervous of. You've spoken to her about her wifely duties?"

"Of course grandmother" I laughed again "she's more frightened of everyone watching her"

"She'll have Andrew at her side to steady her, that's what fathers do, even step fathers, and of course her intended will be at her other side. My grandson is a very sensible young man"

"It's not physical support she requires. She wants to go away somewhere quiet with just her and William to be wed, and the reverend of course"

"Silly girl!" grandmother exclaimed "spoil our fun and joy of seeing the eldest daughter of our house be wed. It's her duty. I'll tell her so"

"I'm sure she's aware of her duty, grandmother" I turned as grandmother looked beyond me at others who joined us on the porch.

"My, what a picture you look Swefling! Indeed the blushing bride you are, blue does so suit you. William will be struck dumb that he's won the heart of so a fair maid"

"Oh grandmother" Swefling giggled "don't tease so, I feel so … I don't know"

"Excited and apprehensive, I have no doubt my dear, only to be expected. And you Rowan, are you calm enough to assist your sister?"

"I believe so Grandmother Eleanor" Rowan smiled looking about her.

"Good, good, and you will have the single young men trailing after you today, you look as pretty as a picture. Both of you. We should have arranged for a portrait to be done"

"I'm glad you didn't grandmother" Swefling declared.

…

What a splendid day it has been, and now my eldest child is a married woman and whilst the young revellers continue their celebrations, Andrew and I have retired to our bedchamber. And yet I am no longer tired as I sit at my writing table adding my words of the day. I can hear Andrew's gentle breathing as he sleeps behind me and all is peaceful in our room and I am reassured. I have strange thoughts though, one of immense loss for Swefling, far greater in many ways than during the time she was away from us with the Indians and I cannot fathom why that should be. Perhaps although she will be just across the creek with William, her life will not be part of ours any longer. We shall see each other daily I expect and in time welcome her children into our arms but the special relationship I had with her, and do still with Rowan and Bettris and Ales, although they are barely more than babies, will be gone. And Rowan will not be long following her sister for as we have observed this day, at least two of the young men invited to the celebrations sought out her company.

But enough of these comments of the passing of time, I should be happy and contented that the first of my daughters is wed, to man she clearly adores and who is likewise with her and my fervent wish for them is that their joy will remain long into their marriage.

The last will and testament of Eleanor Ales Rebecca Otley Cobbold, widow of Sir William Mortimer David Cobbold Bt, late of Cobbold Hall, Swefling in the countie of Suffolk, Great Britain and latterly of Cobbolds, Middle Parish, Virginia in the British Colonie of America, being of sound mind but weak and feeble of limb and body, in the 93rd year of her life.

To my dearest companion Marian Scrivenor, now the wife of Philip Archer, my grandson of Jamestowne, I give and bequeath my inlaid black wood table, she oft remarked favourably of and the mirror that hung above it in my chamber.

To my son in law John Archer, son of Sir Felix Archer late advisor to her Majestie Elizabeth, Queen of England, and widower of my dearest daughter Ales Rebecca Cobbold,

I give and bequeath the French bureau at present in the small sitting room at Cobbolds, the home of my grandson William M D Cobbold and the entire contents therein for his use in whatever manner he believes correct.

JNR

To Richard Tye, of Tye House, Swefling in the countie of Suffolk, and his heirs and successors, the grandson of Richard Tye, the dearest man who ever walked this earth,

I give and bequeath one hundred acres of land from Cobbold Hall, to be determined and agreed upon at his will in consultation with the lawyers representatives in England.

To my lawyer Justin Makepeace of Makepeace and Gordon of Middle Parish, I give and bequeath the painting of Otley Hall he oft times admired and a case of

Geneva.

To my dear friend Margaret wife of Sir Francis Wyatt, Governor of the colonie of Virginia, I give and bequeath the ornamental plates on the dresser at Butlers, she has long admired.

To my grandchildren William Mortimer David Cobbold, the son of my only son William Mortimer David Cobbold, deceased, John Archer of Ipswiche, Middle Parish, Virginia, Philip Archer of Jamestowne, Virginia and Swefling Archer Butler now the wife of Andrew Butler of Butlers, Middle Parish, Virginia, the children of my only daughter Ales Rebecca Cobbold, deceased and her dearly beloved husband John Archer, I give and bequeath equally and jointly all my worldly possessions, goods and chattels, not referred to above that reside in the home of my grand son, William Mortimer David Cobbold referred to above. Additionally, all which infers and purports to be the property of myself, in other words: Cobbold Hall, Swefling in the Countie of Suffolk, England, Otley House, Otley in the said Countie of Suffolk, 93a Cheapside in the City of London, England, together with their entire contents, and land pertaining to the same, excepting as described above and the vessel named as "Ales Rebecca" and her cargo, currently on the high seas.

My bodie is to be wrapped in finest linen and placed in an oak casket as I have discussed with John Archer senior and buried under the willow tree across the track between Cobbolds and Butlers and marked by a granite headstone.

Signed: Eleanor Ales Rebecca Cobbold on this day, May 29 in the year of our Lord one thousand six hundred and forty three
Witnessed her hand by: Jeremiah Gordon – lawyer,
Simon Tumilty – Justice of the Court of Virginia,
Francis Wyatt - Governor of the Colonie of Virginia

The lawyer placed the parchment down on the table and removed his spectacles and with a flourish withdrew his lace edged handkerchief and mopped his brow before lifting his glass of Geneva to his lips and taking a sip. The day was, I had to agree with him, exceedingly warm and all the more so in the dining room with all the windows closed, but whether it was the heat of the April day or the emotion of the reading of the will of my grandmother I could not estimate. I wanted to ask many questions but felt it inappropriate in the silence as we watched the lawyer, until my brother John coughed and cleared his throat.

"One of us has to speak" he said looking at Philip, William and I. I'm certain we have many questions and much surprise at Grandmother's will"
"Your grandmother came from an important countie family" Papa reminded us "and married into another, the Otleys and the Cobbolds as you well know"
"Lady Eleanor required it be your determination how the properties are to be divided" Mr Makepeace advised us.
"We have no use for property in England" I declared even before I discussed it with Andrew but the look of agreement on his face confirmed my assumption.
"Me neither" John agreed.
"I have a hankering for the ship, the 'Ales Rebecca'" Philip declared not I am sure to anyone's surprise.
"It's value is reputed to be considerably less the properties"

we were told.
"I'm sure we will be able to make suitable arrangements" John declared "William? What say you?" and we looked at our cousin.

"I grew up in Cobbold Hall but I have made my life here in Virginia I have no use for it. The farms are profitable but I would wish us to have some consideration for the folk there and at Otley House though I suspect the Otley family will wish to reclaim the House for the Hall. I believe we should dispose of the properties, obtain an inventory of the contents and use Philip's vessel to bring to our houses those items we wish to keep"

The four of us looked around the table at our family but we knew the decisions were ours and there was no reason not to follow the path William had suggested.

"Mr Makepeace?" Philip enquired of the lawyer "are you in a position to assist us further?"
"I am indeed, my family have offices in Fleet Street in the city of London, they will conduct the business on your behalf. I suggest you discuss further the matter and advise me in due course and I will ensure instructions are forwarded without delay"
"I do believe that will be satisfactory" William smiled at us and reached for his glass "I also believe a toast to our grandmother in order, God rest her soul" and following his example we all raised our glasses to Lady Eleanor in thanks for her life and our inheritance and sadness at her passing.

But I did have one question, I kept for myself at that time, who on earth is Richard Tye? For that more than anything else was the one thing that puzzled me.

"You simply cannot tell my daughter she's not welcome here Andrew" I declared, wiping my tears roughly from my eyes "I will not forgive you for as long as I live"
"You will not threaten me Swefling. Your daughter maligned our son, and cast a slur over our house. She should have considered that before she and her husband made their pronouncements"
"What on earth did William tell you?" I asked, for I was still somewhat in the dark although I believed it concerned Richard, who chose that moment to come wandering into the room.
"Richard leave us" Andrew told him most fiercely.
"Papa?" he grinned in surprise believing Andrew was jesting.
"I said leave us!" Andrew growled at our son, his face growing red with rage.

Andrew took several deep breaths as Richard quietly did so bidden and closed the door behind him as he left, and in the silence that followed, as I watched, Andrew seemed to lose his stature, as if all the troubles of the world were bearing down on him.

"I believed when we left Jamestowne and all the upset caused by Lucy Martin, our lives would be calm and peaceful" he said.
"We have calm and peaceful lives" I said, calmer myself now.
"You consider this calm? All this upset. William and Swefling speaking ill of my son. It is not right"
"What did William say?" I asked again.
"You will not wish to know"
"Tell me Andrew for goodness sake" I demanded feeling my anger rising again.

Andrew looked at me steadily for a moment or two as if deciding on his course of action. He nodded then and sighed as he spoke.

"William reported that Richard has been seen fornicating in public places and in the vestry"
"Why is that a reason to throw Swef out" I said.
"William declared Richard has fathered two children, with Ruby the African house maid. Why would they tell such lies? What jealously is there within him?"
"Have you considered it might be true?"
"Of course it is not" Andrew stared at me. "I do not wish to discuss it further Swefling. Your daughter and her husband are no longer welcome in my house"
"They will have a reason for telling us Andrew" I suggested but he looked away "how will we see our grandchildren if Swef and William are not welcome? Have you thought of that?"
"We shall make the sacrifice. Now enough of this nonsense"
"Nonsense?" I flared up again "Nonsense" I screeched "I will not remain in this house if you prevent me from seeing Swef and the children and I'll take Bettris and Ales with me" I threatened.
"You will not Swefling. You are my wife and you will remain here in your place"
"You can not make me Andrew Butler" I screamed "You can not"
"Be quiet woman before I take my belt to you"
"How dare you threaten me. You're a wicked man. Stay with your precious fornicating son. I will not remain with you"

As I spoke Andrew grabbed hold of one of my arms and pulled me towards him and with the other firmly slapped my face. We stared at each other for several moments heavy in the silence, until I felt the pressure on my arm lesson as Andrew released me. I continued to look at him as tears came to my eyes and then I turned and fled from the room.

"Swefling I'm sorry" I heard Andrew call after me as I ran into the hall and practically fell into Richard who appeared to be hovering around, perhaps listening to our conversation.
"Get out of my way" I cried pushing past him and heading up the stairs.

I threw myself on the bed but my tears had stopped and I just lay there wondering how we had come to this sorry state of affairs. My daughter and her husband and children banned from our house and Andrew and I screaming at each other. And he had hit me! Andrew had never touched me or the children before, well sometimes the boys on the backs of their legs when they were young and up to mischief, but never once out of anger and I had never been hysterical before in my entire life, even in the worst moments when Crispin and our sons died and Sweffie was taken by the Indians. I had been calm and collected, now I was like a rampaging bullock and I didn't care for my behaviour either. Nor did I understand.

The awful thing was, I knew what William had reported about Richard was true, that he had fathered two children with our free African employee and I assumed Andrew knew too, but he had not acted on the matter or spoken to Richard as far as I was aware, nor had we discussed it. How could we? And now it had come back to haunt us. Andrew and I were in disarray and Sweffie and her family, her dear daughter Swef and the boys were barred from me and I didn't care for that either, not one bit.

But what to do about it, that was the difficulty. I would not go to Andrew and apologise for my behaviour. I would not and he certainly would not come to me. And what of Richard and his behaviour? It was too late to tell him of our displeasure at his behaviour for he would not listen to our words, as he had never done, for he always knew best and now he was a man of over twenty years he had to take responsibility for his own actions and not divide our family. But we had been too soft over our eldest son for he had never taken any such responsibility and now it was too late for us all.

May 25 1651

I really hoped Andrew would relent and allow us to be reconciled with Sweffie and William before Rowan's wedding, but he seems to have grown more and more stubborn as the months have passed and even Rowan's pleading with him have fallen on deaf ears and come to nought. But at least there will be some peace in our house later today it is promised, although I know Andrew was hurt that Rowan refused to allow him to lead her down the aisle to Thackeray and accepted the fact that Papa would do so. For myself, I have made a determination and endeavour not to bicker with Andrew and spoil the day for I am becoming something of a harpy.

Sweffie, I am certain, will be devastated not to be present to witness her sister being wed but William is perhaps as stubborn as Andrew and would not come to request permission for his wife and children, if not himself to be present. Perhaps too William is right in the matter, for we hear only this last week, that Andrew and Richard are to be brought to the court to give witness regarding Susie Taylor and Ruby on charges of prenuptial fornication and Ruby additionally, for bastardy.

Of course Andrew is not involved but as the master of Butler's, it is his responsibility to ensure everyone behaves in a seemly manner. Andrew nevertheless despite the apparent evidence will not accept the truth of the matter and argues with us all, refusing to believe our son is guilty of anything and now it is to come to court in a number of weeks, believes Swefling and William guilty of bringing the charges. I know it is not so for it was Thackeray who advised them of the matter and they were most surprised and distressed at the news, so I know it was not them.

...

Rowan looked most happy this afternoon when she wandered about the garden on Thackeray's arm after they were married in Butlers church. She smiled at most everyone and I am most delighted she has found the love of a good and kind man, after the blackard her first husband, Jackson Bowden turned out to be. I have no doubt Thackeray will treat her well, for he is an easy going man, a peacemaker too if I'm not at all mistaken, for during the course of the activities I saw him glance across the creek to Sweffie's house and whilst I could not see them I knew the family were on their porch. Without a moment's hesitation, Thackeray whispered in Rowan's ear and she too looked across and arm in arm they turned and headed towards the footbridge between the two properties.

"Where do they think they're going?" Andrew asked

as he stood beside me with Gabriel who was taking a breather from the dancing with Kate. Neither of us spoke for it was more than obvious and we watched as Rowan and Thackeray stood in Swef's gardens as her sister came running towards them her arms outstretched, followed at close quarters by William and the children.

"At least someone has some sense" Gabriel declared looking bravely at his Papa.

"What's that supposed to mean?" Andrew asked not matching our son's humour.

"This is Rowan's wedding day Papa, a happy time when families should be together"

"Not when traitors are abroad"

"Andrew, don't" I began "Please not today"

"I'll say no more, and you'll mind your business Gabriel" and without more ado Andrew wandered away towards Bettris and Ales who were sharing a glass of some amber liquid they'd somehow gotten hold of.

"Sorry Mama" Gabriel smiled sadly at me as we watched his father with his youngest sisters.

"It's alright, just leave Papa be" and my glance left Andrew and the girls and turned to the group across the creek who were clearly enjoying a brief moment together and I found tears come to my eyes.

...

As the evening wore on the musicians took up their instruments once more and much dancing ensued, more especially from the younger folk but Andrew and I, in an attempt to bury the hatchet, did take one turn about the floor, for if we remained at the edge, we managed well enough for Andrew's leg troubled him far less these days. I had been sitting to one side with Kathren when Andrew wandered over to us.

"Will you dance?" he asked me most formally. I looked up at him about to ask why he thought that was a suitable invitation for his wife when I felt Kathren's elbow nudge me.

"Alright" I agreed and took his offered arm as I stood.

"I was pained" he said as we stood at the edge of the dance floor waiting for a space to join in "when Rowan refused to allow me to escort her down the aisle"

"Andrew" I began "not today"

"Let me finish please Swefling" he sighed "I am at odds with everyone but Rowan is right. She is true to her sister and that's how it should be, whatever the rights and wrongs of the other matter"

"You believe now what they say about Richard?"

"I have not said so, but ….. it's for the court to decide but Swefling and William should not have laid the charges or become involved"

"Andrew you know they had nothing to do with the court finding out" I said stopping our dancing and drawing him away "neither of them are vengeful people you know that, but it is beyond doubt now Ruby has a second child and she does not deny Richard is the father of both, the one who died as well"

"Dear God, Swef listen to yourself, he is just twenty, how could that be so?"

"Oh Andrew" I laughed then "he's a lusty young man"

"You approve?" he sounded incredulous at my words.

"You know I do not. We should have kept him under tighter control"

"Me you mean?"

"No! Us! Really Andrew this is not about you" I said exasperated but found myself slipping my arm through his "it is about our family, all our family" I emphasised.

"You believe I am wrong over Swefling and William" it

was a statement not a question.

"Yes I do, you know how I feel, and you feel it too"

"But it can not be undone"

"Of course it can. You just have to go to Cobbold's and explain or write them"

"No! They told the court. Announced it to the world. Richard and I will both be charged"

"Is that what you believe they did? Really?"

"I don't know anymore Swef. Nothing makes any sense. You and I at odds, I don't like it"

"Neither do I" I smiled at him, glad we were having this conversation even if the time and place could have been better chosen, but we were soon to end our discussion for Rowan and Thackeray were coming our way.

"Mama" Rowan beamed "we are to leave, the carriage is waiting. Thank you for our day" she smiled and gave me a hug as she kissed both my cheeks. She looked at Andrew as we drew apart. "Thank you for allowing us to be wed here"

"You are our daughter Rowan" Andrew said uncertain if to hug her or not. He chose a hug, brief though it was before turning to Thackeray, who bowed most formally and kissed my hand.

"Thank you for Rowan" he said "I will do all in my power to keep her as happy today being my bride all though our lives together"

"Oh Thackeray" Rowan and I said together "be off with you and take good care of Rowan" I beamed desperately trying to fight off my tears.

May 1 1652

I woke to the sounds of screams and it me took a moment to focus, before I realised they were not screams of despair or anxiety. I opened my eyes and saw Andrew also awake.

"What is it?" I asked throwing back the covers and stretching my legs before standing.
"The girls" he said for it clearly was Bettris and Ales making all the noise. Their screaming had stopped now and we heard their feet running along the hall and pounding down the stairs in the distance. I climbed from the bed and crossed to the open window and peered out.
"Oh the dear Lord be praised" I sighed a wide smile on my face.
"What do you see?" Andrew asked.

"Come and see, Oh Andrew come and see" I briefly turned and looked at him before I looked back and saw Bettris and Ales running barefoot in their nightshifts across the grass to where Swefling and William were making very slow progress up the garden from the footbridge. Andrew joined me and together we peered out and watched our daughters hug and kiss each other for the first time in over a year. Then to our dismay we saw William and the girls help Swefling onto the grass.

"The baby!" I cried "the baby it's coming" and as if to confirm my words Bettris came running back to the house screaming for me. I was already throwing my clothes on as she burst into the room and very soon I was ready.
"Baby! Swef! Baby!" Bettris gasped most breathlessly.
"I saw" I smiled "go tell Kate and Mistress Harkness and bring pillows" I urged her and with a quick look and a smile at Andrew, halfway to his own clothing, I hurried from the room after my daughter.

Swef was in such an emotional state when I arrived,

as much from the imminent arrival of her child as our reunion and it was some moments before I was able to ascertain how soon a delivery might be made and I was most surprised for I could see the baby's head already.

"Bettris stuff those pillows behind Sweffie's back. William you help, the babe is almost here" and suddenly there was an outburst of giggling from Bettris and Ales which became most infections and we were all thus occupied when Kate and the housekeeper joined us, followed a measured distance away by Andrew. William looked up seeing himself beset by women who knew much more about birthing a child and with a brief peck on Swef's cheek he made a timely withdrawal and joined Andrew observing from a distance.

It was not many minutes afterwards, surrounded by the women of our family that Swefling gave birth to her fifth child and fourth son, a noisy, healthy child who was to be named Gabriel Philip. His arrival was the most perfect way for us to be reunited as a family and as Kate, Bettris, Ales and I watched Swef hold her son, we all shed tears of joys.

Later, in the day when Swef was rested somewhat and her children had met their brother, with much disinterest from the boys and marginally less so from her daughter, we were joined on the porch where Sweffie lay covered in a quilt to keep off any chill, by Kathren and Edward and Joane and Joseph, and of course Papa and Mary, and we had one of those unforgettable family gatherings, that were so special to us.

The time was not yet right for Swef and I to talk at any length for we were both too emotional and she had a baby to care for, but I knew in the days to come we would spend hours filling in the gaps of our lives since we'd been apart and I'd tell her that not for once did I believe she was wrong or that I didn't regret I was unable to come to her and make things right or nurse her when she was sick or in distress with the tutor. It was a time when I should have been there to console my daughter but I had been found wanting for my loyalty to my husband, who I was nevertheless most angry with, had outweighed that to my daughter in just the same way, I realised as her loyalty was to William first, and then her children and then me.

But that was done with and now we were together just as we should be and that was all that mattered.

October 14 1660

The day of our celebrations dawned warm and fair despite the time of year, and I slowly came awake and stretched and reached out for my husband. He rolled over and opened his eyes, a smile on his face, as he moved to kiss me.

"Thirty years Swef" he said, "who'd have though it, you and me together still after all this time"
"Hasn't it been grand though Andrew. You're just as handsome as the day I first saw you, when we were no more than children"
"Our children's children are not much younger than we were, do you realise that? And Swefling and William's girl older yet"
"I know. I remember when they wed, grandmother Eleanor asking where all the years had gone"
"They slip by so fast, but everyone of them a delight with you, my dear" Andrew said kissing me again "We'll

have to begin planning for when we go, there's so many children of ours to consider" he laughed.

"Not for a time Andrew, not yet. We have many more years I hope. Look at our families, your parents and papa all over eighty and grandmother was ninety four when she passed"

"Well, we shall continue to say our prayers, living well and not be too excessive and who knows we might beat the old lady, but for now I think we should just lie here until the time is come for the festivities to begin, do you agree?"

"What could we do to pass the time do you suppose?"

"I'm not sure if I remember exactly" he laughed, "'tis all of eight hours since I last made love to you, but I believe I should put one hand here and my lips on yours and see what happens"

"It seems a very good idea to me" I murmured as he did so.

…

Throughout the morning family and friends began to gather in the house and the gardens and on the porch as we had done on many occasions since our arrival at Butlers. It seemed as if we'd always lived here now after twenty two years. The house was well lived in, the plants in the garden mature and stately and all around us new folk moving out of Jamestowne and settling along the road to Middle Plantation. Across the road where Kathren and Joane lived were numerous other cottages where the workers from our properties had their homes and planted their own gardens, so our own community was growing fast.

I wandered down to the edge of the stream, some time during the morning where divers grandchildren were paddling, much to the consternation of their mothers, fearful their offspring were in danger of drowning or other such dreadful mishap but apart from getting a little wet about the edges of their clothes no harm came to any of them.

When all of our elder sons and daughters were arrived, around thirty adults sat down to eat at the long table set out under the trees and piled high with dishes prepared in the kitchens of our house and Cobbolds, and much drink to refresh us. An even larger number of children from infants up to twelve years took their meal elsewhere, supervised by various nanny's and helpers, much to the disgust as always of the older children but for several hours much chatter and laughter was heard about the garden. When we finally rose from our chairs the infants and younger children were taken inside the house to lay down for a time to rest and one or two older members of our gathering, papa and Mary and Andrew's parents especially, likewise. The rest of us sat about in groups talking and dozing and so the afternoon passed in peaceful harmony.

As the evening drew on our neighbours and the workers from Cobbolds, Ipswiche and Butlers joined us for the music and entertainment we arranged ~~for the eveni~~ng and much dancing took place amid noisy laughter, some tears of course from the children who grew over tired and more food and drink. Grandmother's Eleanor's favourite Geneva remained a most popular libation together with rum and ale as well and thus there were many sore heads the following morning.

Late into the evening Andrew and I stood to one side of the dance area, where we had been taking a turn and caught our breath, watching the youngsters enjoying themselves.

"How wonderful this is Andrew" I smiled at him, "all our children and grandchildren, except Richard, about us and enjoying each other's company with hardly an argument between them"
"And some new friendships being formed" he smiled.
"Who? Who have you seen?" I asked eager to know with whom our offspring were taking an interest.
"Our John, dancing with a very comely lass, and Ales with one of the Chessingham's, don't know which they all look alike, and our granddaughter"
"Not Sweffie, already" I giggled "she's just a baby"
"She is just the age you were when you wed Cris" Andrew reminded me "She is spending a lot of time flirting with the younger Hopkins boy"
"Thomas you mean?"
"Probably"

I smiled at all the liaisons beginning under our noses, pleased, in fact delighted for our Ales, who thus far had shown little interest in anyone of the opposite sex.

"I am glad Ales is taking an interest. I would hate for her to be an old maid and not have the joy of being wed" I smiled.
"Swefling, our daughter is twenty two" he laughed" just because you couldn't wait to be wedded, and bedded, doesn't mean they all do"
"Andrew! What a thing to say" I laughed though, "but I want all my children to be happy"
"As happy as we've been Swef eh? As I said to you this morning we've done very well for ourselves, you and me together and given them all a good start in life. Even

Richard"

As we stood and watched the activities before us, we were joined by papa and Mary, both stooped now with age, but bright as two new pins.

"You dancing papa?" Andrew asked as I wrapped an arm around my father's waist.
"No, we'll leave it to the younger ones, the spirit is more than willing but the flesh is weak" he chortled.
"That's all you ever say" Mary teased.
"There's no call to be crude Mary, in front of my little girl" papa teased likewise.
"I wasn't" she grinned at us.
"Stop arguing the two of you" I laughed, "anyone would think you were old and beyond such ……… activities"
Papa looked at me, a grin on his face.
"I will ignore your remark daughter, I have no notion from where you get your manners, surely not your Mama and I. I will speak with your husband, he will keep you in order"
"Never been able to yet papa" Andrew declared "you know how difficult it is with someone as wilful as Swefling"
"And your daughters are the same, how you have put up with them all these years I cannot imagine?"
"I learned to keep quiet and let them get on with it" Andrew laughed "it's the only way to survive"
"Mary and I will leave you two nagging fishwives if you carry on" I grinned at them.
"No stay with us Swef" Papa grinned "we need your protection from those wicked grandchildren of ours" he said spying Bettris and Ales coming our way. I'm an old man and I wish to see those girls wed. You must do something"
"Oh leave them be John" Mary laughed "they're far too

comfortable at home to be thinking of seeking husbands. I wouldn't wish to leave"

"Enough of this" Andrew declared "this is a celebration of married bliss let's not have disharmony, even in jest"

"Well said" Papa agreed.

November 2 1661

The grey days of November are with us once more and I am confined to my bed yet again. The sickness has returned and I feel weak and listless much of the time. Last week though when the sun shone, John and Gabriel carried me down the stairs to the porch. A rug was wrapped about me and when I felt the warm sun on my face my spirits lifted. Andrew joined me mid morning and we took our coffee together and Jenny brought some fresh biscuits, warm still from the oven, but since then I've remained in our bed.

There is a constant stream of visitors, but the grandchildren are tiring and forever clambering over the bed wanting hugs and kisses and forever asking why I am sick. I wish I knew for perhaps I could take steps to alleviate some of the pain, but it grows steadily worse. What began in the spring as a cough didn't leave and now oft times my handkerchief comes away from my mouth with spots of blood. Andrew, I think, knows I am dying but he hides his sorrow well, smiling as always, chirpy and full of plans for us, but in the quiet of our room at the end of the day, when he lies beside me I hear him sob when he believes I am asleep and I can do nothing to console him.

I do not wish to die just yet, my papa is still with us and Mary too, as lively as ever, but if my God says it's my time then I must go and go quietly and bravely without argument. I think to my son Crispin, all those years ago when he was called, he went fighting, protesting almost, but even so he was called and went. Will I see all those who have gone before I wonder? All my sons with Cris, are gone to him, but not our girls, Swefling and Rowan, how healthy they are. Was it Lucy's curse that took them before their time I wonder? I shouldn't think so, she didn't mean what she said. She was just a tortured poorly girl, who's mind had gone. And what of Cris will he be waiting? It is strange to consider that. We had such a passion for each other in the few years we were together but now I cannot remember how he looked. How strange that is.

I have so many questions now to fill my days, how do we chose our partner, that's one that often crosses my mind, for I have loved both Crispin and Andrew, and they me and all I wanted was to be with them forever. Only with Andrew have I succeeded for the rest of my life and we have been most happy and content together, except for that dreadful time when our Swefling was sent twice from our lives but now all is well except my life draws towards its end.

November 17 1661

The lawyer has recently departed with details of my last will and testament for it has to be done, I intend to depart this life with everything ordered and in its place. I wished to make a few small bequests to each of my children, something personal from myself to them and a word of comfort for Andrew. I will leave him my love, for even when I am gone, I will love him and wait for him to join me. I do not want to wish his life away but I do not want to be apart from him for too many years.

For Swefling my eldest I shall leave her this, the journal of my life, my thoughts, my emotions and experiences and trust she will find solace in my words. She will also have the jewellery grandmother Eleanor gave to my own mama as we boarded the Agnes Rose in Ipswyche in 1616.

But these will be my last words I suspect, for I cannot face the pain of writing of my imminent death.

I have had a good life with kind and loving parents who guided my brothers and I and prepared us well for the old world and the new one we came to and made us good citizens. I believe I have lived an honest life. I have worked hard to the best of my ability, and never knowingly done a cruel act or said a harsh word to a living creature. I have loved two men well, one with a passion and one with deep affection.

And now I am prepared to meet my Lord in heaven.

Swefling Eleanor Archer Butler

Printed in Great Britain
by Amazon.co.uk, Ltd.,
Marston Gate.